RANGER'S TRAIL

FORGE BOOKS BY ELMER KELTON

Badger Boy
Bitter Trail
The Buckskin Line
Buffalo Wagons
Cloudy in the West
Hot Iron
The Pumpkin Rollers
Ranger's Trail
The Smiling Country
The Texas Rifles
The Way of the Coyote

RANGER'S TRAIL

ELMER KELTON

A TOM DOHERTY ASSOCIATES BOOK
NEW YORK

RANGER'S TRAIL

Copyright © 2002 by Elmer Kelton

All rights reserved, including the right to reproduce
this book, or portions thereof, in any form.

This book is printed on acid-free paper.

A Forge Book
Published by Tom Doherty Associates, LLC
175 Fifth Avenue
New York, NY 10010

www.tor.com

Forge® is a registered trademark of
Tom Doherty Associates, LLC.

ISBN 0-765-30571-2

First Edition: September 2002

Printed in the United States of America

0   9   8   7   6   5   4   3   2   1

Dedicated to Nat Sobel, agent, friend, and
a good judge of a story

RANGER'S TRAIL

⊕ 1 ⊕

The election had gone smoothly except for certain extra-legal shenanigans perpetrated by both sides. Those were a normal feature of Texas politics and came as no surprise. By contrast the aftermath was chaotic enough to try the patience of saints, if there had been any. Rusty Shannon had encountered few saints in reconstruction Texas.

He slow-trotted his dun horse westward along a rutted wagon road skirting the edge of the Colorado River and wished he were back home on the farm where he belonged. On one side of him rode Sheriff Tom Blessing, in his sixties but still blacksmith-strong, solid as a block of oak timber. On the other, Andy Pickard whistled in a country boy's youthful awe and marveled at the town just ahead. His urban experience had been limited to a few small crossroads settlements.

Andy declared, "I had no idea Austin was this big. Must be three—maybe four—thousand people here. I never saw such a place in my life."

No one knew exactly how long a life that had been. Andy had been orphaned before he was old enough to retain clear memories. Rusty's best judgment was that he might be eighteen or nineteen, allowing some leeway on one side or the other. Strenuous outdoor labor and the excesses of Texas weather had given him a mature appearance beyond his years. He had a young man's seasoned face but had not lost the questing eyes of a boy eager to ride over the hill and see the other side. Girls seemed to consider him handsome. Andy seemed to have no objection to their thinking so.

Rusty turned up his frayed old coat collar against a cold wind coming off of the river. He had been wearing that coat for more than ten years, always intending to buy a new one someday when he felt he had a few dollars to spare but always "making do" for one more winter. He said, "San Antonio's bigger. I was there once."

His face, browned and chiseled with premature lines, was that of a man forty or more. Actually he was in his mid-thirties, but most had been hard years spent in sun and wind, riding with frontier rangers or walking behind mules and a plow. He said, "Got no use for San Antonio, though. It's overrun with gamblers and whiskey peddlers and pickpockets."

Tom Blessing declared, "Austin's worse. It's overrun with lawyers."

Andy had seen little of gamblers, whiskey peddlers, pickpockets or lawyers, but he was itching to start. He told Rusty, "You always say I need more learnin'. I'll bet I could learn a lot here."

"Mostly stuff you oughtn't to know."

Andy was well schooled in the ways of nature, but Rusty had worried about his limited book education. Andy had caught a little here and a little there as country teachers came, stayed a while, then drifted on. Rusty, in his time, had had the advantage of coaching by a foster mother. There had been no woman to help teach Andy. At least he could read a newspaper, and he had an aptitude with figures. He was not easily cheated, nor was he a forgiving victim. Most who tried once never cared to do it a second time.

Andy said, "I doubt I'd get bored in a place like this. Bet there's somethin' goin' on all the time."

In Rusty's view, that was the trouble. His idea of a perfect day was a quiet one. He had finally begun having a lot of those, thanks to the farm. "Most of it you wouldn't want any part of. Country folks couldn't abide the crowdin'. You soon get tired of people trompin' on your toes all the time."

He was here against his will and better judgment. He had planned a journey north toward old Fort Belknap to visit the Monahan family and to bring Josie Monahan back with him as his wife. But Tom had asked him to make this trip, and it was against Rusty's nature to refuse a good friend. Tom had ridden often with Daddy Mike Shannon in old times when there was Indian trouble. He had introduced Rusty to the rangers at a crisis point when Rusty had badly needed somewhere to go. Rusty often said he would follow Tom into hell with a bucket of water. He had, once or twice. Austin might not be hell, but Rusty did not consider it heaven, either.

He wished he had not given in to Andy's plea that he be allowed to come along. He dreaded the temptations this town might present to someone no longer a boy but not quite yet a man. Rusty had taken on the responsibility of a foster brother after Andy's nearest known relative, an uncle, had rejected him. At times, like now, it had been an uneasy burden to carry.

He surveyed the town with apprehension. "Tom, reckon how we'll find your friend amongst all those people?"

"Maybe we'll get lucky and stumble into him. Otherwise, he's likely puttin' up at a wagon yard. We'll ask around."

Tom had been a county sheriff before reconstruction authorities threw him out of office for having served the Texas Confederate government. The recent election had restored his badge after the former Confederates finally regained their right to vote. Another sheriff, a friend of his, had sent word that he was badly needed in Austin. He had not explained his reasons. He had just said to hurry and to bring help. Tom had immediately called on Rusty, respecting his law enforcement experience before war's end had caused the ranger companies to disintegrate.

Andy had jumped at a chance to quit the farm a while and see the city. To Rusty he had argued, "You're liable to need somebody to watch your back. You made some enemies while you were a ranger."

Rusty suspected Andy's motivation had less to do with protectiveness than with an urge to see something new and enjoy some excitement.

Because it was the dead of winter, Rusty and Andy had little farmwork that could not be postponed. Last year's crop was long since harvested, and this year's planting had to await warm ground. It would have been a good time for Rusty to get his red hair trimmed, then take a several-days' ride up to the Monahan place and ask Josie a question he had postponed much too long. Instead, he found himself approaching Austin and wondering why.

During ranger service that often took him far from home, Rusty had remained at heart a farmer with a strong tie to land he had known since boyhood. Andy empathized but had never been that dedicated to the soil. A tumultuous boyhood had given him a restless spirit. He welcomed any excuse to saddle Long Red and travel over new ground, to cross rivers he had not previously known.

"It's the Indian in him," Rusty had heard people say. "You never saw an Indian stay in one place long unless he was dead."

Andy was not Indian, at least by blood, but when he was a small boy the Comanches had taken him. They had held him through several of his vital formative years. Rusty had found him injured and helpless and returned him to the white man's world. But Andy had never given up all of his Indian ways.

Rusty hoped youthful curiosity would be satisfied quickly. He doubted that Andy would remain contented for long in a city like Austin any more than he was likely to be content spending all his life on the farm.

A squad of black soldiers drew Rusty's attention. He and Andy and Tom had drawn theirs as well. He murmured, "They're studyin' us like we might be outlaws."

Tom muttered in a deep voice, "They're lookin' at our guns. They're always afraid some old rebel may take a notion to declare war again." A few had, from time to time.

Rusty half expected the soldiers to stop them, but they simply watched in stone-faced silence as the three riders passed by and turned into a long street, which a sign on the corner said was Congress. At the head of it, well to the north, stood an imposing wooden structure larger than any other Rusty could see.

Andy's eyes were wide. "Is that the capitol? The place where they make all the laws?"

Tom said, "That's the place. Fixin' to be a lot of different faces there now that we've elected a new governor. Be a lot of carpetbaggers huntin' new country."

Rusty had mixed feelings about the outsiders who had crowded into Texas after the war, hungry for opportunity. On the positive side they had brought money to a state drained dry after four years of debilitating conflict. On the negative side some had brought a bottomless hunger for anything they could grab and went to any lengths of stealth or violence necessary to satisfy it.

Now thousands of ex-Confederates, disenfranchised after the war, had finally recovered their voting rights. By a margin of two to one they had defeated the Union-backed reconstruction governor, Edmund J. Davis. They had voted in Richard

Coke, a former Confederate army officer and one of their own. Perhaps that transition accounted for the large numbers of men standing along the street as if waiting for something to happen, Rusty thought. It did not, however, account for so many being heavily burdened by a variety of firearms.

Andy grinned. "Looks like the war is fixin' to start again." War had been a central fact of life among the Comanches, often sought after when it did not come on its own.

Rusty frowned. "I'm commencin' to wonder what we've ridden into." He reined his dun horse over to a man leaning against a cedar hitching post. "Say, friend, what's the big attraction in town?"

The man straightened, fixing suspicious eyes on Rusty, then on Andy and Tom. "I reckon you know, or you wouldn't be here. Did Governor Davis send for you?"

"I wouldn't know Edmund J. Davis from George Washington."

The man said, "A lot of Davis's friends have come to town includin' his old state police. They're all totin' guns. I see that you are, too."

Rusty kept his right hand away from the pistol on his hip, avoiding any appearance of a threat. "We brought our guns because we came a long ways. We didn't know what we might run into, or who."

"Just so you ain't one of them Davis police."

Mention of the Davis police put a bad taste in Rusty's mouth. "I used to be a ranger, but I never was a state policeman."

The governor's special police force—a mixture of white and black—had been organized as part of the state's reconstruction government, replacing the traditional rangers. Excesses had given the force a reputation for arrogance and brutality, arousing enmity in most Texans. Rusty had always felt that a majority were well intentioned, but a scattering of scoundrels overshadowed the law enforcement achievements of the rest.

A new legislature had recently abolished the state police to the relief of the citizenry and the consternation of Governor Davis.

The man said, "Local folks are naturally stirred up about so many strangers bringin' guns to town. Coke has been sworn in as governor, but Davis won't recognize him. Word has gone around that he has no intention of givin' up the office."

"But the people voted him out."

"He's declared the election unconstitutional."

Tom's face reddened. "He can't. That's not legal."

"He claims he's got the authority to say what's legal and what's not. Thinks he's the king of England, or maybe old Pharaoh."

The occupying Union forces had given their handpicked governor dictatorial power. He had instituted worthwhile improvements, particularly to the educational system, yet Texans resented his issuing punitive executive orders from which they had no recourse. Though Davis was a Southerner and a longtime citizen of the state, most former Confederates felt that he belonged to the enemy. He had fled Texas early in the war, eventually becoming a brigadier general in the Union army. The governor's office had been his reward.

Now it appeared that he did not intend to give it up.

Tom said, "We hold no brief for Davis. We voted for Coke." He glanced questioningly at Rusty. "At least I did."

Rusty nodded. He, too, had voted for Coke because he felt it was time to shed the smothering reconstruction regime so Texas could work its own way back to order and stability.

"Then I'd advise you to either join Coke's militia or take care of your business and move out of town before the roof blows off of the capitol yonder."

Pulling away, Rusty muttered to Tom, "I think I see why your sheriff friend asked you to come and bring help."

"I've known him a long time. I couldn't turn him down."

Tom's loyalty to a friend was such that he had reluctantly left an ailing wife at home to come on this mission. Rusty's loyalty to Tom did not allow him to refuse Tom's request, though he had planned to be marrying Josie Monahan about now. He said, "We're liable to get pulled into a fight that ain't ours. That whole damned war wasn't really ours."

Like the late Sam Houston, Rusty had never favored secession from the Union, nor had he ever developed any allegiance to the Confederacy. One reason he had remained with the frontier rangers throughout the war was to avoid conscription into the rebel army. Even so, he had come to resent the oppressive federal occupation.

Tom frowned. "I wouldn't have asked you to come if I'd known we were ridin' into a situation like this. Maybe you and Andy better turn around and go home."

Disappointed, Andy said, "We ain't hardly seen the city yet."

Rusty said, "We've come this far, so we'll wait and size things up. Then we can go home if we're a mind to."

Initially Tom had harbored reservations about the wisdom of the war, but once it began he had given his loyalty to Texas and the South without looking back. He said, "Davis got beat fair and square. If he was a proper gentleman he'd recognize the will of the people. He'd yield up the office."

Andy said, "The Comanche way is simpler. A chief can't force anybody to do anything. If the people don't like him anymore they just quit payin' attention to him. No election, no fight, no nothin'." He snorted. "And everybody claims white people are smarter."

Andy's sorrel shied to one side, bumping against Rusty's

dun. Two men burst off the sidewalk and into the dirt street, wildly swinging their fists. Immediately another man joined the fray, then two more, cursing, wrestling awkwardly. Foot and horse traffic stopped. Onlookers crowded around while the fight escalated.

Andy asked, "Whose side are we on?"

Rusty said, "Nobody's." He saw little difference between the combatants except that some might be drunker than others. He said, "We'd best move on before some fool pulls a gun." He found the way blocked by men rushing to watch the fight.

Faces were bloodied and shirts torn, but nobody drew a pistol or knife. Whatever the quarrel was about, the participants did not seem to consider it worth a killing.

A city policeman strode down the street, gave the situation a quick study, then stepped back to observe from a comfortable distance, hands in his pockets. Shortly a blue-clad army officer trotted his horse up beside the policeman. His sharp voice indicated he was used to people snapping to attention in his presence. "Aren't you going to stop this?"

The policeman did not take his hands from his pockets. "A man can get hurt messin' in where he wasn't asked. Long as they don't kill one another, I say let them have their fun."

"You are paid to enforce the peace."

"Not near enough. Ain't been any peace around here since this governor business came up. You want to stop the fight, go ahead."

"The army is not supposed to interfere. This is a civilian matter."

"And this here civilian is goin' into that grog shop yonder to have himself a drink. If anybody gets killed, come and fetch me." The policeman turned away. The officer watched him in frustration, then turned his attention to the ongoing fight.

A couple of the brawlers had had enough and crawled away to sit on the edge of the wooden sidewalk, there to nurse their wounds while the altercation went on. They were not missed.

Andy's eyes danced with excitement as his fists mimicked the movements of the belligerents. He had been in plenty of fights himself, usually instigated by other young men making fun of the ways he had learned from the Indians.

Rusty knew a good scrap when he saw one. This was not a good one. It was slow-footed and clumsy, loud but not likely to produce anything more serious than loose teeth, bruised knuckles, and maybe a flattened nose. He decided the policeman had been right in leaving bad nature to run its course.

Onlookers' comments bore out his assumption that some of the fighters were Davis men. Others supported Coke. The fight slowly staggered to a standstill. The Coke men appeared to carry the victory, such as it was. They moved away in a triumphant group, weaving toward the grog shop the policeman had chosen. Their opponents dragged themselves to the sidewalk and slumped there, exhausted.

The fight had energized Andy. He said, "Some folks take their politics serious."

Tom Blessing nodded grimly. "With good reason. Davis's men tromped on everybody that got in their way. Stole half the state of Texas. Now comes the day of reckonin', and they ain't willin' to 'fess up."

The three rode north up the wide street, Rusty warily eyeing the armed men scattered all along. He saw no reason anyone would shoot at him on purpose, but he had learned long ago that the innocent bystander was usually the first one hurt. The more innocent, the more likely.

They reined up short of the capitol building. Several men stood shoulder to shoulder at the front door, holding rifles. They had a military bearing but did not wear uniforms. Rusty surmised they were former Confederate soldiers who had not forgotten the regimens learned in war.

He said, "Looks like they're guardin' the state treasury."

Tom said, "Too late for that. Talk is that Davis's adjutant general slipped away with it and sailed for Europe." He stepped down from the saddle and lifted the reins for Andy to hold. "You-all better stay here so we don't accidentally provoke somebody into somethin' rash. I'll walk up there and see what the game is." He unstrapped his pistol belt and hung it over the saddle horn as an indication that his intentions were benign.

Andy gazed southward back down Congress Avenue, where substantial buildings lined each side. Rusty assumed he was marveling at the variety of merchandise available here for anyone who had the money to buy it. That was the catch. Texas was just emerging from the economic devastation of war and its aftermath. Not many people other than opportunistic outsiders had much money to spend. Most of what Texans needed, they produced for themselves or did without. But Austin had been something of an oasis, money flowing more freely because of the Union soldiers and the state's reconstruction government based here.

It dawned on Rusty that Andy's attention was focused on two young women who stood in front of a nearby saloon. It was obvious they were not Sunday school teachers.

He warned, "Don't let your curiosity get stirred up too much. I don't expect we'll be stayin'." It occurred to him that he had taught Andy a lot about plowing straight rows but not enough about avoiding society's pitfalls.

Tom returned, his jaw set grimly. "Governor Davis has got himself barricaded in the capitol basement with a bunch of his old state police. The Coke men and the legislature have got the upper floor."

"A Mexican standoff," Rusty said.

"Maybe not for long. Davis has sent a wire to President Grant. He's askin' him to order the troops in. Wants them to throw out the Coke crowd and keep him in office."

That news troubled Rusty. "If he does, there's apt to be an awful fight."

Andy had no problem with the notion of a fight. "I wish old Buffalo Caller could've seen this." Buffalo Caller was the Comanche warrior who had first captured him and kept him for his own. "He would've given a hundred horses to watch white men battle one another instead of fightin' the People. And it would've been worth every one of them."

Tom declared, "You're white. That's a scandalous thing to say."

Andy said, "Was it to happen, I'd cheer for the old Texans to win. But not too quick. I'd like to see the fight stretch out a while."

Tom shook his head. "Scandalous." He looked back toward the capitol. "I've offered to do my part and stand with Coke. This ain't none of you-all's fight unless you want it to be."

Rusty said, "We're here now. We wouldn't go off and leave you by yourself."

Tom seemed pleased. "You sound like your old Daddy Mike. But I won't be by myself. There's several of my friends up there from way back. There's a bunch of old rangers, too. Friends of yours, I'd warrant."

Rusty's interest quickened. "Rangers?"

"Yeah, but like I said, it don't have to be your fight. I wouldn't want a young feller like Andy on my conscience. Or you, either."

"We came of our own accord. We're grown men." Rusty glanced at Andy. "*I* am, anyway."

Tom nodded. "There's a wagon yard down yonder. Would you take my horse for me?"

Rusty jerked his head. "Come on, Andy."

Andy led Tom's mount. Rusty guessed there must be a hundred horses in the several corrals to the side of and beyond the large wooden barn. A droop-shouldered liveryman slouched in the big open doorway, waiting for customers. He limped out a few paces and spat a stream of brown tobacco juice at a bedraggled cat, missing by a foot. A bit of the spittle remained in his stubble of gray-and-black beard. He said, "You're supposed to be in there chasin' mice. They're fixin' to carry off the whole shebang, barn and all." He looked up at Rusty. "What can I do for you-all?"

"Got room for three more horses?"

"If there ain't room enough we'll just stack them like cordwood. I expect you-all are in town to see the excitement?" It was a statement, but he made it sound like a question.

"We didn't know about it 'til we got here."

"I ain't takin' sides, you understand, but I hope the Coke people give that Davis crowd a hell of a lickin'. I've had a gutful of them thieves."

Rusty smiled. "Sounds like you *have* taken sides."

"I reckon, but if the shootin' starts I'm keepin' my head down. I taken a Yankee ball in my leg durin' the war. Convinced me I ain't no fightin' man."

"But you're willin' to take money from either side?"

"I take care of horses, and horses don't know nothin' about politics. I do business with any and all, long as the money is genuine." He extended his hand, the palm up. "And paid in advance."

Rusty took his time counting out the coins, for he did not have enough that he could afford to spend them needlessly. "We'll want to bed down here in the wagon yard tonight. We've got no money to waste on a hotel."

"Hotels are all full, anyway. Spread your blankets anywhere you can find an empty space. And be careful with your matches. You don't want to buy no burned-up barn." He dropped Rusty's coins into his pocket. They clinked against silver already there.

The capitol standoff was good for business.

The liveryman looked behind him as if to be certain he would not be overheard. "Couple of fellers were talkin' back of the barn. They're waitin' for Coke to give the word to make a rush against the capitol and put Davis out on the street. Could be a right interestin' show."

Rusty glanced uneasily at Andy. "Tom could get hurt. He's a shade old to be mixin' in a bad fight."

Andy said, "He's never run away from one yet. That's why they made him sheriff again."

"He ought not to've let them put that badge back on him. I've got a notion to try and talk him into goin' home before somethin' happens. That sick wife of his needs him more than anybody here does."

Andy had not seen enough of the town. "Gettin' kind of late in the day. We couldn't go far before dark."

"We could get out of gunshot range."

Andy resigned himself to disappointment. He patted Long Red's neck. "You better eat your oats in a hurry." He followed Rusty out the door.

Rusty told the liveryman, "Don't turn our horses into the lot just yet. We're liable to be leavin'."

The old man shoved his hands into his pockets. The coins jingled like tiny bells. Reluctantly he said, "I guess you'll want your money back. You still want me to feed them some oats?"

"I wish you would." Rusty was more willing to spend on the horses than on himself.

He saw a crowd of nervous-looking men standing around the front of a hotel as if waiting for someone to assert leadership and take them somewhere . . . anywhere, to do something . . . anything. A familiar voice called his name, and a man pushed through the cluster. Len Tanner was tall and lanky, in patched trousers that hung loose around a waist thin as a slab of bacon. He always looked as if he had not eaten a square meal in a month. In truth, he could put away an alarming amount of groceries when the opportunity presented itself.

Rusty exclaimed, "Len! Thought you were back in East Texas, visitin' your kin."

"Ain't much excitement in seein' kinfolks. Here's where the fun is at."

Rusty had ridden with Tanner during his ranger service. Since the war, Tanner had spent much of his time at Rusty's farm when he lacked something better to do. He was not addicted to steady employment. Tanner said, "There's a bunch of our old ranger bunkies here ready to run the carpetbaggers out of town on a rail. But Coke keeps holdin' back, hopin' Davis will cave in without a fight."

"What if he doesn't?"

"After fightin' the damned Comanches, this oughtn't to make us break a sweat." Tanner frowned at Andy. "Sorry, button, I didn't mean nothin' personal."

Andy shrugged. "I take it as a compliment to the Comanches."

"They're honest enemies, at least. They come against you face-to-face. Carpetbaggers sneak up behind you and kill you with affydavits." Tanner's family had lost their farm to confiscatory reconstruction taxes, though he, like Rusty, had never actively supported the Confederacy. He said, "I know why Davis wants to keep that office. There's some of Texas that his cronies ain't stole yet." His momentary dark mood fell away. "Speakin' of old friends, I'll bet it's been a spell since you seen Jim and Johnny Morris."

"Sure has." Rusty looked around eagerly. "Are those rascals here?"

The Morris brothers had served in the same ranger company as Rusty and Tanner until they went into the Confederate army late in the war.

Tanner said, "Me and them are plannin' on a little sortie tonight. Goin' to aggravate some Yankee soldiers."

That did not surprise Rusty. Like Tanner, the brothers had always gloried in a fracas. If they could not find a fight already in progress they had occasionally instigated one.

Rusty and Andy followed Tanner through the crowd. Two men of roughly Rusty's age shouted his name and pushed their way to him. They could be taken for twins, though Jim was a year or so the oldest. He declared, "Glad to see you're still alive." He gripped Rusty's outstretched hand with a force that could crush bones. "Me and Johnny figured you'd worked yourself to death on that wore-out farm."

"I've come awful close."

Jim turned to Andy, his manner jovial. "You'd be the Comanche button Len's been tellin' us about."

The brothers' being friends of Tanner's did not automatically assure Andy's acceptance. He regarded them with an element of doubt. "Len's been known to lie a little, once or twice."

Johnny Morris grinned. "We've caught him abusin' the facts ourselves. But only when he's awake." He jerked his head, beckoning Rusty and the others beyond the edge of the crowd. In a low voice he said, "Rusty, you're just the man to help us do a little job tonight."

Rusty felt misgivings. As much as he liked Tanner and the Morrises, he remembered times when they had acted first and considered the consequences later, if at all. Events had not always worked to their advantage. "I'd want to hear the particulars before I say anything." He already leaned toward saying *no*.

"The army's brought up a cannon from San Antonio."

Rusty's jaw dropped. He had not considered that the dispute would come to this. A cannon could blow a big hole in the capitol building. He thought immediately of Tom Blessing, standing guard somewhere in or around it.

He protested, "Hard to believe the army would fire on the capitol while Davis and some of his people hold the basement floor."

"No," Johnny said, "but they'd fire into the crowd if a bunch was to try and rush the buildin'. We figure they're just waitin' for Grant to wire them the orders."

"But a cannon . . . what could you do against a weapon the size of that?"

Jim said, "Me and Johnny and Len are goin' to spike it."

Andy demanded, "What do you mean, 'spike' it?"

Johnny explained, "You drive an iron spike into the touchhole. They can't fire 'til they get it out, and that can be hell to do if it's pounded in there hard enough."

Rusty said, "Don't you know they'll be guardin' it? You'll get yourselves shot."

"Len'll distract the guards. Won't take us but a minute to fix the cannon and be gone. You could help him."

The idea was much too simple. Rusty could see a dozen holes in it, most of them potentially lethal. "You're crazy, all three of you."

Andy said eagerly, "Let's do it, Rusty. We can run rings around them soldiers."

"*Four* of you are crazy. You're too young to be mixin' into a thing like this."

"How old were you the first time you rode with the rangers?"

"That was a long time ago. Times were different." It struck Rusty that his foster father, Daddy Mike Shannon, had said the same thing to him once, to no effect.

Johnny Morris turned. "Yonder come some of them bru-
nette Yankees." A small squad of black troopers marched up
the street, led by a white officer on horseback, the same one
Rusty had seen earlier. "At least they ain't brought their cannon with them."

Jim said, "Washington still ain't given them permission
to mix in. That's all they're waitin' for."

The presence of black troops had been a thorn in the sides
of ex-Confederates during the reconstruction years. Texans
were convinced that the victorious Union intended to humil-
iate them by putting them under the authority of former
slaves. The effect had been more of outrage than of humilia-
tion.

Several in the crowd began catcalling, shouting racial and
political insults at the soldiers and their officer. One man
stepped out past the others and shook his fist, loudly cursing
all Yankees and their antecedents from the poorest foot soldier all the way up to President Grant. His slurred speech
indicated that he had imbibed a good measure of liquid courage.

The officer unbuttoned his holster and drew a pistol. He
pushed his horse up close and brought the barrel down across
the heckler's head. The man went down, his hat rolling in the
dirt.

The officer turned in the saddle. "Arrest him. Two of you
men take him to the bull pen."

Len swore under his breath. "That old boy was too drunk
to know what he was sayin'."

"He knew," Rusty said sternly. "But loud talk is no reason
to break a man's skull."

A noisy protest arose from the crowd, but no one made
a move toward the well-armed soldiers.

Jim Morris said, "Whatever happened to free speech?"

Johnny replied, "It ain't free anymore. And the price keeps goin' up."

Rusty gave way to rising anger as two troopers dragged the half-conscious man away. He looked into the faces of his friends and saw the same reaction.

Andy demanded, "Don't you think we ought to do somethin'?"

Rusty said, "Like what? The South already lost one war."

Tanner said, "At least you can look the situation over with us. Help us figure out how we're goin' to do it."

"I guess I can go that far. But this is a dog fight, and me and Andy have got no dog in it."

The liveryman did not get up from his rawhide-bound chair, but he eyed Rusty with regret. "Fixin' to go? I done fed your horses some oats, so I can't give all your money back."

Rusty said, "We're not leavin' town yet."

Cheered, the liveryman pushed away from the chair. "I'll show you where they're at."

Andy lagged behind, nursing his disappointment. Rusty had told him he had to stay at the wagon yard. He saw no need for Andy to take chances by joining Tanner and the Morrises.

The liveryman led Rusty into the barn to a small pen where his horse, Andy's, and Tom's still nuzzled a wooden trough, seeking stray bits of grain stuck in the cracks. Rusty wondered if they had actually been fed as much as he had paid for.

He led his dun out into the fading daylight. As he prepared to mount, Rusty heard a familiar voice. "How's my young Comanche friend?" It was addressed to Andy.

Andy considered his answer, then said firmly, "I don't remember that we was ever friends, Farley Brackett."

Brackett was a large man with a scar from the edge of his eye down to his cheek. War had scarred him even worse on the inside, turning him into an outlaw, at least in the eyes of the state police. As Brackett approached, Andy took half a step back before standing his ground.

Brackett pointed his chin at Long Red. "I see you've still got my sorrel horse."

Andy bristled. "He never was your horse. Your daddy gave him to Rusty, and Rusty gave him to me."

"He wasn't my daddy's to give. He was mine."

Andy stiffened. "So you say, but your daddy's dead. We can't ask him."

Rusty intruded. "You're runnin' a risk, Farley, showin' up in public. The state police don't forget."

"They've had their fangs pulled, but I haven't. Any of them tries to mess with me, he'll get what they gave my old daddy." State police had mistaken the father for Farley and had killed him.

Rusty said, "Anyway, you leave Andy alone. We're not here to fight."

"Everybody else is." Brackett looked back at Andy. "I still say he's my horse. You've just got the loan of him. For now." He walked away, toward the milling crowd that stirred dust along Congress Avenue.

Worriedly Andy asked, "He can't take Long Red back, can he?" Andy thought more of that horse than of any human. Almost any human, at least.

Rusty said, "He's got no claim. His daddy gave me that horse to replace one Farley stole when he was on the run."

"If he tries to take Long Red, I'll shoot him."

Rusty suspected Andy would at least try. But Farley Brackett had shown the reconstruction authorities he was a hard man to kill. "You shouldn't talk loose about killin'. It can lead to more than just talk."

"Just the same, I'm keepin' a close eye on Long Red. Farley had better not so much as look crossways at him."

Rusty met Tanner and the brothers where the three had dropped their blankets near the river. Johnny pointed. "The troops made camp down thisaway."

As they rode, Rusty heard a horse loping up from behind. Andy pushed to overtake them.

Rusty turned in anger as Andy pulled in beside him. "I told you to stay behind."

"That Farley kept hangin' around the stable. I decided the best way for me to keep an eye on Long Red was to be ridin' him."

Rusty knew that was more an excuse than a reason. "All right, but don't be gettin' any foolish notions."

He saw several rows of tents lined in military order. Johnny said, "They got the cannon placed back of the tents."

A hundred yards beyond the tent line stood a set of wooden pens. The troops were infantry. Rusty surmised that the few horses he saw were for the officers. He counted four draft mules. Drawing the cannon would be their job.

He shivered at the thought of such a weapon being fired into a crowd. For that purpose artillerymen would probably load it with scraps of metal and pieces of chain. Those would damage more rioters than a single cannonball.

Tanner muttered, "A mean piece of business. And all on account of politics."

Rusty said, "The whole war was because of politics."

He was not surprised to see two black soldiers standing guard on either side of the cannon. He was a little surprised there were not more. "You think they'll stand by idle while you-all drive your spike?"

Tanner said, "When the time comes I'll see to it that they ain't there."

"You wouldn't kill them? The army would run you to the ground and hang you from the tallest tree they can find. If they didn't just shoot you outright."

Johnny said, "We wouldn't hurt a hair on their heads. Len is goin' to draw them away."

"How?"

"We hoped you'd help us figure that out."

Rusty studied the cannon and everything around it. He saw a stack of hay near the horse pens. He said, "I don't see anybody guardin' that hay yonder. If it was to accidentally catch afire, . . ."

Jim nodded, his eyes brightening. "That's the same stunt me and Johnny pulled on some Yankees just before the end of the war. Got away with a bunch of their horses. They didn't need that many, anyway, since their hay burned up. They didn't have anything to feed them."

Andy had listened quietly, but excitement built in his eyes. Rusty sought to head him off. "You're not goin' along with them. You're too young, and it's too dangerous."

"I've been in dangerous places before. My Comanche brother Steals the Ponies could tell you that."

"But he's not here. If he was, he'd be welcome to help. But not you. I didn't spend all these years raisin' you to lose you in a fight that's none of your business."

Rusty expected more argument. Andy simply shrugged and said, "Here come some soldiers to see what we're about. You want to talk to them?"

Four troopers and a white officer were marching toward the five Texans. Rusty said, "I don't believe we've got anything to talk about." He reined his horse around and started back toward the brothers' camp, careful not to move faster than a walk. He did not want to arouse suspicion by appearing to run away. The others followed him. The troopers soon stopped.

Tanner asked, "You reckon they suspect us?"

Rusty said, "They suspect everybody, and have since the first day they came into Texas."

Tom Blessing walked to the wagon yard about sundown, tired and burdened with worry. "Hard to guess what's fixin' to happen," he said. "Governor Coke has got a bunch of his old rangers at his side. Governor Davis has called out the Travis Rifles to help him hold the capitol. Some of them have come over to us, but there's enough left to give us a right smart of trouble. And we still don't know what President Grant will do. If he orders the troops in, with their cannon, . . ."

Tanner declared, "Don't you worry yourself about that cannon. It's fixin' to be took care of."

Rusty frowned at Tanner and looked about to see if anyone might have overheard. Most people around here were strangers. He had no way of knowing which side they were on. He said in little more than a whisper, "The Morris boys figure on spikin' that cannon tonight."

Tom was not relieved. "They're liable to get spiked themselves."

Rusty said, "Len Tanner's goin' to help."

"That's no big relief." Tom nodded toward Andy. "Surely you're not lettin' the boy go."

"He's stayin' here with me."

Tom said, "Good. We're dealin' with people who are used to absolute power. If they got him in their sights, they wouldn't take his youth into account."

Andy spoke up. "If I was still with the Comanches I'd be looked at as a warrior now. I sure wouldn't let a bunch of bluecoats scare me."

Tom said, "They scare *me*. I just hope Grant doesn't set them loose. You know they arrested the mayor today."

Rusty said, "I hadn't heard that."

"Roughed him up some, then turned him loose because it looked like a riot was fixin' to break out. They still haven't got their orders from Washington."

Rusty walked to the door and stared out into the street. Everywhere he looked little clusters of armed men stood waiting, watching. The tension was electric, much like the atmosphere before a thunderstorm. "Wouldn't take but one good spark to touch off the powder. I wish we'd gone back home."

Tom said, "For my wife's sake, I wish we'd never been asked to come in the first place. She needs a woman to be with her 'til she gets her feet back under her. I ain't been able to find one who'd stay."

Rusty kept a disturbing thought to himself. What would become of Mrs. Blessing if a bullet brought down her husband? "We could start home right now. It won't be full dark for another hour."

Tom shook his head. "We finally got back the right to vote. It's time to get off of our knees and stand on our feet."

"No matter what it costs?"

"We're at a fork in the road. One way follows the law. The other twists the law to whatever it wants it to be."

Rusty smiled. "First time I ever heard you make a speech."

"I don't often feel the need, especially with you."

Rusty did not intend to go to sleep so early, but it had been a long day. Soon after he lay down on his blankets he dozed off. He awakened suddenly to the squealing of two horses nipping at one another. He saw that Andy's blankets had been thrown back. Andy was gone.

Damn fool kid, he thought. He's gone to help Tanner and the Morrises.

The stableman was asleep on a steel cot in a small office at the front of the barn. Rusty aroused him to ask when Andy had left. The man sat up, blinking rapidly, swinging his bare feet over the side. His voice was sour. "Don't you people know what the night is meant for?"

"That boy who was with me, did you see him leave?"

The man ignored the question. "Night's a time for rest. If you want your horse, you know where he's at. Catch him yourself. And you can put him back for yourself when you come in. If you're too drunk to unlatch the gate, just tie him to the fence."

"How long has it been since the kid left?"

"I didn't look at my watch." The man scratched his backside. "What kind of a critter is that button, anyway?"

"What do you mean?"

"He come stealin' in and got his horse. I wouldn't have knowed he was here if the horse hadn't snorted just as he passed my door. Wouldn't surprise me none if that boy's got Indian blood in him."

"I'll admit he acts like it."

The stableman said, "Probably snuck off to find him a sportin' gal. I did when I was his age. 'Spect you did, too. I got no quarrel with it as long as they let a man sleep."

Rusty saddled his horse while the stableman returned to his blankets, muttering all the way.

The kid's got more nerve than judgment, Rusty thought darkly. As bad as Len Tanner.

He rode in a long trot to the Morris brothers' camp at the edge of town. He found the fire burned low. No one was

there. He was sure he knew where they were, and Andy with
them.

Damn Len Tanner. He knew I didn't want Andy to be
any part of this.

He rode toward the soldier camp under a dark sky, the
moon hidden by a heavy cover of clouds. Unable to see much,
he almost rode upon two men sitting on horseback. Johnny
Morris demanded, "Who the hell are you?"

"It's me, Rusty. Where are Len and Andy?"

"They've snuck off down yonder to set the hay afire.
While everybody's runnin' to fight the fire, me and Jim will
fix the cannon." He showed Rusty an iron rod. Jim carried a
blacksmith's hammer across the pommel of his saddle.

Rusty said, "Why didn't you-all turn the boy back?"

Jim said, "His mind was made up. We couldn't have
stopped him if we'd hit him over the head with this hammer."

Rusty knew how stubborn Andy could be. "Maybe I can
head him off. You-all be careful. Some Yankees are good
shots."

He rode down toward the camp. He could not make out
the shape of the haystack, but he knew more or less where it
should be. He felt a chilly dampness moving up from the
river on the south wind. He shivered and pulled his old coat
more tightly around him. A couple of fires flickered in the
soldier camp. He envied the men warming themselves there.

The cannon guards had a fire of their own. Rusty took
that as a good sign. Glare from the flames would diminish
their ability to see through the darkness.

He saw a match flare, then flicker out. Andy and Tanner
must be having poor luck getting the hay to catch fire. Both
were single-minded enough to keep trying, even if soldiers
swarmed over them.

A hostile voice demanded. "Who goes there?"

Rusty realized the challenge was directed at Andy and Tanner. He put spurs to the dun horse, urging him into a long trot.

A rough voice shouted, "Who are you? Speak before I blow your head off!"

Tanner's answer was defiant. "I'm Robert E. Lee and I'm here to whup some Yankee sons of bitches."

Rusty saw a quick movement and heard a thud as a soldier struck Tanner in the stomach with the butt of a rifle. Rusty did not give him a second chance. He rode in, swinging his pistol. He felt the barrel connect with a trooper's head. The trooper fell, firing his rifle by reflex. Tanner wrestled with another soldier but was losing ground. Rusty grabbed a handful of uniform and pulled the man off of him. He swung the pistol but missed.

He heard a shout. "Corporal of the guard! Post number two!" It came from the direction of the cannon. He heard more soldiers running toward him. A rifle cracked. Rusty fired his pistol into the air, hoping to confuse and perhaps discourage the soldiers. "Forget the fire," he shouted. "Get out of here."

The troopers guarding the cannon came on the run, silhouetted against their fire. Rusty aimed a shot in their general direction, slowing them. One discharged his rifle into the darkness but had no clear target. Rusty leaned low to be sure he did not present one.

Andy came riding out, leading Tanner's horse. "Here, Len. Get on him quick."

Rusty heard the whisper of bullets passing much too close. Len staggered. Andy swung around to help lift him into the saddle. The three set their horses into a run.

The firing continued behind them. Rusty said, "You two stirred up the whole Yankee army."

Andy laughed. "Didn't we, though? But we couldn't get the fire started."

Len lamented, "Damned hay was wet. All I burned was my fingers."

Rusty said, "It was a fool notion in the first place."

Andy said, "Only thing wrong with it was that it didn't work."

Rusty did not see the Morris brothers, but he figured they were old enough to take care of themselves. They always had. Andy was young, eager, and still needed watching. Tanner should have known better, but he was inclined to create trouble even where there had been none. He had long maintained that a good fight was more invigorating than a double shot of whiskey.

Rusty led Andy and Tanner along the river until he was sure they had shaken off pursuit by the foot soldiers. Then he circled back in the direction of the Morris brothers' camp. Andy was still laughing.

Rusty decided it was time for the lecture. "Now listen here—"

Andy cut him off. "I know what you're goin' to say, so there ain't no use sayin' it. I didn't have any business bein' out here. But I figured Len needed help. By himself, he was apt to get killed."

"You could've both been killed."

"We weren't, and I had more fun tonight than I ever got followin' a mule across a field. Len, you're lookin' kind of sick."

"Took a rifle butt in my ribs. I'm goin' to be awful sore in the mornin'." He moaned. "Every time a man gets to feelin' smart, somethin' comes along and kicks him in the belly."

Johnny and Jim arrived in camp just ahead of them. "Everybody all right?" Johnny asked worriedly. "What went wrong out there?"

"Damp hay," Rusty said. "Looks like it ruined you-all's plan."

The brothers grinned at one another. "Not really," Johnny said. "Len and the boy set out to draw attention away from us. They sure did that."

"You managed to spike the cannon, after all?"

"The only way it could hurt anybody now would be if it fell on him."

Rusty grunted, surprised but pleased. The troops could do a lot of damage with their rifles if they were called into the dispute, but at least they should not be able to use artillery against the crowd.

He said, "If you-all don't mind a little company, I think me and Andy'll bed down here instead of goin' back to the wagon yard. The stable keeper needs his sleep."

With only their saddle blankets for cover against the night chill, Rusty and Andy lay near the campfire. Rusty poked a little fresh wood among the coals and watched the flames rise up before he stretched out on the ground. He lay awake, replaying the evening's action in his mind.

Tanner was soon snoring. Andy rolled onto one side, then moved to the other, pulling his legs up tightly. Rusty asked, "Can't you sleep?"

"I'm a little cold. And there was too much excitement, I guess. Got my blood all stirred up."

"I'm not havin' much luck myself." Rusty arose to put more wood on the fire. Instead of lying down and rolling up in his saddle blanket, he squatted on his heels and stared into the fire.

"Been doin' some thinkin', too," he said. "How would you like to have a cabin of your own?"

"What do I need a cabin for? There's plenty of room in yours."

"Maybe not for long."

Andy stared at him in puzzlement. "How come?"

"I've been plannin' a trip up to the Monahan farm. Been wantin' to see how everybody's gettin' along."

"Especially Josie?"

"Especially Josie. I'm figurin' on askin' her to marry me."

Andy grunted. "It's about time. She's been askin' *you* long enough."

"Things weren't right before. I never knew what the carpetbaggers might throw at us. They tried once to take the farm, and I was always afraid they might do it again. But things'll settle down now that we've got a new governor."

"We've got two governors. We don't know which one will win out."

"I've got a feelin'. Old Preacher Webb always said if you keep the faith, good things will eventually come to you."

After a campfire breakfast of bacon and black coffee, all five rode up onto Congress Avenue to see if anything had changed overnight. A large group of men had gathered some distance below the capitol building. Rusty recognized several as former rangers with whom he had ridden at one time or another. Tom Blessing walked out from among them and hailed Rusty. He said, "Word has come from Washington. President Grant won't order the troops to help Davis. Told him the election is over, he lost, and he had just as well yield like a gentleman."

Rusty accepted that as good news, but not the ultimate answer. "He hasn't given up though, has he?"

"Not yet, but he must be feelin' like a mule has kicked him in the ribs. He can't call in the army. All he's got backin' him now is a bunch of his old state police and some officeholders who know they're fixin' to be out of a job."

Rusty was still trying to absorb the fact that the troops were not to be involved. That meant they would not have used the cannon even if it had not been spiked. Last night's wild sashay had been unnecessary.

Tanner had waked up with sore ribs and belly from the blow he had taken. He would hurt even more when it soaked in on him that he had taken the punishment for nothing.

Tom said, "We're waitin' for Governor Coke to show up and lead us on a march to the capitol."

"And if Davis won't give up?"

"We'll burn that bridge when we get to it."

Richard Coke was tall and heavyset, his white beard neatly trimmed. He wore a suit well tailored to his bulk and projected a sense of dignity the way a governor of Texas was supposed to, in Rusty's view. In a booming voice he shouted, "Let's go."

Flanked on either side by ex-rangers and Confederate officers Rip Ford and Henry McCulloch, he led the parade of determined men up Congress. In front of the capitol stood a line of well-armed Davis men, appearing just as determined. Coke acted as if he did not see them, never breaking stride. The defenders looked to one another for guidance, for someone to take the initiative and do something. No one did. The Davis men stepped back grudgingly, and the Coke procession marched into the capitol.

A tall, gaunt, defiant Davis awaited them in the hallway outside of his office. The door was closed. He stared sullenly at Coke.

Coke said, "Governor Davis, the new legislature has convened and canvassed the vote. They have declared that I am the rightful holder of this office. I respectfully request that you honor the wishes of the people of Texas."

Davis glared, his gaze sweeping over the men who faced

him. "I do not recognize the election as legitimate. But I see that the laws of the state have been trampled underfoot. The rule of the mob has prevailed."

He strode past Coke. His opponents moved aside to let him pass. He did not look to right or left but focused his gaze straight ahead.

An audible sigh of relief arose from the men clustered in the hallway. One of Coke's lieutenants tried the door to the governor's office. "Locked," he said. "Davis did not turn over the key."

Another lieutenant said, "Break it open."

Tanner and a couple of others put their shoulders into the task. The door splintered. Tanner stepped back, gripped his belly, and grimaced in pain.

Inside the office, Davis's secretary of state still sat at his desk. The lieutenant who had tried the door said, "It's over. You can leave."

The man sat in stubborn silence.

The lieutenant said, "Some of you escort him outside."

A momentary clamor arose as several in the crowd suggested throwing the man out the window, but Coke overruled the idea. "That is the way of the old regime. As of today Texas is steering a new course."

Three men lifted the secretary from his chair and hustled him outside. Tanner did not volunteer to join them. He was still holding his stomach.

The people of Austin, and most of the visitors, celebrated far into the night. Rusty thought of the stable keeper. He wouldn't be getting much sleep.

Tom Blessing sat on the ground near the Morris brothers' campfire, chewing a piece of bacon. He told Rusty, "I'm ready to start home come daylight. You and Andy seen enough of the big city?"

Rusty glanced at Andy, who put up no argument. "I was

ready before we came. But now that it's over, I'm glad we were here to see it. It'll be somethin' to tell our grandchildren about someday."

"Andy's too young to be thinkin' about grandchildren. And you ain't even married."

"I'm figurin' on fixin' that."

Tom stopped chewing. He seemed a little perturbed. "You sure bein' a ranger is a proper thing for a married man?"

"I'm not a ranger anymore."

"But you could be again. Governor Coke says one of the first things he plans to do is reorganize the rangers. He'll be lookin' for men of experience."

"I've *had* plenty of experience," Rusty said ruefully. "More than I ever looked for. I'm not sure I want any more like it."

"It gets in your blood, like sheriffin' got into mine. You'll want to study on it before you take to double harness."

L en Tanner stood with hands in his pockets to keep them warm. He watched as Rusty and Andy lifted blankets, provisions, and Rusty's saddle into the bed of the wagon. The sun was just breaking over the eastern horizon, looking crisp and frosty through a thin blanket of gray winter clouds.

"I don't see why you want to take the wagon," he said. "You'd get there a lot sooner if you rode horseback."

"Josie'll be wantin' to bring all her things," Rusty said.

"How do you know she'll even come? You ain't asked her yet."

"She'll come." Rusty looked toward a new single log cabin standing halfway between the older double cabin and the livestock pens. "I hope you don't mind finishin' the roof on Andy's cabin."

"I got nothin' better to do. And Shanty's comin' over to help me build the chimly." Shanty was a former slave who lived a few miles away. Age had bent his slender frame, but his hands were still those of an artisan. "We'll have the place ready for the button to move in by the time you-all get back."

Andy had been torn about making the trip. He wanted to stay and help finish the cabin, but Rusty had persuaded him that the Monahans would be eager to see him. They had come to look upon him as a member of the family.

Andy saddled Long Red and tied Rusty's dun horse behind the wagon. "Reckon we got it all?"

Rusty said, "If we don't, we'll do without it." He shook Tanner's hand and climbed onto the wagon seat.

Tanner said, "Tell that cute little Alice girl I said howdy."

Rusty grinned. "We'll tell her."

"And watch out for Indians. They may not all know they're Andy's friends."

"I doubt they'll come far enough south for us to see them. They've got their hands full fightin' buffalo hunters."

Rusty had heard talk that large numbers of hide hunters had filtered down onto the Texas high plains from Kansas during the fall and winter. They had decimated the herds farther north in Cheyenne country. Now they were invading the Comanches' best hunting grounds. The Comanches were not feeling generous.

The news had disturbed Andy. His first thought was of his Comanche family and how the buffalo slaughter would affect them. "I thought there was a treaty that said the hunters couldn't come south of the Cimarron River."

Rusty said, "The treaty was with the federal government, on federal land. The federals have no right to make agreements about Texas land."

"I doubt that Steals the Ponies knows where the line is or that he would give a damn. Land is land. The Comanches figure they own all of it they're strong enough to hold."

"That's what counts, bein' strong enough."

Rusty had not tried to argue Texas's case. Andy had strong feelings where Indians were concerned. Trying to alter his views was like trying to stop a flowing river with a leaky bucket.

Andy looked back as they started away. He said, "I like my cabin, but a good tepee would serve me just as well."

"You won't feel that way when you've got a blaze goin' in the fireplace on a cold night. I hear the reservation Indians have started buildin' houses."

"Yes, but a lot of them put up tepees beside their cabins. They like to sleep next to Mother Earth. She gives them their strength."

"I've spent a lot of my life sleepin' on the ground. All I got from Mother Earth was rheumatism and a likin' for an honest-to-God bed."

They crossed the Colorado River at a ford. The water was higher than it would be in spring, when winter-dormant vegetation came back to life and sapped much of the underground moisture before it had a chance to seep into the river. Rusty pushed hard to keep the team moving forward briskly enough that the current would not pick up the wagon and carry it away.

He had ridden this trail many times, going to or from the Monahan farm or in the course of his ranger duties. Andy had ridden it, too, once when he was almost too young to remember. On that first trip he had traveled northward as captive of a Comanche raiding party. He had ridden again as a half-grown boy, this time heading southward to join his adopted brother as a participant in a horse-stealing foray. Fate in the guise of a fallen horse and a broken leg had dropped him back into the white world. There he had remained, though not willingly at first. He had never completely relinquished the heritage of his Comanche years.

Some people considered him unreconstructed, a streak of the savage locked forever in his heart. Andy had found he could use such people's attitude against them, keeping them at arm's length as a measure of self defense. His friends accepted him as he was. He was not troubled by what others thought.

Andy rode alongside the wagon, talking at intervals, then silent for long stretches. He was especially quiet after they made the first night's camp. Rusty recognized the dark moods that came over him now and then and did not push him for conversation. As they hitched the team next morning, Andy asked, "We goin' by the grave?"

Rusty had suspected this had been heavy on Andy's mind. "We can if you want to."

"I reckon I want to."

The grave was above the north bank of a small creek, just off the wagon track. At one end of a stack of stones a wooden cross had fallen to the ground. Rusty moved the wagon a little beyond and stopped. He got down, but he stood back, letting Andy have his time alone.

Andy dismounted and removed his hat, his head bowed. After a while he wiped a sleeve across his eyes, then straightened the cross. He pulled off a small wad of dark hair. "Buffalo," he said. "They knocked it over, scratchin' their itch."

Many of the stones lay scattered. Andy placed them neatly back over the mound. "Someday," he said, "I'm comin' back and puttin' a fence around this." When he was satisfied with the appearance of the grave, he straightened. Rusty joined him, hat in his hand.

Andy said, "I wish we had Preacher Webb with us. He'd know the words to say."

Rusty nodded. "He already said them, when we first buried her here." He shuddered, remembering.

Andy bit his lip. "I can't quite remember what my mother looked like. I sort of remember her voice, but I can't see her face in my mind. I like to think she was pretty."

"I expect she was, but she'd been poorly treated by the time we found her."

The memory chilled Rusty. It had been his first time to ride with the rangers, though they were little more than a loose band of local militia at the time. They had trailed after marauding Comanches who had killed several settlers and swept away all the horses they could find. They had kidnapped a small boy and his mother. The rangers had found the mother here, dead. The boy had disappeared. He was not seen again until Andy turned up years later, left behind in the wake of another Comanche raid.

Andy said, "I guess a lot of folks wouldn't understand. I don't myself, sometimes. The Comanches killed my mother here. Then they took me as one of their own. Some would say I ought to hate them, but they became my people. They're still my people."

"I like to think we're your people, too, me and Len and Shanty, and the Monahans. Tom Blessing, too."

"You are. Guess there ain't many like me with people on both sides of the fence. Not blood kin, but even better." Andy turned toward his horse.

Rusty said, "We don't have to be in any hurry if you'd like to stay a while."

"I've said all I know to say to her. Stayin' and wishin' won't bring her back. It won't even bring back a clear memory." Andy mounted the sorrel and started out.

Rusty remembered the first time he had seen the Monahan farm. Preacher Webb had escorted him there on his way to join the rangers at Fort Belknap. The place had looked like paradise after a long ride up from the Colorado River. Paradise was lost during the strife of war, but fragments had been regained in the years since.

Andy asked, "You nervous?"

Rusty was. The nearer they came to the farm, the less

certain he was of what he should say, how he should approach Josie. In his view, one thing had always stood between
them. He had once loved her older sister Geneva, but she had
married another. For a long time he had feared that his growing feeling for Josie came only because she had begun to re-
semble her sister so much. The years had gradually erased
his doubt, but he was afraid Josie might not be so certain.

He saw two men working with a young horse in a corral,
trotting him around and around at the end of a rope. A boy
sat on the fence, watching. He raised his arm and pointed,
then jumped down and began running toward the two visitors. One of the men called after him. "Billy!"

The boy seemed not to hear. He cried, "Andy! Andy!"

Andy dismounted and swept the boy into his arms,
swinging him halfway around. "You derned little Indian,
you've grown a foot."

"I ain't no Indian. But I *have* grown. I'm near as big as
you are."

He was not, but the point did not merit an argument.

Rusty said, "Howdy, Billy."

The boy replied, "Rusty," and gave his attention back to
Andy.

He thinks Andy's the one that hung the moon, Rusty told
himself, smiling. Billy was Geneva's son, and Evan Gifford's.
While Rusty had been away serving as a frontier ranger, Evan
had come back from the war, gravely wounded. Geneva had
nursed him, and a strong bond had developed between them.
Rusty recognized Evan in the corral, along with his brother-
in-law, James Monahan. Evan climbed over the fence and
walked out to meet the visitors. He was smiling, but his voice
was stern.

"Billy, we've taught you not to go runnin' off by yourself
that way. You don't always know who's comin' in."

Billy said, "I could see it was Andy. Couldn't you see it was Andy?"

"My eyes aren't as sharp as yours." Evan grasped Andy's hand as if to crush it. "Good to have you back." He looked up at Rusty. "You, too. Bring your wagon on up and we'll unload it."

Rusty looked toward the main house, hoping to see Josie come out onto the porch. Evidently she did not know he had arrived.

"Is everybody all right?" he asked.

He caught the serious look that came over Evan's face. Evan said, "Didn't anybody write you about Clemmie?"

Clemmie was the family matriarch, mother of Josie, Geneva, and the youngest sister, Alice.

Rusty felt a sharp foreboding. "Our mail goes astray a lot. What's happened to Clemmie?"

Evan jerked his head in the direction of the main house. "Yonder comes Preacher Webb. It's more his place to tell you than mine."

More than thirty years ago, circuit rider Webb and farmer Mike Shannon had found the orphaned Rusty wandering bewildered in the wake of an Indian battle. Mike had become Rusty's foster father. Webb had been like a benevolent uncle, poor in the world's goods but generous in spirit and rich in friends. He had married the widowed Clemmie Monahan three years ago.

He seemed older now than he actually was. He had lived a strenuous life, most of it in the service of others. Rusty felt a rush of sympathy as the tall, gaunt minister walked slowly toward him. Every step seemed to bring pain. Rusty hurried to meet him, to spare him from having to come so far. He was conscious that Andy followed him, eager to hear about Clemmie. She had become like a grandmother to him.

Rusty was careful how he grasped Webb's gnarled hand, knowing arthritis afflicted him. "It's good to see you, sir. What's this about Clemmie?"

Webb's face was grave. "The Bible tells us that even the just must suffer times of tribulation. Clemmie has had a stroke. Her limbs are paralyzed on one side. She cannot so much as leave her bed without someone to support her. She even has trouble in speaking."

Rusty was momentarily speechless. Clemmie Monahan was a little woman, weighing scarcely a hundred pounds, but she had always reminded him of a willow. Ill winds had bent her more times than was her due, but never, it had seemed, could they break her. It always shook him to see infirmities catch up with people he had considered invincible, like Daddy Mike and Preacher Webb and Clemmie. Such occasions forced him to consider his own vulnerability.

He asked, "Can't anything be done?"

"James fetched a doctor out here all the way from Sherman. He gave her some medicine, but I think it was more to bring the family's hopes up than to fix what's wrong with her. I've lost count of how many times I've prayed over this."

"I wish there was somethin' I could do."

"She'll be cheered that you've come." Webb put an arm around Andy's shoulder. "Andy, seein' you will be better medicine than anything a doctor could give her. She looks on you as one of her own."

Andy said, "I wish I was."

Rusty said, "I wonder what brought this on."

Webb frowned. "Just one trouble too many, I reckon. I don't guess you knew that Alice ran off with a cowboy."

Alice was the youngest daughter. Len Tanner had long had eyes for her. This news would be a sad disappointment to him. "Any idea where they went?"

"We had a letter. Said they got married down at Fort Griffin. James swore he'd go and fetch her back whether she wanted to come or not. He was killin' mad. Clemmie had to talk hard to stop him. That's when the stroke hit her."

"How did Josie and Geneva take Alice's runnin' away?"

"Better than their mother did, but that's not sayin' much."

Rusty could not wait longer without asking, "How *is* Josie?"

"Bone tired. Besides bein' nurse, she's takin' on all the work Clemmie used to do. I've been afraid she'd wind up sick herself. You'll be like a dose of tonic to her."

"I'd have come earlier if I'd known."

"Josie wrote to you. I guess you didn't get her letter."

"Never did." He had lost Geneva because of a lack of communication during the last part of his ranger service. She had thought him dead. Evan Gifford had come along, an answer to her loneliness.

Josie heard footsteps on the porch and came to the door. She stared at Rusty in pleased surprise, then self-consciously reached up to check her hair. It needed combing. She said, "I must look a sight." She seemed to consider retreating back into the house, then stepped out onto the porch and into his arms. He held her tightly and said, "You look beautiful."

"You're a terrible liar."

"I'd have come sooner if I'd known about Clemmie."

He stepped back without releasing her. As Webb had said, she looked tired and drawn. Even so, she was still a pretty woman. Josie's blue eyes glistened. "I wrote you a letter," she said.

"I never got it. I ought to've come sooner anyway."

Webb asked, "Is Clemmie asleep?"

Josie shook her head. "She woke up when she heard Billy holler. She'll feel better, seein' who's come." She kissed Rusty again. "So do I." She led him to a bedroom. Andy and Webb followed.

Rusty wanted to say something that might pretend cheer-fulness. Seeing Clemmie lying there even thinner than nor-mal, her mouth twisted by the stroke, he could think of nothing that would not sound flippant and false. "I'm sorry, Clemmie." That was all he could say before he choked.

Her left arm was still and useless. She raised her right arm, and he took her hand. She struggled with her words. "The heart . . . ain't quit beatin'." Her eyes cut to Andy. "How's . . . my Indian boy?"

Some people could call him that and he would take it as a compliment. Others said it and he was ready to fight. Clem-mie could call him anything she wanted to.

Andy seemed to have as much trouble with his words as Clemmie did. "I'm . . . I'm just fine." He leaned down and kissed her on the forehead. His face was pinched. Rusty sensed that only a strong will held back Andy's tears.

She squeezed Rusty's hand and looked at her daughter. "Take Josie . . . take her out into the sunshine. Make her smile."

Josie protested, "What if you need somethin', Mama?"

"Warren . . . ," she nodded toward her husband . . . "he can get it. Or Andy." She touched the boy's arm. "You stay with me, Andy."

Andy cleared his throat. "Sure. I ain't goin' nowhere. You want somethin', you just tell me."

Josie seemed hesitant, but Clemmie dismissed her with a motion of her hand. Rusty put his arm around Josie and walked her out onto the porch. They seated themselves on a bench. She took a deep breath and expelled it. "The fresh air does feel good. I haven't had much time outdoors since this all happened."

"Preacher Webb is worried about you. I'm sure Clemmie is, too."

"There's nobody else here to care for her in the things it

takes a woman to do. Alice is gone. Geneva's got her own family to see after. Preacher Webb and James do what they can, but the rest is up to me."

"You've got your own life to live."

"I wouldn't have a life if it wasn't for Mama. She always took care of me. Papa would turn over in his grave if I didn't take good care of her."

The family had never entirely recovered from Lon Monahan's death early in the war. Radical secessionists had killed him for his Union sympathies, and a young son had died with him. After many hardships and indignities, the surviving Monahans had found shelter and protection at Rusty's farm on the Colorado River. There they had remained until the war ended.

Then, at least, Rusty had known how to help them. He felt useless now.

He said, "I suppose you can guess why I came."

The look she gave him seemed strangely defensive. "I think I might."

"Things are in good shape down at the farm. They came near takin' it away from me once, but that's over now. I'm askin' you to go back down there with me."

The sadness deepened in her eyes. Tears welled before she turned her head and wiped them away. "For years I waited for you to ask me. Even a few weeks ago, I could've said yes. Now I can't. I can't leave here while Mama's in this shape."

Rusty could not have said the answer surprised him, but it shook him nevertheless. He could have come earlier. Once last fall's crops had been gathered he could have made the trip at any time. But he had waited, uncertain of the future, uncertain he would continue to own the farm when others wanted it and were more favored by the reconstruction government.

"We've built a separate cabin for Andy," he said, realizing how feeble an argument that was, how little it must mean to her in the face of hard reality.

She said, "You can see, can't you, why I can't go with you? Even if I'd gone with you before, I'd have had to come back. There's no debt as heavy as one you owe to your blood kin."

Rusty had no blood kin that he knew of. He had been a nameless orphan, left wandering in the wake of an Indian raid. But he understood what she meant by debt, for since boyhood he had felt a deep obligation to those who had given him a home and selflessly cared for him as if he had been their own.

"Clemmie would want you to be happy," he said. He knew that was another weak argument.

"I couldn't be happy knowin' I hadn't done right by her. No, Rusty, we'll have to wait . . . wait 'til Mama gets over this stroke, or 'til . . ." She did not finish.

He tried to keep his voice from betraying the disappointment he felt. "You've got to do what you think is best."

She leaned against him. "I wasn't sure you'd understand."

"I understand."

"I always said you're the best man I ever knew, Rusty, except maybe for Papa and Preacher Webb. I'll just have to wait some more. I hope you can."

He could. He had to. In all his life he had loved only two women. One had been lost to him. He would go to any length to avoid losing this one.

"However long it takes," he said. "I just wish there was somethin' I could do for Clemmie."

"The best medicine she could have would be to see Alice come back. Or at least to know she's all right."

"Why wouldn't Alice be all right?"

"It's that man, Corey Bascom. I never did trust him. I don't think anybody did except Alice. James wouldn't have hired him if he hadn't been desperate for help in breakin' horses. I could see that Alice was taken with him, but I never once suspected they might run off together."

"It's hard sometimes to tell what's in young folks' minds." Rusty often had difficulty in reading Andy's intentions. He could be as inscrutable as an Indian.

Josie said, "Alice got a thrill out of havin' all the young bachelors around here come and pay court to her. That's why I can't figure why she settled for Corey. He had an air about him like he was hidin' somethin'. Maybe it was the mystery that attracted her."

Rusty considered a while before he offered, "What if I was to go and look for her? Maybe I can find out if she's all right and bring her home if she's not."

Josie's eyes flickered with momentary hope that quickly gave way to doubt. "I always felt like there was somethin' a little dangerous about Corey. Nothin' I could put my finger on, nothin' he ever exactly said or did. Just a strong feelin'. He might hurt you."

"There's been others tried."

"What if he doesn't want to be found? What if Alice wants to come home but he doesn't want to let her?"

"I'll just have to persuade him."

Misgivings were strong in her eyes. "It's too much to ask of you, Rusty."

"You're not askin'. I'm offerin'."

"I wouldn't want you to put yourself in harm's way for this family."

"I've been in harm's way most of my life. And you-all and Andy are the nearest thing to family that I've got."

"At least talk to James. And to Evan. They worked with Corey. They'll know the most about him."

"I'll do that. It's best you don't say anything to Clemmie. If I don't find Alice, she'd just be hurt all over again."

Josie remained on the porch while he walked toward the dusty corral where James and Evan were working with a young horse, sliding a saddle blanket along its back, getting it used to the strange new feel. Geneva Gifford stood outside the fence, watching them. Her son, Billy, and a young daughter were beside her. Turning as Rusty approached, she extended her hand. She attempted a smile but could not quite bring it off. She said, "Billy told me you and Andy had come. I guess you've seen Mama."

"I wish I'd known sooner."

He could never look at Geneva without feeling a sense of loss, though he had gradually come to terms with that loss a long time ago. He had taken comfort in the fact that her marriage was a good one. She had a husband who was worthy of her. Childbearing had matured her. She carried more weight than when he had courted her, but she was still handsome.

She said, "I saw you on the porch with Josie. Did you ask her this time?"

Geneva had always been able to read him as if his thoughts were written across his face in block letters. He replied, "She said no. On account of her mother."

"You can't blame her."

"I told her I'd try to find Alice."

"I'm not sure that's a good idea."

"It's the only idea I've got."

James released the horse and walked over to the fence. Geneva told her brother, "Rusty says he's goin' to look for Alice."

Rusty's relationship with James had always been shaky. Ranger service had put him at cross-purposes with Josie's brother more than once. The end of the war had brought them to a truce, but earlier disagreements had left a lingering aftertaste like burned coffee on the tongue.

James demanded, "What's Mama say about this?"

Rusty said, "She doesn't know. It's best to leave it that way."

James frowned. "In other words, you're not sure you can do it."

"All I'm sure of is that I'll try."

James said grimly, "I wanted to go myself, but Mama wouldn't hear of it. She thought I'd more than likely shoot the son of a bitch. And I would've, if he gave me any excuse."

Rusty pointed out, "He did marry her, at least. He is Alice's husband."

"A son of a bitch, just the same. A good rider but rough on horses. Used his spurs too much. A man rough on horses is apt to be rough on a woman, too." He motioned, and Evan came over to the fence, carrying a coiled rope. "Evan worked with him as much as I did. His opinion is the same as mine."

Geneva told her husband what she had told James. Evan said, "I was always uneasy while Corey worked here. I suspicioned that he planned to steal some of our horses. I never thought that he might steal Alice instead."

James said, "I never was plumb sure that Corey Bascom was his real name. Wouldn't surprise me if he borrowed it someplace."

Most of the aliases Rusty had come across seemed to be simple names such as Smith or Jones or Brown, not unusual enough to be memorable. "You have any idea where he came from, or where he might've gone with Alice?"

James and Evan glanced at one another. James said, "All we know for sure is that Alice sent her mother a letter from Fort Griffin sayin' she had got married."

Evan added, "He told me one time that his family had a stock farm over east someplace. I think he mentioned the Clear Fork. But I guess there's several of those in Texas."

Rusty said, "He could've meant the Clear Fork of the Brazos. It flows past Fort Griffin and spills into the main Brazos farther east."

James grunted. "That's a long ways from here. But if it was closer I'd've gone after Alice no matter what Mama said."

Evan asked, "You want somebody to go with you?"

Rusty caught the misgivings in Geneva's face. "There's no need in that. You-all have got enough to worry about right here."

Geneva looked relieved. She reached through the fence and clutched her husband's arm. Evan did not argue the point.

Geneva bit her lip. "One thing, Rusty. If you find Alice, don't give her the notion that she caused Mama's stroke. There were so many things that piled up . . . the stroke might've come even if Alice hadn't run away."

James said, "And maybe it wouldn't. Alice hasn't exactly been a sweet little angel. Maybe she *ought* to feel guilty."

Rusty shook his head. "It's not my place to blame her *or* to forgive her. I'll just see if she wants to come home and bring her if she does."

James added, "And don't kill anybody you don't have to. Mama wouldn't like it."

Rusty tightened the cinch on his dun horse in the frosty light of the winter sunrise. Andy led Long Red to where his saddle rested on the top rail of a fence. The sorrel's breath made a small cloud in the crisp air.

Rusty demanded, "What do you think you're doin'?"

"Fixin' to go with you."

"I want you to stay here. Make yourself useful to the Monahan family."

Andy lifted his saddle from the fence. "You don't know what you may be ridin' into. You're liable to need help."

"I doubt it. If I do I'll go to the local law. You stay here." Rusty mounted and rode away, looking back. Andy stood with the saddle at arm's length, watching him.

"You stay," Rusty hollered back.

He had ridden half a mile when he heard a horse coming up behind him. He stopped and turned the dun around as Andy approached. He said, "I told you I'm goin' by myself."

"And I'm goin' by *my*self. I just happen to be travelin' the same direction you are."

Rusty wanted to be angry with him but couldn't. "As I remember it, you trailed after your Comanche brother once

when he told you not to. Got yourself in bad trouble." That
had been the time Rusty had found him lying helpless, his
leg broken after his horse fell.

"I was just a kid then."

"By my lights, you're still a kid."

"But too big for you to whip. Are we movin' on, or do
we just sit here and talk?"

Rusty saw that neither reason nor threat would change
Andy's mind. He had a stubbornness that Daddy Mike Shannon would have appreciated. "I guess we can argue and ride
at the same time. Come on."

He carried supplies rolled up in a blanket tied behind the
cantle of his saddle. Andy had brought nothing but an extra
blanket. Rusty knew they would have to be sparing of his
coffee and flour and bacon. He said, "Keep a sharp eye out
for game or we'll be awful lank by the time we reach Fort
Griffin."

"You don't know what hungry is 'til you've ridden with
the Comanches. They can go for a week on a chunk of sun-
dried meat the size of your hand."

"I've done it, but I never liked it."

Fortunately Andy's sharp eyes picked up some antelope
that afternoon, and his keen marksmanship brought one
down. Antelope would never replace beef in Rusty's opinion,
but it was better than fat hogback.

Preacher Webb had told him about an army chaplain he
had met in Fort Griffin. "When he wasn't ministerin' to the
soldiers he was takin' the gospel to others that needed it. The
good Lord knows there's a lot of them that need it around
Fort Griffin. The ground over there is soaked in whiskey."

Andy asked, "Is Fort Griffin really as bad as Preacher
makes out?"

Rusty said, "From what I hear, one minister isn't near
enough."

It was not much of a village. Its main clientele was soldiers stationed at the post on a flat-topped hill just to the
south. It catered also to ranchers and farmers of the area and
to freighters passing through. Whatever resentment the old
Confederates might harbor against Union soldiers, they were
never averse to profiting from them.

Rusty had found from experience that a saloon was a
good place for information, though sometimes it required a
modest investment in goods from behind the bar. He tied the
dun in front of a crudely constructed frame building and told
Andy, "You don't belong in there."

Andy smiled. "Neither one of us does. Looks like a place
where you could get your head stove in for two bits."

"Or maybe less," Rusty agreed. "You stay here while I go
ask a question or two."

Andy moved his head in a manner that said neither yes
nor no. But he took a position out in front, by the door, where
he could hear what was said inside.

The saloon keeper reminded Rusty a little of the stableman in Austin, middle-aged, thin, a red-tinged face indicating
that he was quite familiar with his stock. He gave Rusty a
piercing study as if gauging his ability to pay. "What's your
pleasure?"

"Depends on what you've got."

The barman waved his hand toward a row of bottles
along the wall behind him. "You see it. Different bottles, same
whiskey. Whichever one you take, you'll wish you'd taken
somethin' else. But there ain't nothin' else."

Rusty liked a little whiskey when it came handy, but he
had never felt any addiction to it. "I'll trust you. Just pour
me one."

The whiskey seared his throat as it went down. He almost
choked.

The barman said, "Told you."

Rusty had no wish for another drink. When his throat stopped burning he said, "I'm lookin' for a preacher."

"You ain't dyin'. My whiskey ain't *that* bad."

"The preacher I'm lookin' for would've married a young couple a while back. I'm hopin' he can give me an idea where they went."

"Probably the chaplain up on the hill. Regular preachers usually take a look at this town and decide it's beyond salvation. Young couple, you say? Name wouldn't be Bascom, would it?"

Rusty stiffened. "That's right, Corey Bascom. You know somethin' about him?"

"Enough not to be talkin' much. He brought a young lady to town with him and got the chaplain to tie the knot. Spent the night camped on the river. Some of the boys thought about goin' down and givin' them a shivaree but decided against it. Them Bascoms are mean all the time. They get *real* mean when they're riled up."

"Do you have any idea where they went from here?"

"The family claims land to the northeast. I doubt it's recorded at the courthouse, but who with any sense is goin' to challenge them?"

"How would I get there?"

"You know where the settlers forted up against the Indians durin' the war?"

Rusty remembered the place. It had been named Fort Davis in honor of Jefferson Davis, disregarding the fact that a military post by the same name existed in mountains far to the west. It had been populated a relatively short time, affording protection to civilians against the Comanches and Kiowas while so many of their young men were away to war.

The barman frowned. "I hope you ain't got trouble on your mind. Them Bascom boys can give you more of it than

you can handle. And old Bessie Bascom . . . she's the devil's
stepmother. You a lawman?"

"Used to be a ranger. I'm not anymore."

"You'd better not let them know you ever was. They're a
grudge-holdin' bunch, and they got a grudge against any
kind of law."

"I'm just lookin' to be sure the girl's all right. She needs
to know that her mother has taken down sick."

"Just the same, you tread softly around that bunch. There
ain't a preacher amongst them."

The barkeep drew a crude map on the back of an out-
dated fugitive poster originally circulated by the state police.
The description on the poster fitted the man himself. He cau-
tioned, "Now, don't you let them Bascoms know I told you
how to find them. I was lucky to live through the war. I don't
know how much luck I got left."

Andy was waiting outside. He indicated that he had
heard everything so Rusty need not repeat any of it. Rusty
said, "I'd ought to leave you here, only this is no place for a
green young feller like you."

Andy said, "Maybe those Bascoms aren't as bad as he
makes out."

Rusty did not attempt a reply.

He had visited the site of Fort Davis while on ranger patrol,
so he had no difficulty in finding it. Old cedar picket buildings, thrown up for temporary shelter, slumped in various
stages of ruin. A stockade fence, started but never finished,
leaned toward its final rest upon the ground. A hungry-
looking coyote slunk away at the far end of the quadrangle,
its ribs showing through a rough coat. Winter had not been
kind.

Rusty said, "Folks here had a hard life. Carried water up from the river in buckets. The men, what there was of them, did their cow huntin' in bunches. Had to watch for Indians all the time. They took care of their farms the same way. There were more women and children than men."

Andy remarked, "The Comanches had just as hard a time of it. If they had ever really wanted to they could've cut through this place like a knife through butter." He spoke with a touch of pride.

The saloon keeper's map was vague. It showed a wagon road leading away from the ruined fort, but Rusty found there were several. He asked, "Which one do your Indian instincts tell you to take?"

"I'm afraid my guardian spirits stayed back at Fort Griffin. I'm not hearin' anything from them."

Rusty chose one at random. "Let's try this."

A couple of miles proved it to be a bad choice. The road showed no sign of recent use. It disappeared where heavy rain had washed it away, taking a deep cut into the topsoil. Rusty decided to strike due east, hoping he might intersect a trail showing more sign of recent travel. He did, after a time, and followed it until he came upon a farmer breaking sod with two mules and a moldboard plow.

He asked if they were anywhere near the Bascom place.

The farmer eyed him suspiciously. "You a friend of theirs?"

"I don't even know them. I'm just carryin' a message." He saw no need to burden the man with details.

"Well, if you don't know them, and they don't know you, it might be better if you don't find them."

"The message is important."

The farmer hunched his shoulders as if to say he had given fair warning. "You follow this road another mile or so, then take the first wagon trail that forks off to the right. Stay with it 'til you get to a long picket house with dirt coverin' on the roof. Better holler good and loud before you ride in so you don't surprise anybody. Them Bascoms don't like surprises. Don't like neighbors much, either."

Rusty thanked him for the information and the advice. He glanced at Andy as they resumed their journey. "Aren't you glad you came with me?"

Andy smiled. "Beats plowin'. They sound like interestin' folks."

If it had not been for Clemmie, Josie, and Geneva, Rusty would not have undertaken this mission. Alice had made her bed, and it might do her good to lie in it a while. She resembled her two older sisters in appearance but not in personality. If anything she was prettier, and she was filled with fun-loving spirit. This in some respects had been to her detriment. It had brought her more adulation than was healthy from starry-eyed boys and young men of the area. As the baby sister she had been petted, sheltered, and catered to more than the others. Too young during the war years to realize fully what was going on around her, she had not had to develop the toughness and steadiness of purpose that marked Geneva and Josie. Much had come easily for her. Rusty could imagine how the dashing manner of a handsome stranger could have turned her head.

In due time he and Andy came to the picket house the farmer had described. Rusty paused for a long look. "I don't see but one horse in the pen. Maybe most of the family is gone somewhere."

"That's just as well. They sound like the kind of folks you'd want to meet one at a time."

The farmer had said the Bascoms did not like neighbors. To Rusty that meant they were probably into some kind of business that did not welcome observation. The chaotic years that followed the war had spawned much of that kind of industry. The state police, often more involved with politics than with law enforcement, had done relatively little to stem such offenses as bank robbery and horse and cattle theft.

He said, "If we ever get the rangers back, this whole country is due for a big sweepin' up."

Andy asked, "Do you figure on joinin' them?"

"Like Tom Blessing said, the rangers is no place for a married man."

"You ain't married yet." As an afterthought Andy added, "Neither am I."

"You're too young to be a ranger."

"How do you know? *I* don't even know how old I am. If I told them I'm twenty-one they'd never know the difference. For all we know, I may *be* twenty-one."

"You're some short of that."

"We don't have to tell them so."

Rusty had not suspected that joining the rangers had even crossed Andy's mind. "We'll talk about it when and if the time comes. The state's broke. It may not have enough money to reorganize the rangers anyway."

"I'm bettin' it will. You saw Rip Ford and Henry McCulloch with Coke when he marched up to the capitol. He didn't pick old rangers like them for nothin'."

Rusty remembered the farmer's admonition to announce himself before he rode up to the Bascom place. He shouted, "Hello the house."

He saw a movement at a window and had a quick impression of a face, though it was gone so quickly he could not be sure whether it was that of a man or a woman. He shouted again.

The door opened. A tall, raw-boned middle-aged woman stepped outside with a double-barreled shotgun pointed in Rusty's and Andy's general direction. The chill wind toyed with her long, stringy hair that showed no familiarity with comb or brush. "I don't know you," she hollered. "You got no business on this property."

"If this is the Bascom place, we're carryin' a message for Alice."

"You're close enough. I can hear you from where you're at. Deliver your message."

Rusty disliked having to shout, but that shotgun did not invite a closer conversation. "It's kind of private. It's about her mother. Is Alice here?"

Rusty caught a quick glimpse of a girl coming up behind the woman in the doorway. The woman shoved her back inside. "You tell me, and I'll tell her what she needs to know."

"Her mother is worried. Wonders if she's all right."

"Of course she's all right. Why wouldn't she be?"

"Her mother's *not* all right. Alice needs to know that she's awful sick."

Alice pushed her way outside toward Rusty, but the woman grabbed her and pulled her back. Alice struggled to free herself. Momentarily distracted by her effort to control the girl, the woman turned the shotgun away from Rusty. He took the opportunity to spur the dun and close the distance. Without dismounting, he wrenched the weapon from her hand. He pitched it to Andy, who caught it and broke it open to extract the shells.

The woman's face flushed with rage. "Who are you to come bustin' in here like this? You've got no right."

"We just came to see Alice and tell her about her mother."

Alice's eyes said she was afraid of the woman. She pulled away. "What's happened to Mama?"

"She's had a stroke. Paralyzed on one side. It's a struggle for her to talk."

"She was all right when I left."

"It happened afterwards. It'd do her a world of good to see you."

The woman's eyes were the deadly gray of bullet lead. "You got no business goin' anywhere. Your place is here with your husband."

"I want to see my mother."

"And ride off with two strangers? I won't stand for it."

"They're not strangers. Rusty and Andy are friends of my family."

"They're men, and you're a woman. A married woman. It wouldn't be decent."

"Decent?" Growing indignation pushed Alice's fear aside. "You call this family decent? You call robbin' and stealin' decent?"

The woman raised her hand as if to slap Alice. "Shut up, girl. You don't know what you're talkin' about."

"Oh, but I do. You think I don't know where Corey and his brothers have gone?"

Rusty saw murder in the woman's eyes. "You shut your mouth or I'll shut it for you. I told Corey he made a mistake bringin' you here."

Rusty felt a strong apprehension. "Alice, you'd better come with us. I already see that this is no place for you."

She hesitated. "I don't know what Corey might do."

"We'll take you back to the protection of your family. There's nothin' he *can* do."

The woman declared, "The hell there ain't. He'll be comin' after you and draggin' you back by the hair of the head."

The girl wasted no more time considering. She said, "I'll gather my things." She went into the house.

Rusty said, "Andy, go saddle that horse yonder for Alice. I'll keep Mrs. Bascom company."

The woman seethed. Rusty was glad she no longer had the shotgun. She scolded, "It's a mortal sin, comin' between a man and his wife. My son and Alice taken the vows before a minister of the gospel and in the sight of the good Lord Hisself. The Book says what God has joined together . . ."

"You don't talk like somebody who'd know much about the Book."

"I know it says an eye for an eye and a tooth for a tooth. You carry that girl away and I'll see to it that my boys take a lot more than an eye and a tooth."

Rusty saw no point in arguing. He let her continue a malevolent harangue laced with profanities the likes of which he had never heard pass a woman's lips and some he had heard from few men.

Alice brought a cloth bag out of the house. Rusty asked, "Is that all you've got?"

"I didn't come here with much. I haven't picked up anything new except bitter experience."

Mrs. Bascom shook a finger at her. "There'll be hell to pay when the boys fetch you back here. And they will."

Alice murmured, "Hell is all I've had since I came."

"You Jezebel!" The woman slapped Alice so hard that a red splotch arose where the flat of her hand had struck.

Alice made an angry cry and drove her fist into Bessie Bascom's face. The woman rocked back, almost falling.

Rusty watched in pleased surprise. Maybe he had underestimated Alice. He said, "Looks like you're your mother's daughter, after all."

Andy led a brown horse up from the pen, a sidesaddle on its back. He boosted Alice up into place. Mrs. Bascom held one hand to her jaw, her eyes blazing from shock and pain and anger.

Alice said, "I've wanted to hit that woman ever since the day I came here."

Rusty asked, "Why didn't you?"

"She'd have killed me, or made me wish she had."

"Well, she can't do anything to you anymore."

Andy still had the shotgun. He pitched it up on top of the dirt-covered roof, raising a wisp of dust. He said, "I hope the law don't get after us for takin' this horse."

Alice said, "It's the one I came here on. It never belonged to the Bascoms."

Rusty said, "Let's git. I wouldn't put it past that old woman to climb up there after that gun."

They rode at a rapid pace for a mile or so, then slowed. Alice looked back with concern. Rusty said, "She wouldn't chase us afoot, not this far."

Alice was not comforted. "You don't know Bessie Bascom. She's liable to take a broomstick and come flyin' after us."

"How long do you think it'll be before her menfolks come home?"

"Hard to say. They've been gone three days. Corey was talkin' about a nice little Yankee bank over east that he said needed robbin'."

"So that's what they do for a livin', rob banks?"

"Part of it. They burgle stores, steal cattle, horses, whatever comes easy to hand. I'm sure now that's why Corey came to our farm in the first place. He had heard about the Monahan horses. But we took a shine to one another, and he carried me off instead."

"Against your will?"

"Not then. I wanted to come with him. But when I got here I found things weren't like he'd been tellin' me. Nowheres near."

Rusty had noticed a blue mark beneath her left eye. "Corey did that to you, I suppose."

"Not Corey. His mother. She reminds me of the wicked stepmothers I used to read about in fairy tales."

"How long has she been a widow?"

"Several years. From what Corey told me, Old Ansel got

surprised by the state police and tried to put up a fight. After that the Bascoms declared war against all authority. The only thing the boys are scared of is that old woman. Anybody who crosses her is fixin' to bleed some."

She plied Rusty with anxious questions about her mother and others of the family. He knew her concern was genuine.

There's hope for her, after all, he thought. Maybe she's smartened up. Perhaps this bitter experience would bring out the strength and will that was her rightful heritage from Clemmie and Lon Monahan.

They rode by Fort Griffin but did not tarry longer than was necessary to pick up a few supplies. Rusty suspected that pursuit would not be long in coming. Bessie Bascom would insist upon it.

They rode by the saloon where he had stopped for information. The barkeeper stood out in front, puffing smoke from an evil-looking black cigar. His eyes lighted with curiosity as he saw Alice riding with Rusty and Andy. He asked no questions, and Rusty did not pause to offer any answers. But he noted that the man looked hard in the direction from which they had come.

He figures like I do, Rusty thought. They'll be coming after her.

"Let's pick up the pace a little," he said. "We can cover a lot of miles before dark."

Rusty did not ride boldly into the Monahan headquarters. He reasoned that Corey Bascom would expect them to head straight for Alice's home. Though it was unlikely, there was a chance that he and his brothers might have pushed hard and gotten here first.

He watched a while to be sure everything looked normal. He saw Evan Gifford riding a hackamored young horse around and around in a corral. The boy Billy sat on the porch and shouted for Billy to come home. He climbed down reluctantly and trotted toward her.

Rusty eased. "I don't see anything amiss."

"Let's hurry," Alice said. "I want to see Mama."

As they rode in, James Monahan came out of the barn, a bridle in his hand. Seeing Alice, he quickly hung the bridle across the top of a fence, then trotted to meet the three riders. "Alice!" he shouted. "Baby sister!"

He had every right to be angry with her, and some recriminations might come later, but now was not the time. He lifted her down from the saddle and hugged her as if she had come back from the dead.

"Mama is goin' to be tickled to see you. She's liable to get up and come runnin' when you walk in the door."

"How is she?" Alice asked anxiously.

"Fair to middlin'. She'll do better now." He looked up at Rusty and Andy. "Did you have to kill anybody?"

"Not yet."

"Where's Corey?"

Rusty looked behind him. "Back that way, somewhere. We figure he'll be comin' for Alice. We just don't know when."

James gave his sister a searching look. "When he does, will you be wantin' to go with him?"

"I'd rather kill him than go back there."

"We'll try to see that you don't have to do either one." James reached up to shake hands with Rusty, then Andy. "Fellers, I ain't got words enough to thank you."

Rusty said, "It wasn't much trouble to get her away. Keepin' her may be somethin' else."

"We'll keep her. We've fought off rebel hangmen and Comanche Indians and horse thieves. Corey Bascom ought not to be that much of a challenge."

Alice said, "You haven't met the rest of his family. Especially his mother."

James frowned. "I don't see how one old woman could give us much trouble."

Andy said, "You'll think different if you see her. When she dies and goes to hell even the devil is liable to take out a-runnin'."

Geneva saw Alice and hurried down from her house, throwing her arms around her sister. "Thank God you've come back."

"Thank Rusty and Andy. I wouldn't be here if they hadn't come and fetched me."

Geneva turned to express her thanks to Rusty. She held onto his arm long enough to stir old feelings he had hoped he had put behind him. He was almost relieved when Evan came up to join his wife.

Josie stepped out onto the porch in response to the racket. Recognizing Alice, she came running. She embraced her sister with tears in her eyes. "You're the best medicine anybody could've brought for Mama." When she released Alice she hugged Rusty. "And you're the doctor who fetched it." She looked up at the boy. "And you, Andy." She turned back to her sister. "Come on, let's go show you to Mama."

The family trooped into the big house. Andy started to follow, but Rusty raised a hand to stop him. "This is for the family," he said.

Andy nodded, seeing the rightness of it. "But you're one of the family too, just about."

"Not yet, not 'til Josie and me stand up in front of Preacher Webb. Right now there's no tellin' when that is liable to happen."

5

C orey Bascom was in a dark mood as he and three younger brothers approached the long picket house that had been their home since soon after they had left Arkansas just ahead of some angry horsemen. The bank for which he had held considerable hope had been a disappointment. With the muzzle of a pistol in his face, the bank's president had stammered that local farmers had made only a mediocre crop the previous fall and most of their money had already been spent. The county government should have had some funds on deposit, but the outgoing officeholders had absconded with most of the money. "We've got nothing but a toenail hold," he had said, "and hopes for a better year."

Frustrated, Corey had promised to come back in the fall, after harvest. "You'd better have somethin' here worth the takin'. Otherwise you'd better start learnin' how to play a harp."

His brother Lacey then forced the sweating banker to go to his knees and beg for mercy. It was a bluff, but Lacey took pleasure in his ability to frighten people. He especially enjoyed it when he could make them wet themselves, which the banker did. Corey sometimes worried that Lacey would get carried away and really kill someone. He had come close. So far the Bascom brothers' crimes had stopped short of murder. So far.

Before leaving town the brothers had paused to rob a mercantile store but found its till was as poor as the bank's.

Lacey shot out a window glass as they left. "Somethin' for them to remember us by," he had explained. It was an unnecessary gesture. Nobody ever forgot a visit by the Bascoms.

The only bright spot Corey could see in this whole trip was the prospect of getting back to Alice. He had enjoyed women before, usually with payment involved, but this girl had awakened a hunger in him that never remained satisfied for long. She had been shy and uncertain the first few times, and he had gotten a little rough. He had occasionally been rough with other women but considered that to be his right inasmuch as he had bought and paid for them. He suspected this treatment was the reason Alice had become increasingly reluctant about his attentions as the weeks passed. He had tried to be gentler, but he didn't know how.

This trip had kept him away for four days—and four long, lonely nights. He hoped his absence would have made her more receptive. He would keep working on the gentleness thing and see if it helped.

He saw smoke rising from the chimney and realized he was hungry for more than Alice. Though Ma's cooking wouldn't get her a job even in a hole-in-the-wall chili joint, when a man's belly was empty her beans and cornbread were welcome. Nobody ever complained, at least where she might hear. Though her sons were grown, she felt obliged now and again to take a quirt to one or another of them just as she did when they were little. To Ma they would always be "my boys," to be praised highly or punished severely, whichever the situation called for.

Praise came sparingly. She had come near taking a quirt to Corey when he brought Alice home unannounced. In her view he had no right to get married without her approval, especially to a pampered girl who was obviously a misfit, unlikely ever to find a comfortable place in this close-knit family. Bessie Bascom had tried hard to weld her boys into an insular unit, mutually shielding one another from the rest of the world. To her it had always been "us against them." Anyone outside of the family was a potential enemy, not to be trusted.

She always preached that old Ansel Bascom had died because he trusted others too much. Someone had betrayed him to the damnable state police. He had died with a dozen bulletholes draining his life's blood into the dirt street outside of a two-bit bank that had not been worth the gamble in the first place.

"Never take nobody into your confidence outside of family," she had told her boys again and again. That prohibition included Alice, whom she regarded as a potential Jonah, if not a Judas.

Corey had been reluctant about being away from Alice so long, leaving her in Ma's less than gentle hands, but family needs took precedence over his personal desires. He would make up for lost time tonight. In his mind he was already in bed with her.

He noticed that the Monahans' brown horse was not in the corral where he had been kept penned and fed, handy in case Ma needed to saddle him and go somewhere in a hurry. The gate stood open, which struck him as odd.

Bessie Bascom heard her sons' arrival and came striding out from the picket house. Her long steps and grim face told Corey that something had gone awry. He had expected her to raise hell when she found out how little money they had brought home, but it appeared she was not going to wait for the bad news.

She went immediately on the attack, shaking her finger in his face. "I told you that little hussy didn't belong here. Well, the buttermilk has done been spilt now. She's gone."

Corey swallowed hard. She could not have hit him harder if she had struck him with a club. "Gone? Where?"

She touched her fingers to her chin. "See this bruise? She put it there. Hit me with her fist, she did, then rode off with two men bold as brass. And they wasn't even her brothers. Told you she wasn't no good."

Corey did not care about the bruise. He cared about Alice. "What men? Who were they?"

"She said they were friends of her family. I told her it wasn't fitten for a married women to do such a thing. I told her it was agin the Book."

Corey struggled to absorb what his mother was telling him. Damn it all, how could Alice just up and leave like that? She belonged to him. She had no right to do anything or go anywhere without his say-so.

"Did they tell you where they were goin'?"

"Back to her folks, they said. But from what you've told me, that's at least two days' ride. That means two nights, layin' out with two men. It don't take much imagination . . ."

The image was too ugly for him to contemplate. He clenched a fist. "Stop it, Ma. She wouldn't do that."

"She did it with you, didn't she? I've heard the two of you many a night, and I've seen you slip into the barn with her in the daytime when your brothers was out workin', like *you* was supposed to be. She's a tart."

"Did you hear her call them by name?"

"I heard her call the oldest one Rusty. The other one was just a big boy, but I expect he's old enough to know what to do with a woman like her."

Corey tried to remember. Rusty. He had heard the Monahans mention that name often. Rusty Shannon, it was. Had an understanding with Alice's sister Josie, as he recalled. He had been a ranger for a long time. Had a farm way down south somewhere. Alice had told him the Monahans stayed on that farm during part of the war, getting away from Confederate zealots who had killed Lon Monahan and a young son named Billy for Unionist leanings.

Corey tried to push his conflicting emotions aside and think. If Rusty Shannon was going to marry Josie, it seemed unlikely he would do anything untoward with Alice no matter how many nights it took them to get back to the Monahan farm. As for the boy, though, he must be the one they said had lived with the Comanches. A boy brought up on Indian ways was something to worry about. There was no telling what he might do.

He demanded, "How long they been gone?"

"Left about this time yesterday. They got a long start on you if you're figurin' on goin' after them."

"Damn right I'm goin' after her."

Bessie nodded. "I told her you would. Told her you'd come draggin' her back by the hair of the head."

"Them Monahans may not give her up easy."

"You better get her back, or else shoot her. She knows too much about our business. If she talks to the wrong people it's liable to cause us a lot of trouble."

"I couldn't shoot her, Ma."

"I could. Wouldn't bat an eyelash. And you'd better be ready to do the same thing. You don't need her. You can buy plenty of women better than her for the price of whiskey."

Corey felt sick at his stomach. He had not dreamed the girl would go off and leave him. "Love, honor, and obey," the chaplain had said. *Obey* was the word that stuck in Corey's mind. She had pledged to obey him no matter what.

As his wife she was property like his spurs and saddle and guns, like his horses. A man didn't let somebody run off with what belonged to him and not do something about it.

He turned to Lacey. "You boys go rustle us up some fresh horses. Soon as Ma fixes dinner we're goin' after Alice."

Lacey grinned in anticipation. "You goin' to take a quirt to her, Corey? That's what you ought to do, is take a quirt to her." Lacey had been on the receiving end of many a smart whipping from Ma, and deserved most of them. He enjoyed seeing somebody else get it.

Bessie said, "Lacey, you and Newley and little Anse bring up a horse for me, too. I'm goin' along with you boys to make sure you do the right thing."

Corey had rather she didn't go. She was not a good traveler, always finding fault. He said, "It'll be a hard trip, Ma."

"I've made many a hard trip before. I want to see you give little missy what's comin' to her. And if you don't do it, by God I will."

Rusty sat on the front-porch bench with Josie and watched as twilight darkened the fields stretching beyond the barn. She laid her head against his shoulder, her fingers firmly clasping his arm. She said, "I've been thinkin' a lot about that farm of yours."

"Ours," he said.

"I remember how it looked when Mama and us stayed there durin' the war."

"It's nicer now. We've fixed it up a right smart, me and Andy and Len Tanner, when Len would stand hitched long enough to help. You'll like it. I'm anxious to take you down there."

"Maybe it won't be as long as we thought. Mama perked

up a lot when you brought Alice home. She's got a stronger look in her eyes, and I do believe her talkin' has improved."

"But you don't want to leave her just yet?"

"Not 'til she's on her feet. Preacher Webb is hopeful this will all pass and by summer she'll be back to the way she was."

"Summer seems like a long time off. Me and Andy will have to go back home and get the plantin' done before that."

"But you're not in a hurry, are you?" Her tone was hopeful. "You *are* goin' to stay with us a while longer?"

"I'm waitin' to see what Corey Bascom does. James and Evan and Preacher Webb will need all the help they can get if he and his brothers come for Alice."

"You've already done a lot. We're all grateful." She kissed him on the cheek. "How many times have I asked you to marry me?"

He smiled. "Lately, or altogether?"

"I guess it's been shameless of me, but you know I wanted you. I've wanted you ever since I was a girl."

"That was when you first asked me."

"I just didn't want to let you get away. I knew I had to speak up because I could see you and Geneva had eyes for one another."

"That was a long time ago. Things change."

"Not my feelin's about you. I love you."

Rusty tried to say what she had said, but the words would not come as he wanted them to. He said, "I . . . I've got the same feelin's."

Geneva came out of her house across the yard, her small daughter at her side. Josie's gaze followed her sister as she seated herself in a rocker on the porch. The girl climbed up into her lap.

Josie said, "Geneva's still a pretty woman."

"Yes, she is." Rusty felt uneasy, talking about her.

"I remember when everybody figured you-all would get married after the war was over."

"That was before Evan came along."

"Some feelin's never die. I can't help but wonder sometimes if you just think you love me because I remind you of her."

Rusty thought hard about his reply, for he did not want to say anything that would reinforce her doubts. Only to himself would he admit that the same question haunted him from time to time. The answer seemed clear as he sat here beside Josie, feeling the pleasant warmth of her cheek, the arousing pressure of her body leaning against him. But away from her, he might wonder again.

He said, "Geneva's got her own family, and she's happy. Whatever was between us once is long gone."

She pulled away far enough to stare into his eyes. "I wouldn't want to find out someday that I'm a substitute for somebody else. Not even my own sister."

"I can't deny that Geneva was the first woman I ever loved. But you'll be the last."

"Show me," she said, and kissed him again. He felt as if the sun was bearing down upon him with all its noonday heat.

She said, "Hold me, Rusty. Hold me like you'll never let me go."

Evan Gifford had been keeping watch and sounded the alarm. "They're comin'," he said, running up from the corrals. "Looks like a bunch of them."

Rusty had seen them from the porch. He squinted. "I count five. You sure it's the Bascoms?"

"That's Corey in the lead. I never saw the rest of his family."

The only rider Rusty could recognize was Bessie Bascom, sitting straight as a fence post on a sidesaddle. She had a determined posture that reminded him of old Captain August Burmeister of the prewar rangers. Rusty was surprised to see her on a mission like this, but after reflection he decided he could have expected it. He had quickly gained the impression that she was mother, father, and supreme commander of her troop.

James and Preacher Webb and Andy came out of the house. James gave the situation a quick study. "I'll stand here and wait for them. I wish the rest of you would scatter the way we talked about." He glanced back at Webb. "Preacher, it might be better if you stayed in yonder with Mama and the girls."

Webb demurred. "Maybe I can talk common sense to them."

"I doubt as they'd pay attention to it. If you're goin' to stay out here with me you'd best fetch a gun. That way maybe they'll be more willin' to listen to the gospel."

Evan trotted to his own house. Geneva came out onto the porch. He waved her back inside and took a position at the corner. Andy moved out to stand beside the woodpile. Checking the load in his rifle, Rusty walked to the corner of the barn and stepped back out of sight. If the Bascoms rode all the way up to the main house they would be covered from all sides.

From his vantage point Rusty studied the faces. He already knew Bessie Bascom's. Her square jaw was firmly set, her eyes fierce like a hawk's. In comparison, her sons looked almost benign. Rusty decided the one riding closest to Bessie must be Corey, for he appeared a little the oldest and had the

most serious expression. The others, Rusty guessed, had probably come along mostly because Bessie had ordered it. He
doubted the strength of their resolve. Alice was not *their* wife.

One of the Bascoms had an ironic smile as if he found the
situation amusing in some off-center way. Instinct told Rusty
that this one might bear special watching.

James stepped to the edge of the porch, a rifle across his
folded arms. "That's about close enough, Corey."

Rusty had been correct in assuming which was Alice's
husband. Corey stopped and leaned on his saddlehorn. He
said, "You know what we've come for."

"You can't have her."

"She's mine. We had the knot tied by a sure-enough
preacher." He nodded at Preacher Webb, standing beside
James, rifle in his hand. "Wasn't no jackleg, neither. Army
chaplain, he was. Had the papers and everything."

James argued, "Bein' married don't make her your property, to be branded and treated like a mare. She's still a free-
born American, with the rights God gave us all."

"Her place is with me. How I treat her is between me and
her. She ain't your business anymore."

"She's my sister, so she'll always be my business. *Our*
business, this family's."

"She belongs to my family now. And I brought them
along to see that she goes back where she's supposed to be.
There ain't enough of you Monahans to stop us."

James frowned. "Maybe you ain't seen everybody yet.
You're just countin' me and Preacher Webb. You're probably
thinkin' a preacher ain't any hand with a gun. You'd be
wrong. He can knock a coyote's eye out at a hundred yards.
And you know my brother-in-law Evan. That's him over on
the porch of his house, carryin' that shiny new shotgun."

All the Bascoms turned to look as Evan stepped away

from the corner of his house, bringing the shotgun up into both hands.

James went on, "Now, if you'll look out yonder by the woodpile you'll see Andy Pickard. Raised by the Comanches to be mean as hell. Crack shot with pistol or rifle. If he runs out of shells, he can get you with a bow and arrow.

"And finally, I want you to make the acquaintance of Rusty Shannon. That's him beside the barn yonder, with the rifle. A ranger for years. Brought many a bad man and several Indians to heel in his prime, and he still ain't got enough gray hair that you'd notice it much." He shifted his attention back to Corey. "You still got a notion you want to tackle this family?"

Corey sat rigid in the saddle, his face reddening. He said nothing.

Bessie watched him, looked at James a moment, then turned back to her son. "Is that the best you can do, Corey Bascom, sit there and let them run a bluff on us?"

Corey did not look at her. Grittily he said, "You better count the guns, Ma."

She turned in fury toward her other sons. "You-all just goin' to let this stand? They've got a woman in yonder that rightfully belongs to your brother. Carryin' his seed now, more than likely. Ain't there any shame in the lot of you?"

Nobody moved. They could count, even if the old woman couldn't.

She shrilled, "I'm glad your pa ain't here to see his family tuck their tails between their legs like egg-suckin' hounds." She pushed her horse forward. "If you-all won't do anything, I will."

Rusty saw hesitancy in the faces of James and Webb. If one of the Bascom brothers had made this move they would have stopped him. But though they raised their rifles, he knew they would not shoot a woman.

The front door opened, and Alice stepped out holding a pistol in both hands. She aimed it at Bessie and shouted, "They won't shoot you, but I will. I got cause enough."

Rusty's lungs burned. He had been holding his breath. The air was cool, but he sweated as if he were digging post-holes.

Corey said, "Better stop, Ma. She means it." He rode forward far enough to grab her bridle reins. "This ain't worth gettin' killed over."

Bessie's face was flushed with fury. "It ain't her. You can buy better than her in any dancehall from here to Arkansas. But the shame she's brought on this family, that *is* worth killin' for, or even gettin' killed."

"Nothin' is worth gettin' killed for, not money, not pride, not even a woman. Come on, Ma. We're startin' home." He had to pull on the reins and forcibly turn her horse around.

She cursed her son as she had cursed Rusty the day he had taken Alice away.

Not until they were a hundred yards out did Rusty pause to wipe sweat from his hands onto his trousers, then rub a sleeve across his face. Andy came to meet him halfway to the house. He whistled in relief. "The Fort Griffin bartender was right. That old woman is the devil's stepmother."

Rusty nodded. "You're a good judge of character."

The Bascoms stopped a half mile from the Monahan place, all but Corey. He kept riding.

Bessie shouted, "Where you goin'?"

"I'm goin' home, and I'm goin' by myself. You'd bitch at me the whole way, and I don't want to listen to it."

"You come back here. We got talkin' to do."

Corey kept riding. Bessie hollered at him again, more of a screech than a shout. "Damn you, come back here!"

Corey gave no sign that he heard. Bessie turned to her other sons, her mouth puckered with fury, her eyes cutting like a knife. "To hell with him then. It's up to us to do what has to be done."

Lacey was the next oldest to Corey. He said, "We could slip back in there and pick off them Monahans one at a time 'til Alice gives up and comes with us."

"One or two of us might get picked off, too. No, there's just one thing to do. That girl knows a way too much about this family and our business. If she was to testify in a court, ain't no tellin' what the law might do. So if we can't take her home, we have to see that she don't talk to anybody ever again."

Lacey almost grinned. "You mean kill her?" He had had no use for Alice since she had blackened his eye one day when he tried to drag her into the barn.

Bessie said, "This won't set well with Corey. She turned his head real good. But he'll get over it. So we'll find us a place to rest a while. Come full dark, Lacey, me and you will go back and do what Corey didn't have the stomach for."

Little Anse, the youngest, asked, "You ain't takin' me and Newley, Ma?"

"Two's enough. More than that might attract attention."

Newley Bascom had had a crush on Alice ever since Corey had brought her home, but he had had the good judgment not to let Corey see it. He said, "Seems a waste, killin' her. She was a lot of help to you doin' chores around the place. Couldn't we just grab her and drag her away before they can stop us?"

"I know what you want her for, and it ain't the chores. She ain't worth the risk. Come on, boys. Let's find us a good place to wait for dark."

*   *   *

Rusty sat on the porch bench, staring off into the darkness, wondering if the Bascoms were really gone. He was aware that Evan sat on his own porch, doing the same.

Josie came out and seated herself beside him. He asked, "How's Clemmie?"

"A little worried the Bascoms might come back. But I guess everybody's worried some or you wouldn't be sittin' out here watchin'."

"It doesn't seem likely they'd try, but with people like them you never know. Main thing is to keep Alice indoors so they can't grab her and run before we can stop them."

"You figure they really want her that bad?"

"Maybe Corey does, that's hard to say. I feel like the old woman is mostly afraid of what Alice knows and what she might tell the law."

"I don't understand people like that. They could probably make a good livin' for themselves if they'd buckle down to honest work, probably better than they're doin' now with the risks they're takin' and the trouble they cause to others. Maybe it's the times."

"You can't just blame it on the times. We've always had people like them, good times and bad. By what Alice has said, Bessie and her husband brought the boys up to see the rest of the world as their enemy. They always hated the law. Didn't make any difference if it was Union or Confederate. Most people raise their younguns to be whatever *they* were. The Bascoms always had a wide streak of outlaw in their blood. The old man and the old woman taught the boys to make the most of it. Used the whip on them if they showed weakness."

She leaned to him, and he put his arm around her. She said, "We won't have a whip on the place, you and me. We'll raise our children with love, like Mama and Papa did."

Rusty remembered the kindness of Daddy Mike and

Mother Dora, treating him as if he were their own. He said, "I can almost feel sorry for the Bascom boys. They weren't raised up, they were just jerked up. Life's too short to do it that way."

From the direction of the barn he heard the snort of a horse, followed by the sound of hooves. He stood up and grabbed the rifle that leaned against the wall. "Stay put," he told Josie.

He walked partway to the barn, pausing to listen. The horses were quiet again. Hearing no more from them, he returned to the porch. He said, "Just a little bitin' match, I suppose. My dun horse never has quite got used to these here."

Josie motioned for him to sit. "I guess even the horses are a little skittish. They seem to sense when things aren't right."

"What you-all need is a couple of real mean dogs to keep watch on this place."

From inside the house he heard a woman's voice. The words were not clear. Josie said, "That's Mama. I guess she needs me."

Rusty grasped her hand for a moment. "I'm hopin' she won't be needin' you too much longer."

She smiled at him. "Don't go away. I'll be back." She kissed him and went into the house.

Moments later he saw a flash from out in the night and heard the crack of a rifle. A windowpane shattered. Josie gave a cry that made Rusty's blood run cold.

He raised the rifle and sent a wild shot in the direction of the flash he had seen. He heard Alice scream. "Josie! Josie!"

Rusty rushed into the house. In the lamplight he saw Alice holding Josie, trying to keep her from falling. Dropping the rifle, Rusty took three long steps and grabbed Josie. His hand against her back felt warm and sticky.

Josie looked up at him with stricken eyes. She gasped for breath. Rusty lifted her up and carried her into the room she shared with Alice. He placed her gently on her bed and found his hands red with her blood. "Josie!" he cried. "Josie!"

She found breath enough to whisper his name once. The light slowly faded from her eyes. He shook her, trying desperately to find life, but there was none.

He heard Alice sobbing. "Rusty, she's gone."

Rusty felt numb, kneeling beside the bed where Josie lay. He did not look up as James and Andy rushed into the room. Alice leaned her head against the wall and cried softly, her back turned.

James shouted, "Andy, blow out the light."

The room fell into darkness. From the next room Clemmie called in a desperate voice, barely understandable, wanting to know what was happening.

James bent to touch his sister, then drew his hand away. "My God. They've killed her."

Rusty heard Preacher Webb's quiet voice, offering a prayer. Andy said, "I'd best see after Clemmie." A moment later Clemmie gave a cry of anguish. Her voice seemed clearer then. "Help me, Andy. I've got to . . . got to go to my daughter."

Still in shock, Rusty managed to push to his feet and make room for Clemmie. She limped painfully into the room, her arm around Andy's strong shoulder. Webb moved to help her. She fell across Josie and wept.

James trembled, his voice breaking. "For God's sake, how many more? First Pa and Billy. Now my sister."

Rusty heard heavy footsteps on the porch. Evan rushed in. Though the room was dark, he immediately grasped the sense of tragedy. "They shot Alice?"

Andy was the only one who seemed to find voice. "No, they killed Josie."

Evan sighed, "God help her." He bent down for a look, then straightened. "I heard two horses runnin' away right after the shots. We all expected them to come for Alice, but why Josie?"

Andy said, "They were out yonder a ways. They saw Josie in the lamplight and mistook her for Alice."

Rusty had been too stricken to reason it out, but he judged that Andy was probably right.

Alice saw it, too. She turned, both hands to her mouth as she stared at Josie's still form in the dim reflected light from the moon. "Then she died in my place. Why couldn't it have been me instead?" She seemed about to collapse. James and Webb both grabbed her.

Webb said, "Hold tight, Alice. Some things we are not given to understand. It was not your fault."

"But it was." She made a weak effort to break free of them, then fell back against the gaunt Webb. "If I hadn't been addle brained, if I hadn't run off with Corey, . . ."

Webb said, "You couldn't have known it would lead to this. You couldn't have known what Corey was capable of."

Corey. The name ignited a flame in Rusty's brain. Bessie Bascom had vowed that her sons would take an eye for an eye. The flame built into wildfire. He said, "Corey Bascom will die for this."

Webb said, "You're in shock, Rusty. Wait 'til you have time to think straight."

"I'm thinkin' straight enough. Corey Bascom killed her. I'm goin' after him."

Andy moved to his side. "Not by yourself. I'll go with you."

Webb showed no more inclination to argue. He bowed his head, his voice breaking. "I prayed for Clemmie, and I prayed for Alice. I never thought to pray for Josie."

James placed his hands on Rusty's shoulders. "Josie was my sister. I've got as much interest in Corey as you have. But let's don't go off half cocked. We need to see her buried first, with the proper words said over her."

"And give Corey a long start? No, I know where he'll go first. I'm not givin' him time to go any farther."

Evan said, "You and Andy may not be enough against that bunch. I'll be ridin' with you."

Rusty argued, "You've got a wife and family to think about."

"This family took me in when I was near dead and gave me a life again. Josie was my wife's sister, and like my own. I'm goin'."

Rusty felt too beaten down to protest more.

Evan said, "But first I've got to break this to Geneva. She's at the house with the kids, probably worried to death. Tellin' her will be as about as hard a thing as I ever did."

Andy said, "I'll go catch up our horses."

James relighted the lamp and turned to Rusty. "You've got your mind made up to go. Nothin' I can say will stop you?"

Rusty found it painful to speak. "I can't do anything to help Josie now. But I can do somethin' about Corey."

"Then I'll throw some grub together for the three of you. You'll need it."

Corey Bascom expected his mother and brothers to return home soon, but they did not show up until near noon of the day after his arrival. He walked to the barn to meet them as they rode in. They were dusty and weary, but his mother had a stern look of triumph about her.

He asked, "What kept you-all? You ought to've been home yesterday."

She fastened accusing gray eyes on him. "We stayed around and finished the job you ought to've done for your-self."

Alarm quickly stirred in him. "What do you mean?"

"I mean your sweet little Alice girl ain't goin' to do no talkin' to the law or anybody, not ever again."

He felt as if his skin were afire. "What did you do?"

"Me and your brother Lacey went back and took care of her."

Corey's jaw dropped. For a moment he could not move. He could only look at her in disbelief. But he knew he had to believe. He felt a fool for not having realized she might do it. She was fully capable of killing anyone who stood in the way of her and the family. He remembered that years ago she had stalked and shot a witness in Arkansas just before the grand jury was to convene and bring an indictment against old Ansel for stealing hogs.

He trembled. "But I loved her, Ma."

"Love!" She spat the word. "Love is what you give to your family, not to some calf-eyed little tart. All your thinkin' lately has been below your belt or you'd have seen what had to be done and done it yourself."

Grief and fury rose together, swelling and spilling over. "Damn you, Ma!" He drew back his hand and slapped her, hard. He had never done it before.

She recoiled in disbelief, then brought up her quirt. She lashed him about the face and shoulders until he grabbed the limber leather end and jerked it out of her hands. He flung it aside and strode beneath the shed where his saddle sat astraddle a rough log rack.

"Where are you goin'?" she demanded.

"As far from you as I can get." He turned burning eyes toward his brothers. "From all of you." He took a rawhide reata and cast a loop around the neck of his black horse.

She shouted, "Corey Bascom, you turn that horse a-loose. You ain't goin' nowhere."

"How are you goin' to stop me? You goin' to shoot me, too?"

Bessie made a gesture at Lacey. Lacey came at Corey with clenched fists. Corey did not wait for him to strike the first blow. He hit Lacey first in the stomach, taking his brother's breath away, then a second time to the jaw. Lacey went down on his knees and spat blood.

"That's for Alice," Corey said. "I ought to kill you." He saddled his horse and rode away, not once looking back.

Lacey pushed to his feet, rubbing his aching jaw, wiping blood on his sleeve. Newley, who had been morosely silent since the shooting, watched his older brother's departure with concern. "He ain't fixed for travelin', Ma. He didn't take so much as a blanket, and no grub at all."

Newley was a fool, she thought, concerned only about Corey's comfort. Because he, too, had a weakness for Alice, he could not see or chose not to see the threat she had presented to them all. She said, "He'll come draggin' back when he gets hungry enough."

"Maybe not. He looked awful mad."

"Then he'll have to take care of himself. He chose that girl over family." She spread her fingers against a face still reddened and burning from Corey's slap. "First time one of you boys ever raised a hand against me. I don't know why the Lord has let the world come to this. Folks are losin' all sense of right and wrong, the way it looks to me."

*   *   *

Bessie recognized Rusty Shannon and the boy Andy on sight. She did not remember the name of the third rider, though she recalled that he had backed the Monahans when the Bascoms had made their first try at recovering Alice.

She looked around to be sure her three remaining sons were close by and armed. They were. She had put years of training into preparing them for a hostile world, though they had fallen short of her expectations in many particulars. Especially the weak-willed Newley, and now Corey. She stood waiting, the quirt in her hand.

Rusty Shannon had a look of death about him. He reined his dun horse to a stop. The boy Andy pulled a long-legged sorrel in beside Shannon. The third man drew up on the other side, a shotgun across the pommel of his saddle.

Shannon's furious gaze swept over the Bascoms. "Where's Corey?"

Bessie said, "You can see for yourself, he ain't here."

"You say he's not, but you could be lyin'."

Bessie felt a quick indignation. She never lied except when it seemed expedient. This time she didn't have to. "He's gone away. What do you want him for?"

"For killin' a woman."

Bessie felt gratified. She had been a little concerned over the slight possibility that Alice might have survived the bullet, though Bessie had seen the blood gush when it struck her in the back. Lacey's aim had been true.

She asked as innocently as she could, "And what woman would that be?"

"Josie Monahan."

Bessie felt as if a bullet had struck *her*. She struggled to control herself lest Shannon read the dismay she felt. "*Josie* Monahan?"

"That's what I said."

Bessie began to shake in spite of a determined effort to take a grip on her emotions.

Shannon seemed to read her thoughts. "I guess you thought it was Alice. But Corey shot the wrong woman."

Bessie's mind raced as she considered the implications of the mistake. Shannon was clearly in a killing mood. It was a good thing Corey had left. Shannon was prepared to kill him or die in the effort. But there was another complication. Alice might or might not have talked before, but her sister's death would make her eager to tell everything she knew about the Bascoms.

Shannon stared at her with a severity she could not handle. She looked away from his blazing eyes. He said, "I'm askin' you again, where's Corey?"

Newley said, "Corey didn't—"

Ma cut him off short. "Shut your mouth, Newley."

Andy brought his rifle to bear on the brothers, and Evan followed his lead with the shotgun. Andy said, "We'll keep these boys off of your back if you want to go search the house."

Without answering, Shannon rode close to the picket house and dismounted, keeping the horse between himself and the dwelling. Rifle in hand, he walked to the door and kicked it open. He rushed inside.

Bessie said to the other two, "Told him Corey ain't here. He left, and I doubt he's comin' back. Ever."

Andy said, "Won't do him any good. Rusty'll hunt 'til he finds him."

"Shannon ain't a Monahan, and neither are you. What was that Josie woman to you-all?"

"Rusty and her were fixin' to get married."

Bessie had no time or inclination to feel sorry for people outside of her own, but she recognized that this made Shannon a lethal threat. She had seen with Corey how much store a man could place in a woman whether she deserved it or not. The mood he was in, Shannon was as dangerous as a den of rattlesnakes. She hoped neither Lacey nor little Anse was foolish enough to try a move against him, not right now. Shannon could probably kill them both and not lose a minute's sleep over it. She did not have to worry about Newley. At the first shot he would probably turn and run like a dog.

Shannon remounted his dun and returned, his eyes as threatening as before. "Whichaway was he goin' when he left here?"

She said, "You know we wouldn't tell you. Look for yourself. Maybe you can find his tracks." She had little concern on that score. There were so many horse tracks around here that he could have no idea which were left by Corey's mount.

Shannon said, "I'll find him. Consider him dead, because I'll find him no matter how long it takes." He jerked his head at his two companions. They rode away in the general direction of Fort Griffin. That was the course Corey had been taking when she last saw him.

Newley was the first to speak. He had looked relieved when he found out Alice was still alive. "Ma, you let them go on thinkin' Corey done it when it was really Lacey."

She lashed him with the quirt. "Don't ever let me hear you say that again. They'd have killed Lacey as sure as he's standin' there."

"But they'll kill Corey if they find him."

"Corey can take care of himself better than Lacey. He's a better shot. But we stand together, us Bascoms. We take care of one another, and we don't point a finger at any of our own. Now gather close and listen." She looked around as if she thought some outsider might hear. They had let Alice hear too much. "You boys have got a job of work to do. Lacey, you heard what he said. You shot the wrong woman."

Lacey was immediately defensive, raising his hands as if he expected her to take the quirt to him. "You know we couldn't get real close to the house. She looked like Alice, the best I could see in the lamplight."

"You was in too much of a hurry to get it over with and run. So now you got to do it again."

"They'll have that place guarded better than it was before. I might not come back."

"If you don't kill that girl there ain't no use in you comin' back. Time she gets through tellin' what she knows, Texas won't be big enough for any of us."

Newley said, "Let me go do it, Ma."

Her eyes narrowed in suspicion. "I got other work for you and little Anse." She knew about Newley's infatuation. He had no intention of killing Alice. If he had the chance he might carry her away to protect her. "You heard what Shannon said. The only way to keep him from huntin' down your brother is to kill him before he can."

Newley betrayed strong misgivings, as she expected. Little Anse seemed eager. "How do you want us to do it?"

"Any way you can. Trail after him. First chance you get, bushwhack him."

"What about them two that's with him?"

"Maybe they'll split up. Even if not, they don't have the killin' fever in their eyes like Shannon has. Get him and they'll probably give up the chase."

Without enthusiasm Newley said, "We'll do our best."

Newley's best wouldn't be worth a Confederate dollar, but little Anse would give it a good try. "Get at it then. Saddle your horses. I'll be puttin' some grub together."

In the house she paused in her task to look at a tintype on the mantel over the fireplace. It was of old Ansel. She kept it there as a constant inspiration to her sons and a reminder that they had to keep their guard up because the world was against them as it had been against their father.

"You was always weak, Anse," she said. "I've tried to make your boys stronger than you ever was, but I swear sometimes I have to wonder. Maybe they got too much of your blood and not enough of mine."

Rusty stopped once they were out of the Bascoms' sight. "I'm afraid I just made a bad mistake."

Andy said, "I didn't see you do anything wrong."

"I talked when I ought to've stayed quiet. They thought Corey had killed Alice. I let them know otherwise. Now they're liable to make another try for her."

Evan said gravely, "I hadn't thought of it that way."

Andy said, "We'd better get back to Alice before they have a chance."

Rusty nodded. "You two go. The Monahans may need all the help they can get. I'll keep after Corey. Maybe I can catch him before he finds out Alice is still alive."

Andy frowned. "By yourself?"

"He's by *him*self."

"You don't even know which way he went."

"No matter where he intends to go, I'm bettin' he'll stop at Fort Griffin first for supplies. Maybe I can pick up his trail there."

"How long do you figure on bein' gone?"

"Don't look for me 'til you see me comin'."

Andy gave Rusty a worried study. "You ain't slept, hardly, since Josie died. You're worn out. If you do catch up with him, the shape you're in, you may not be a match for him. You could get yourself killed."

"I lost a lot of sleep in my rangerin' days. Never got killed yet." Rusty stepped down and tightened the cinch. Josie's image came to him suddenly and unbidden. He swallowed hard and turned to Evan. "There's somethin' I want you to do."

"Anything you ask."

"It won't be hard." Rusty's eyes burned. He blinked away the tears that came to cool them. "When you get home, you take Geneva in your arms and hold her like you'll never let her go."

He could hardly expect Corey Bascom to be waiting for him on the street in Griffin Town, but he watched closely just the same. He saw everything that moved. He rode up to the saloon where he had stopped the time he had asked directions to the Bascom place. He found the same dour bartender wiping dust from glasses and placing them on a shelf behind the bar.

The bartender gave him a critical study. "I know you, but you look different."

"I'm huntin' for Corey Bascom."

"I told you the last time where he lives."

"He left there. I thought he might've come this way."

The bartender grunted thoughtfully and went back to dusting glasses. "Any special reason you're lookin' for him?"

"He killed a woman."

The barman stopped what he was doing and studied Rusty with a more critical eye. "*Your* woman?"

"She was."

The man turned to retrieve a bottle from a shelf. He poured a glassful and set it in front of Rusty. "The look on your face tells me you need a drink."

"What I need, I won't find in that bottle."

"But it might help. Drink it."

Rusty took the contents of the glass in two swallows. The initial burn was followed by a healing glow.

The bartender said, "I don't ordinarily mix myself in other people's problems, and I sure don't go around givin' out information on other people's business. But I reckon this case justifies an exception. Corey was in here late yesterday. Bought supplies at a store down the street, then he stopped in here and got him two bottles of whiskey. Said he needed them for the road. Sounded like it was goin' to be a long one."

"Do you know which way he went after he left here?"

"No, swear to God I don't. I never watched him. There's lots of trails out of here. He could've gone south toward the Conchos and Mexico. Could've gone east, toward Arkansas, or even north, toward the Indian nations. There ain't no tellin'. With all the travelers who come and go, I doubt anybody paid him much mind."

The barman poured another drink. "Down this one. For what you been through, you ain't hardly started."

Rusty hesitated, then tipped the glass.

The barman said, "Couldn't nobody blame you if you went and got yourself staggerin' drunk."

"But then I couldn't do what I came for." Rusty paid him for the drinks. "Do you know what kind of horse he was ridin'?"

"It was a black one. That's all I can tell you."

"Thanks for the help."

He went down the street to the general store. The clerk, like the bartender, was meticulous about not minding other people's business. He was evasive until Rusty told him he knew Corey had bought supplies. He admitted, "Yeah, I sold him some stuff . . . coffee, bacon, salt, cartridges, and a wool blanket. I took it he was figurin' on a long trip, but I didn't ask any questions and he didn't offer any information."

"Did you see which direction he went leavin' town?"

"With customers like the Bascoms I make it a point not

to see anything they do after they walk out this door. For all I know, he just evaporated."

Rusty recognized the futility of further questions. He walked back out to his horse. He rode around the tall hill on which the army post stood and hit the military road that led southward toward distant Fort Concho. Fresh wagon tracks covered any trail Corey might have made, if he had even ridden this way. Rusty swung back to the Clear Fork and looked at the wagon road that led eastward. It had the same abundance of fresh tracks as the other. The north road toward Forts Richardson and Sill would be no different.

He came upon a pair of heavily laden freight wagons creaking their way down from the north, the hubs badly in need of a greasing. He asked the first teamster if he had come upon anybody riding a black horse. The teamster considered, then said, "A troop of them dark-complected cavalry soldiers is all. Talked like they was lookin' for Indians, but I suspect they wasn't lookin' very hard."

Rusty scouted around until dark but knew his search for tracks was futile. Corey could have put on wings and flown away for all the trace that could be found now. He returned to the saloon, weary and sick at heart.

The bartender knew by the look on his face. "I told you. You ready for another drink?"

Rusty placed two coins on the bar. "A whole bottle."

He rode along the Clear Fork a while until full dark caught him. He unsaddled the dun, staked him on a long rope, then considered fixing a little supper. He had not eaten anything today. He built a fire but decided he was too weary to cook any of the bacon he carried. He opened the bottle and took a couple of long drinks.

He stared into the flames, feeding in dead wood to keep the fire going. The need for sleep weighted his eyelids and the whiskey churned his empty stomach, but he feared the dreams that might assault him. He concentrated on the flames. They went in and out of focus as he turned to the bottle from time to time. An old arrow wound in his leg began to ache. It often did when he was tired.

He kept seeing Josie's face in the flickering coals. He imagined Josie's voice, assuring him they would not have to wait much longer. He dwelled at length on the plans they had made for a long life together. Gone. Torn away from him in an instant.

After a time, from grief and sleepiness and the whiskey, he became confused. Was it Josie's face he saw, or Geneva's? Somehow they started looking alike.

He had loved two women, and he had lost them both.

Sleep overwhelmed him. He sprawled on the ground and fell away into a troubled darkness.

The bottle tipped over. The whiskey trickled out and soaked into the dry earth.

He boiled a can of coffee and forced himself to broil some bacon on a stick for his breakfast. At least the Clear Fork's water was good. A lot of water in the rolling plains was barely fit to drink. He felt better rested, but his head hurt from the whiskey. He wondered at the weakness that had allowed him to drink it. Normally he seldom drank, and on the rare occasions that he did it was more for sociability than for enjoyment.

Josie's image was much on his mind, and he was less alert than he should have been. At mid-morning he became aware that two riders had fallen in three or four hundred yards behind him. He gave them little thought at first because the trail showed signs of frequent travel. But after a time he noticed that when he slowed, they slowed. They seemed deliberately trying not to catch up to him. He sensed with rising alarm that they were waiting and watching for the right place to overtake and trap him.

He wondered who they might be. He considered the possibility that Corey had doubled back to the family place and brought one of his brothers to help.

Under other circumstances Rusty would be content simply to elude those who followed him. The thought that one might be Corey made this situation different. He began looking for a chance to swap places with his pursuers, to employ a double-back trick Indians sometimes used against those who would trail them. Corey might be too shrewd to fall for it, but the chance was worth taking. All Rusty wanted was to get close enough to place Corey in his sights.

He edged into the timber that lined the creek, trusting that it would hide him from the two riders' view. After a couple of hundred yards he crossed the creek and rode back in the opposite direction. He hid himself in heavy foliage and dismounted, drawing his rifle from its scabbard. He placed his hand on the dun's nostrils to prevent it from nickering at the other horses should it feel moved to do so. The dun was not particularly sociable with its own kind.

Through the heavy leaves he watched the two men on the other side of the creek, one leaning from the saddle to observe Rusty's tracks.

He felt a sharp disappointment as the pair came into clear view. Neither was Corey. But they were Bascoms, a couple of Corey's brothers. When they rode past him, he remounted and brought the rifle up high enough that he could place the stock against his shoulder in an instant. He put the dun across the creek and closed the distance. The murmur of the creek masked the sound of his horse's hooves.

He ordered, "Turn around and raise your hands."

The voice startled the two. One of the brothers complied, carefully reining his horse about, then lifting his arms. The younger hesitated.

Rusty shouted, "I won't say it again."

The youngster made a grab at the pistol on his hip, at the same time jerking on the reins, trying to turn his horse around to give him a clear shot. Rusty did not allow him time to complete the move. He fired the rifle. Dust puffed from little Anse's shirt. The impact drove him backward as the horse took fright and jumped to one side. Anse tumbled from the saddle. The horse turned and ran a short distance before the dangling reins became entangled in the underbrush.

The younger brother lay in an awkward heap, just as he had landed. He hardly quivered. Newley Bascom's face seemed drained of blood. He trembled.

"Please, Shannon, don't shoot."

"I won't unless you give me reason. Fish your six-shooter out of the holster and pitch it into the creek."

Newley complied.

Rusty said, "Now the rifle under your leg." Newley tossed it away, too. It made a splash and quickly sank to the bottom.

Rusty demanded, "Who sent you-all after me? Was it Corey?"

Newley fought to keep his frightened voice under some measure of control. "We ain't seen Corey since he left home. It was Ma sent us."

That did not surprise Rusty. "Corey hasn't been back? You're not lyin' to me?"

"I wouldn't lie, not when you got that rifle in my face. And my baby brother layin' there on the ground."

"There was four of you brothers. Where's the other one at?"

Newley was reluctant but finally replied, "Ma sent Lacey out to do another job."

Rusty knew what that would be: to finish Alice. "All right, get down real careful and go fetch your brother's horse."

Newley freed the bridle reins and led little Anse's mount back. Rusty dismounted and picked up Anse's pistol. He started to pitch it into the creek to join Newley's but reconsidered and shoved it into his waistband. An extra weapon might come in handy.

"Put your brother's body up on his saddle. Tie his hands and feet so he won't slide off."

Tears streamed down Newley's face. In a breaking voice he said, "I don't know how I'm goin' to tell Ma about this. She's goin' to take it mighty hard."

Remembering the woman's ruthless nature, Rusty could muster no sympathy. "Tell her it's her own fault, sendin' you-all out to do a dirty job."

Only as he watched Newley lead away the horse with his brother's body tied on it did Rusty succumb to any sense of remorse, and that only because of little Anse's youth. The boy was a member of an outlaw family. Even with the best of luck he had probably been fated to an early death by bullet or perhaps by hanging. It was likely that Bessie Bascom would live to mourn all her sons unless her machinations somehow resulted in her own death beforehand.

He considered what Newley had said about the third brother, Lacey, being sent to kill Alice. That came as no surprise; Rusty had expected another try. He had warned Andy and Evan to keep a close watch. Now he began to reassess his own mission, the search for Corey Bascom. This endless riding was getting him nowhere. He might travel a thousand miles and get no nearer to Corey than he already was. Even if he found Corey and killed him, that would do nothing for

Josie except avenge her death. The best thing he could do for Josie at this point would be to help keep her younger sister alive.

He decided to return to the Monahan place. He would not give up his search for Corey, but he would reluctantly defer it for a while. Vengeance would have to wait.

He approached the farm, his shoulders hunched, his body so tired he held himself in the saddle by force of will. The dun horse seemed to falter in its step. It needed long rest and many generous helpings of grain.

James Monahan walked out from the barn. "My God, Rusty, is that you? You look like hell."

Rusty rubbed a hand over his unshaven face. "I've been through hell and out the far side. I'd swear I've ridden this poor horse a thousand miles."

"He shows it. Find any sign of Corey?"

"Not one. He could be in Mexico or Colorado or California for all I found out. How are things here?"

"Grim."

"Is Alice all right?"

"She's feelin' low. Blames herself. Still wishes it had been her instead of Josie."

So do I, Rusty thought with a rush of bitterness, then felt guilty for it. "The Bascoms made any more effort to get her?"

"One. Somebody tried to sneak up to the house a couple nights ago. Andy challenged him with a shotgun. Whoever it was, he turned and ran. Andy gave him a blast and heard him holler."

"All the Bascoms except Corey know Alice is alive. Far as I can tell, though, he still thinks she's dead." Rusty told about his encounter with the two younger Bascom brothers.

James said, "Maybe losin' that boy will convince the old

woman to take what's left of her family and leave the country."

"You ever see a hurt snake get so mad it bites itself? She'll probably be meaner than ever, and more determined. All the way back, I've been thinkin' we need to get Alice away from here."

"Where could she go that they wouldn't find her?"

"My old friend Tom Blessing has a wife who's ailin'. He's been wishin' he could find a woman to help take care of her 'til she's back on her feet. It's a long ways down there. The Bascoms would have no idea how to find her."

"Mama's still in bad shape. I don't know as Alice would want to leave her."

"Clemmie's lost one daughter. What would come of her if she lost another?"

James mulled that over. "Then we'll send Alice away with you whether she wants to go or not."

"Me and Andy can take her out of here after good dark. Even if the Bascoms find out she's gone, they won't have any idea where she went."

"Don't you think you need to rest a day or two first?"

"We don't know how much rest the Bascoms are takin'. I can rest after I get home."

Alice was strongly opposed to leaving, as Rusty had expected her to be. But even Clemmie urged her to go. In a strained but determined voice Clemmie told her, "I don't figure on stayin' in this bed forever. I'll still have Warren and Geneva and James. They'll see after me. You go and see after yourself."

Alice gave in. Clemmie beckoned Rusty to her side and took his hand. Her grip was weak. This woman had been heart and soul of the Monahan family. He hated to leave her now when she was ill.

She said, "I know you're hurtin'. We're all hurtin'. But I've been there before. It passes, with time."

Rusty's eyes burned. "I hope so, because it sure hurts right now. You-all are the nearest thing to family that I've had since my folks died."

"You'll always be family to us."

Preacher Webb walked with him up to the little Monahan cemetery. A bare new mound had appeared beside the grassed-over plots where Lon Monahan and his son Billy had been buried years before.

He felt Webb's comforting arm on his shoulder. As far back as he could remember, Preacher Webb had been around to offer spiritual strength when he needed it.

Webb said, "She's not really here, you know. She's gone on to a better world."

Rusty took no comfort in the words. "I wanted her here, in *this* world. If your God is so merciful, why does He let things like this happen?"

"People have asked that ever since time began. I don't know the answer to it. I just know there is sunlight and there is dark. There is good and there is evil. It's up to those of good heart to try and end the evil."

"I'll put an end to Corey Bascom if I ever find him. And I'll find him!"

"The Bascoms have taken away somethin' precious to you, but don't let them take away your soul. You don't stop evil by doin' more evil. Whatever you do, do it within the law."

"It's been a long time since we've had real law in Texas."

"But we'll have it again. Be a part of it, like you used to be."

"Like in the rangers?"

"Like in the rangers. I hear they're comin' back."

7

B essie Bascom had been preparing to milk the cow when she first saw the oncoming rider. So long as she was outdoors, she missed very little that moved. She had watched the horseman now for half an hour, hoping he would prove to be Corey. Her eldest was the only one she felt was capable of lifting the darkness that had befallen the Bascoms. Sure, he was the one who had brought it upon them in the first place, fetching that girl Alice here, making her privy to the family's doings. And sure, he had taken it badly when he thought his brother Lacey had killed her. But she felt he would come around to his mother's way of thinking eventually. He was family. When the chips were down, the Bascoms always pulled together. Her sons had rallied like troopers when old Anse died at the hands of the state police. They would rally now.

She knew the rider was one of her sons. She knew them by the way they sat in the saddle, the same way their father had done before them. In time she became aware that he led another horse. It appeared to be carrying a pack. That was strange. She had not sent the boys for supplies. She had ordered Newley and little Anse out to trail the man named

Shannon. She had dispatched Lacey to finish the job he had botched the first time, killing Josie. He had returned in pain, barely able to sit in the saddle. She had spent more than an hour digging buckshot out of his backside while he howled like a hurt dog.

Not until the horseman was within a hundred yards did she recognize him as Newley. Her heart began to race as she realized that what she had thought was a pack was in reality a body tied across a saddle. She went running, screaming. "Little Anse, my baby. Oh Lord God, my baby."

The horses spooked at the wailing and the flare of Bessie's skirts. Newley had to hold tightly to the reins.

Bessie threw her arms over the body and kissed the still, cold face. She wept bitter tears while Newley dismounted and stood awkwardly, his head down. He rubbed his sleeve over his face.

Bessie turned on him. Accusation overrode the grief in her eyes. "What happened?"

Newley took a step backward in fear of her. "Wasn't no fault of mine, Ma. He oughtn't to've tried to draw on that Shannon. It was over before I could move."

"I'm guessin' you never moved at all. I'm guessin' you just sat there."

"Wasn't nothin' I could do. Shannon come up from behind. He had the drop on us before we even seen him."

"But your little brother drawed on him just the same?"

"He oughtn't to've."

"Why didn't you draw, too? You could at least have shot Shannon while he was busy shootin' your baby brother."

"He'd have shot me, too. You got no idee how fast he is."

"Maybe it would've been better. You'd've been spared the shame of bringin' this innocent baby boy back here dead while you don't appear to have a scratch on you."

Newley turned away, tears running down his cheeks. "I'm sorry, Ma. I done the best I know how."

"I ought to take a quirt to you, but it wouldn't do no good. Wouldn't make you no smarter, nor braver. Wouldn't bring little Anse back to us. I'm just glad old Anse ain't here to see this. One son dead. One son gone off to God knows where. Two other sons dumber than dirt, can't even take care of a simple job. It's a mean world we've come to."

Newley drew himself up with what pride he could muster. "I'll go find that Shannon, and I'll kill him."

Bessie was gratified that Newley had that much pride, but she knew pride would soon give way to fear. "No, we'll give your brother a decent buryin' first. Then I'll want you to go find Corey and bring him back here."

"Ain't no tellin' where he's at."

"He's somewhere. You'll find him."

"What's Lacey goin' to do?"

"When he's able to ride again I'll send him back to watch for another chance at that girl. It's your job to find Corey before Shannon does."

Newley brought himself to look at his mother for only a moment, then he cut his eyes away. "Do we *have* to kill Alice?"

"Get them silly romantic notions out of your mind. You know it's her that's at the root of all our trouble. It's like she's cast a witch's spell over this family. Trouble will keep throwin' its shadow over our door 'til we've got rid of her.

"Now go carry your baby brother into the house. I'll be washin' him while you and Lacey dig a proper grave. We'll send him to glory in style. And when the time comes, we'll send Shannon to hell."

*   *   *

Looking back in the rosy glow of sunup, Rusty saw that the wagon wheels were cutting deep tracks through the winter-brittle grass. The days were warming, but the nights still brought chill enough to delay the green-up. Riding Long Red alongside the wagon, Andy looked back with concern. "Even a blind Apache could follow our trail."

His Comanche upbringing had given him a dim view of the Apache. The Comanche considered himself superior to all other beings, especially the Apache.

Alice sat on the wagon seat beside Rusty. He had not spoken to her and had hardly looked at her since they'd left the Monahan farm about midnight. Dense clouds had hidden the moon. He had counted on darkness to hide their leaving.

He said, "There's other tracks besides ours, freight wagons and such."

He had left his weary dun horse at the Monahans', trading for a bay to take its place. It was tied to the rear of the wagon.

James had said of the horse, "He's a good one. Come to a chase, he's about as fast as anything I've rode in a long time. Got some wild spirit left, though, so you have to stay awake and watch him. Now and then he'll bog his head and pitch for no cause except he wants to throw you off. You'll like him."

Andy kept looking at the back trail, not convinced that no one was following. He glanced at Alice from time to time, his face troubled. Out of her hearing, he had expressed to Rusty his concern that people might question the propriety of her making this long trip with two men. Rusty had said, "You can be her chaperon."

Andy's Indian upbringing had subjected him to a lot of speculative gossip over the years. "I don't care when it's just me," he had said. "I'm used to it. But folks will mean-talk a woman whether she deserves it or not."

"Maybe she does deserve a little of it." Rusty immediately regretted what he said and was glad nobody except Andy had heard. Andy had too much honor to repeat it.

Alice looked back from time to time. "It's goin' to be tough, not knowin' how Mama is gettin' along."

Rusty had fought against his resentment toward Alice and tried to keep it out of his voice. "Your mother isn't much bigger than a banty hen, but she's got a will like iron. If she makes up her mind to get on her feet, that bed won't hold her for long."

He could see some of Clemmie's strength in Alice, though she still had a young woman's voice. He wished she had employed that will against Corey's entreaties and had not gone off with him in the first place.

Perhaps caring for Mrs. Blessing would help keep Alice's mind off of her mother. He remembered a strong nurturing instinct in Clemmie and her two oldest daughters. Geneva had stayed close by Rusty years ago while he recovered from a bad arrow wound incurred in ranger service. Later, Josie had nursed him after he took a bullet in the back. He hoped Alice possessed the same instincts, though he had seen nothing to convince him that she did.

They took a long noon rest. Rusty slept despite pain from the old wound. He was still weary after his long search for Corey Bascom. He suspected that Andy did not even try to sleep, watching their trail for sign of pursuit. Moving on, Rusty felt better for having had a little rest. Andy's shoulders drooped a little.

Rusty said, "You ought to've slept while you had a chance."

Andy's answer was curt. "Somebody had to watch."

"They don't even know we're gone."

"Maybe not. And maybe they do. That old woman has

got an evil spirit sittin' on her shoulder. For all we know, it's tellin' her everything."

Rusty frowned. He had tried for years to turn Andy away from notions left over from his life with the Indians. They still cropped out from time to time. "What does an evil spirit look like?"

"It can look like anything. Most of the time you can't see it, but you can feel that it's there. Did you hear the owl last night, just before we left?"

"There's been owls around the Monahan place for years."

"Not like that one."

One owl had always sounded like another to Rusty, but he knew owls were a symbol of ill fortune, sometimes death, to the Comanche people.

Andy said, "For all we know, that owl could've been the old woman herself, watchin' us. There's some people can do that, you know, turn themselves into somethin' else. I knew a medicine man once who could turn himself into a wolf."

"Did you see him do it?"

"No, but I talked to people who said they saw him go into a cave, and a wolf came out. He could howl like one. I've heard him start, and wolves would answer him."

"That doesn't prove anything. I've known a few white people who could do that. It helped them hunt down wolves."

Andy said nothing more for a while, his feelings wounded a little. Argument over such matters was pointless. Neither he nor Rusty would change his mind.

Alice had held quiet for the most part. Finally she said, "This far south, do we need to worry about Indians?"

Rusty suspected Andy's talk about spirits had prompted her to wonder. "You never stop watchin' for Indians, wherever you are. But the odds are that most of them are still

in winter camp north of us. The way the country is settlin'
up, they're bein' crowded off of a lot of their old stompin'
grounds."

Andy broke his silence. "And losin' their buffalo to the
hide hunters. Damn shame, people killin' buffalo for the skin
and leavin' the meat to rot. What do they expect the Indian
to do?"

Rusty said, "I expect most would like to see the Indians
all evaporate, like a puddle of water in the sunshine."

Andy's voice became strident. "Well, they won't. They'll
take just so much crowdin', then they'll raise up and fight."
He sounded as if he wished he could join them. Over the
years there had been times when Rusty feared he might do
just that. But Andy had left enemies as well as friends in the
Comanche camps. Going back would be fraught with risk.

Alice took in a sharp breath and pointed. "If there aren't
any Indians around here, what's that yonder?"

Rusty saw a dozen horsemen moving toward them out of
the west. He knew at a glance that they were Indians.

Andy said, "Next time I talk to you about owls, maybe
you'll listen."

Rusty did not waste time with argument or denial. He
said, "We'll head for that buffalo wallow yonder. Maybe they
haven't seen us."

Andy said, "They probably saw us before we saw them.
Anyway, that hole's not deep enough to hide us."

It would give them a better defensive position, however,
if this meeting turned into a fight. Sometimes a good position
and a show of weapons would turn away a hunting party
that was out mainly for meat and not for scalps. A war party
would be something else.

He took the wagon into the dry-bottomed wallow and
stopped. "Help Alice down," he told Andy. "She's too good

a target up on this wagon." When Andy had done that, Rusty said, "Look in my saddlebag. You'll find that Bascom boy's pistol. Give it to her."

Worriedly Andy said, "We don't want to kill any of them unless we're forced to. Some might be friends of mine."

"Then they'd better act friendly."

Alice checked the pistol's load. She appeared more determined than frightened. Rusty asked her, "You sure you know how to shoot that thing?"

"Mama taught me to shoot before she taught me how to sew. Said every country girl ought to be able to use a gun because there wouldn't always be a man around to do it for her."

The wallow was not deep enough to hide even the wagon, but its shallow bank would provide cover for a person lying on his stomach and sighting a rifle up over the edge. Rusty said, "Andy, your eyes are sharper than mine. Are they wearin' any paint?"

Andy observed them a minute before answering. They had stopped a hundred yards out and seemed to be considering their options. "I don't see any. Probably just out huntin'."

"But they wouldn't pass up three scalps and four horses if they thought they would come easy."

Andy's expression indicated he didn't like what he saw. "I'm afraid that's just what they're thinkin'. They act like they're fixin' to give us a try." He handed Rusty his rifle. "I'm kin, of sorts. I'm goin' out and see if they'll parley."

Rusty thrust the rifle back at him. "You don't look like anybody that's kin to them. They're liable to kill you before you can tell them you're a cousin."

Andy refused the weapon. "If they're bound to kill me they'll do it anyway. Three of us ain't got a chance against them all." He climbed up out of the wallow and paused to add, "Told you about that damned owl."

He moved toward the Indians, his hands in the air to show he was unarmed. Rusty held his breath. An old image flashed into his mind: the sight of Andy's dead mother many years ago, butchered in the cruelest manner. He made up his mind he would not let that happen to Alice. If he saw they were about to be overrun, he would put a bullet through her head.

Some of the Comanches raised their bows. At least three had rifles or shotguns. Andy began making sign talk, and Rusty caught remnants of his words as he spoke. The Indians surrounded Andy. For a few moments he was out of sight. Rusty checked his rifle again. It felt slick against his sweating hands.

Alice said nothing. She held the pistol ready, the hammer cocked back. Her jaw was set like Clemmie Monahan's.

Andy emerged from the circle of Indians. He walked slowly and confidently toward the wallow. The Indians followed at a respectful distance, offering no overt threat. Andy signaled from fifty yards that everything was all right and motioned for Rusty and Alice to lower their guns. Rusty did, but not by much.

Andy stopped at the edge of the wallow. "Told you it was better to talk than to fight. Turned out I know a couple of them. We used to play at stealin' horses together."

"They're past the age for play-actin'. They look like they mean business."

"They're huntin' for buffalo. First thing they wanted to know was if we are, too. They thought maybe the wagon was for haulin' hides. Seems like there's a lot of white hunters workin' the buffalo range north of here. It's got the People pretty mad."

"Tell them those hunters are mostly out of Kansas. We're Texans."

"They don't like Texans, either."

Two of the Comanches ventured up close enough to look down into the wallow.

Rusty warned, "Don't let them see fear, Alice. If they've got mischief on their minds it'll encourage them."

The pair focused their attention on her. She still held the pistol cocked and ready, though she diverted the muzzle a little to one side. She looked cocked and ready, too, if they made any direct move toward her.

Andy said, "It's all right, Alice. It's not often they see a white woman up close."

She said nothing. Rusty suspected she knew her voice would be shaky, and she did not want to reveal that she was frightened.

Andy said, "They asked for tobacco, but I told them we don't have any. They'd settle for some sugar. You don't find much of that in a Comanche camp."

Geneva had bagged sugar and coffee and salt for use on the trip to the Colorado River. Rusty said, "Give them the sugar, Alice. We can do without it." He liked sugar in his coffee when he could get it, but more often than not he had to drink it straight. He did not consider that a hardship. Through the war years he had gone for long stretches without even coffee.

Some sugar granules clung to the outside of the bag. An Indian wet his finger, ran it through the sugar, then touched the finger to his tongue. He broke into a broad grin.

Andy said, "Alice, you've made a friend for life."

The one holding the bag spoke a couple of words that Rusty assumed were the equivalent of "thank you," then reined his horse around and set off toward the rest of the party in a long trot. His companion followed but did not catch up to him.

Alice finally found voice. "Are they goin' to eat it right out of the sack?"

Andy said, "Sure. Hasn't everybody done that?"

When Andy had first returned from the Comanches he gorged himself on hog lard and raw sugar. The lard evidently made up for some nutritional deficiency. Sugar had been a new and exciting experience. At the time it was still scarce even in the Texas settlements.

Andy went on, "They don't seem as fearsome when you just see one or two up close, do they?"

Alice looked at him askance. "They look scary enough for me."

"You have to get used to them, is all. They're people just like everybody else, except a little different."

Rusty burned to be on his way, but he was hesitant about leaving the dubious shelter of the buffalo wallow until the Indians were out of sight in a direction other than south. He watched them pass the sugar sack around. Apparently there was some dissatisfaction over the fairness of the division, for the last man angrily threw the empty sack at the one who had offered it to him.

Andy said, "See what I told you? They're just like everybody else."

Not until the Indians were out of sight did Rusty motion for Andy to help Alice back onto the wagon. "They may be friends of yours, Andy, but we're travelin' 'til after dark tonight."

Andy said, "I'd worry a lot more about them Bascoms than about my Comanche kinfolks. Them Bascoms ain't civilized."

They paused briefly at the grave of Andy's mother. The

marker was down again, buffalo tracks all around it. Even if Andy carried out his vow to build a fence around the site, Rusty knew the buffalo would not respect the fence any more than they respected the marker. They would rub their itchy hides against it until they knocked it down. If the Kansas hunters kept moving south, that problem would be eliminated over time. He would not mention that to Andy, however. It would just raise the young man's hackles.

Alice knew Andy's background, but she had never been here before. Seeing the grave brought the old tragedy to a reality she had not quite grasped earlier. She offered a prayer, spoken so softly that Rusty could not hear most of it. She asked Andy, "Do you remember any of what happened here?"

"A little." He grimaced. "A little too much."

She reached out and touched his arm, then drew her hand away.

Rusty felt impatient. "We can still make some distance before dark." They moved on.

They reached the farm just at sunset. Rusty said, "It's too late to go on to Tom's tonight."

Alice surveyed the place with keen interest. "You've built it up some since we stayed here durin' the war. Broke out some more land and built another cabin."

Rusty said, "The new cabin is Andy's. I thought he ought to have a house of his own when Josie and me . . ." He did not finish. He cleared his throat. "Wonder if Len Tanner is around. Be like him to've gone off on another *pasear*."

Tanner appeared on the dog run of the larger cabin, stretching his long frame as if he had been napping. "Howdy. You-all are just in time for supper. All you've got to do is fix it."

The garden showed signs of fresh work. Evidently Tanner had kept himself at least moderately busy. He had no real obligation to do so because he was not a hired hand. He was not drawing wages. He simply had a home here whenever he wanted it, and in return he contributed a share of the work when he was around. He was free to tie his meager belongings behind his saddle and ride off at any time he felt like it, which was fairly often.

Sight of Tanner momentarily lifted the melancholy that had fallen upon Rusty. "Len, I was afraid you'd be off to hell and gone again."

"I would've been if you hadn't got home when you did."

"Where to this time? Thought you'd seen all you wanted of your kinfolks."

"I have. But now I got other things to do." Tanner looked up in surprise at the girl on the wagon seat. "Alice? Is that you?"

"It's me." She gave him a tentative smile. He had flirted with her and her sisters in the past but had shied away from anything more serious than a stolen kiss, which once had earned him a quick slap in the face.

He said, "You're gettin' to where you look more like your sisters every time I see you. How're they gettin' along?"

Rusty had to look away. Andy said quickly, "Josie's dead. I'll tell you about it later."

Tanner's jolly mood was gone. He stared as if struck by a club. "Damn but I'm sorry." He reached to help Alice down from the wagon.

Andy asked, "You seen any strangers around here?"

Tanner set Alice on the ground. "Gettin' to be a lot of traffic around this place. Sometimes two or three people a day goin' one direction or another. Country's settlin' up to where it don't hardly seem the same anymore."

Andy persisted, "These people would likely have asked about Rusty or Alice."

Tanner shook his head. "Nary a soul."

Rusty said, "The Bascoms couldn't have gotten here ahead of us even if they'd known where we were goin'. For all they know we headed north for Colorado, or east for Arkansas, . . . if they've even found out we're gone."

Andy said stubbornly, "That old woman knows."

Tanner looked from one to another, confused but content to wait until someone saw fit to explain.

Rusty asked, "Know anything about Tom Blessing's wife?"

Tanner said, "She's still poorly. Shanty was here yesterday, helped me plant some tomatoes and okry. He'd been by to see the Blessings a couple of days ago."

Shanty was a former slave. His little place lay between Rusty's farm and the Blessings'.

Rusty said, "I brought Alice to stay with Mrs. Blessing and try to help get her back on her feet."

Tanner nodded his approval. "She's a grand old lady. She'll perk up just from havin' the company."

Rusty knew that Tanner had been smitten by Alice for a long time. He was not sure about Andy. He was aware that Andy had been watching women. For a while he had become somewhat attached to a neighbor girl named Bethel Brackett. That involvement seemed to have faded, probably because of his antipathy for her brother Farley.

Rusty told Alice she could have the bedroom side of the double cabin. As she went inside Tanner said, "I told you to tell her hello for me. I didn't mean you had to bring her all the way here."

Rusty told him as much as he figured Tanner needed to know for the time being. Tanner nodded gravely. "I *am* mighty sorry about Josie. If any of them Bascoms come pokin' around here lookin' for Alice, I'll blow a hole in them you could put a wagon through."

Andy said, "Just a little hole would be enough, long as it's in a place to do the most good."

A hundred times Rusty had imagined himself confronting Corey Bascom. He thought he could probably shoot him in the heart without flinching once. Someday, some way, he intended to do just that.

Tanner said, "Fact is, though, I won't be here. I've just been waitin' 'til you got home. I've joined the rangers."

The word brought Rusty and Andy both to full attention. Rusty said, "The rangers?"

Tanner nodded. "You probably ain't heard. Governor Coke is callin' up a lot of the old hands. The Morris brothers brought the word to me. They've joined up, too."

"Those Morris boys are liable to get you shot."

"I'm too skinny to be hit. I can hide behind a fence post. Anyway, them boys have got their hearts in the right place."

"It's not their hearts that worry me. It's their heads."

Andy spoke up. "How old do you have to be to join?"

Tanner shook his head. "Can't rightly say. If it's the way it used to be, you're old enough now. Got to furnish your own horse and your own gun."

"I have those."

"Don't know what the pay'll be. It doesn't matter much anyhow. I'm used to not findin' anything in my pockets except my hands."

Rusty felt uneasy about Andy's eagerness. "You'd better take a long look before you jump, Andy. It can be a hard life."

"I've never had no featherbed."

*   *   *

Rusty decided upon the wagon to take Alice to the Blessing place. The things she had hastily gathered from home were already in it. That would save having to pack them on a horse. He left Andy with Tanner to clean up the place. Tanner's housekeeping had been of the lick-and-a-promise variety.

They went by Shanty's farm; it was but little out of the way. Shanty had no real last name, though when he had to put his X on legal papers he adopted the surname of his late owner, Isaac York, who had willed him the farm.

Shanty was in his garden, hoeing out shallow trenches and planting seeds, then covering them lightly. His years weighed heavily upon his thin shoulders. He straightened slowly, with obvious back pain. Recognition of his visitors brought him to the garden gate. He removed his hat in deference to Alice, or perhaps to both of them. Old slave habits died hard.

"You-all git down and come in the house," he said.

His house was a cabin built of logs to replace one burned by night riders who had resented the idea of a black man owning a piece of land in their midst. Firm talk by Rusty, Tom Blessing, and other friends had put an end to that kind of devilment. A few neighbors still did not like his being there, but they had been buffaloed into silence.

Rusty said, "We're headed for the Blessing place. You remember Alice?"

Shanty smiled. "I do, but it was a long time ago, and she weren't much more than a thin saplin'. She's growed into a fine-lookin' young lady."

"Alice is goin' to help Mrs. Blessing."

"The Lord will smile on her for that. I been worried about Miz Blessing."

"But one thing, Shanty, . . . if some stranger should come

askin' about Alice, you haven't seen her. You don't have any idea where she's at. You don't even know who she is."

Shanty's smile faded into a frown. "Hard to believe some-body'd mean harm to this young lady."

"They do. That's why I've brought her all the way down here." He explained briefly about the Bascoms and Josie's death.

Shanty nodded sadly. "I'll just act like I don't know nothin'. They generally figure that way anyhow." Long years in servitude had taught him how to tell white people what he thought they wanted to hear or to pretend total ignorance, whichever the circumstances called for.

Rusty thought Shanty looked more tired than usual. That concerned him. "You feelin' all right? You haven't been wor-kin' too hard and gettin' yourself too hot?"

"Work and me been friends all my life. And friends know not to crowd one another too much."

Rusty took the remark as a sign that Shanty thought he had been working too hard and not getting enough rest. "We'll be gettin' on to the Blessings'."

"May the Lord walk ahead of you and smooth the road."

8

Tom Blessing's dog announced the wagon's coming and trotted to meet it, tail wagging vigorously. Tom stepped out onto the opening between the two sections of the log cabin and shaded his eyes with his big hand. "Git down," he shouted. "Git down and come in."

Alice looked a little apprehensive. She had gotten to know the Blessings when the Monahan family stayed at Rusty's farm during part of the war years, but she had been only half grown. She had not seen them since. "What if it turns out they've already got somebody to stay with Mrs. Blessing?" she asked.

Rusty suspected that question had been on her mind for some time, but this was the first time she asked it. He remembered the way Tom had answered a question once. He said, "We'll burn that bridge when we get to it."

His comment served only to increase her concern.

Tom raised his strong arms to help her down from the wagon. "Is this Josie?" he asked, smiling. "Lord how you've changed."

"I'm Alice, Mr. Blessing. I've come to stay and help take care of your wife."

"Alice? Then you've *really* changed." He looked expectantly at Rusty. "You left here aimin' to get married. Leave the bride at your place?"

Even after all these days, Rusty still found it difficult to speak about her. "Josie's dead. I'll tell you about it in a little while."

Tom's face fell. His eyes pinched in sympathy. He seemed about to say something to Rusty, but he could not bring it out. He turned back to Alice. "Come on in, girl. Mrs. Blessing will be tickled to see you."

Rusty busied himself unloading Alice's few belongings, placing them in the dog run. He could hear her voice from inside the cabin. It sounded like Josie talking. He leaned against a wagon wheel and stared across Tom's field, but the image was blurred.

Tom came outside in a few minutes. He said, "Alice and the Mrs. are goin' to hit it off real good. It was mighty thoughtful of you to bring her."

"I had a reason. She needs you-all right now as much as you need her. More, maybe." Painfully Rusty explained what had happened to Josie and why he had felt it necessary to bring Alice so far from home.

Tom nodded, his eyes sad. "I reckon this is about as hard a thing as man ever has to take in this life."

"Another hard thing is knowin' that the man who did it is runnin' loose. But he won't stay loose forever. I'm goin' to hunt him down like a hydrophoby dog."

"How you goin' to do that? You've got no idea where to start. He could be ten miles from here or a thousand."

"I'll just give up everything else and hunt 'til I find him."

"That could take years."

"I don't know what else to do."

Tom frowned, deep in thought. "Did Len tell you he's signed up for the rangers?"

"He told me. Andy's itchin' to do the same thing."

"It's not a bad idea. The rangers could be the answer to your problem."

"I don't see how."

"Think about it. You're just one man, lookin' for another man who could be anyplace. If you were a ranger you could put him on the fugitive list. Instead of just one man lookin' for him there'd be a hundred or two, however many rangers there are. And I can send word out to sheriffs around the state to be watchin' for him."

"But I want to be the one who gets him. I want to look him square in the eyes and tell him he's fixin' to die."

Tom frowned. "What's more important, bringin' him to justice or takin' your own personal revenge?"

"The way I feel, I want to do it myself."

"Revenge can poison the soul, Rusty. The man on the receivin' end dies just once, and generally quick. The man out for revenge may die a little every day as long as he lives. Remember after Daddy Mike was killed? You almost let it get the best of you that time."

Rusty remembered. He had been roughly Andy's age. Tom had enlisted him in a frontier ranger company to get him away from home, saving him from killing the wrong man.

Tom said, "Even a justified killin' can eat on a man like slow poison. Say you kill this Corey Bascom but destroy yourself in the doin' of it. Do you think that's what Josie would want?"

"There's no way to ask her."

"Deep down, you know."

"All I know for sure is that I want to see Bascom dead."

"Then at least go about it a right and proper way. Do it through the law."

That, Rusty recalled, was more or less what Preacher

Webb had said. It was as though he and Tom had conspired together.

Tom persisted, "You could do a lot of good, bein' a ranger. There's still Indian trouble up north. And what the Yankees called 'reconstruction' spawned enough outlaws to overstock hell. It'll take some strong-minded lawmen to put them down."

"Is that why you let them make you sheriff again?"

"I looked around and didn't see anybody I thought fitted the job. Except maybe you, and you had your hands full with that farm."

"I still do. That's the reason I can't join the rangers."

Tom's frown deepened. "But you'd leave in a minute if you got a lead on Bascom."

"That's different."

The sound of a running horse drew Rusty's attention to the wagon road that led from town. He saw a rider pushing hard, waving his hat. Rusty began to hear his shouting though he could not make out what the man was trying to say.

Tom stiffened. "Nobody's ever come ridin' in that fast to bring me good news." He walked out to meet the horseman. Shiny with sweat, the horse slid to a stop.

The man shouted, though he was close enough that he would not have needed to. "Sheriff Tom, there's been a shootin' in town. And a robbery."

Tom accepted the information with a grave expression. "Slow down, get your breath, then tell me about it."

The rider had the look of a clerk, his shirt white except where sweat had soaked through and attracted dust. His string necktie was hanging askew. He leaned heavily on the horn of his saddle, struggling for air. "Two men. Strangers. Held up the general store. When Mr. Bancroft reached under the counter, they shot him."

"Kill him?"

"I'm afraid so. He was still breathin' when I left, but he looked like a goner." The man pointed. "They rode out headin' west, across country. I followed their tracks part of the way here. They was pretty plain."

Tom grunted. "I ought to be able to cut across and pick them up." He asked for a description, but the one given was vague enough to have fitted Rusty himself, and half the men he knew.

Tom looked back at Rusty. "See what I told you about lawlessness? It's got mighty close to home."

The words popped from Rusty's mouth before he allowed time for consideration. "You want me to help you?"

"I'd be much obliged."

"I'll need to get back home and swap this wagon for my horse. Need to tell Andy and Len, too, or they'll worry about where I'm at."

"I'll swing by your cabin and pick you up after I get a line on them tracks. Want to say adios to Alice?"

Rusty had not had much to say to Alice during the trip. He knew nothing to say to her now. "You do it for me. I'll be gettin' started." He climbed into the wagon and put the team into motion. Looking back once, he saw Alice standing in the dog run, watching him with a big question in her eyes.

Two men. Robbing stores was one of the Bascom brothers' specialties, Alice had said. He knew it was wildly unlikely that they had been the perpetrators here, but the thought was intriguing enough to set his imagination to racing. He pictured himself confronting Corey Bascom. The thought set his skin to burning with impatience. Flipping the reins across the team's rumps, he yelled them into a hard trot.

Approaching the home place, he wondered that he saw no one in field or garden. Long Red and Len's horse were nowhere in sight. Len's in particular was something of a barn lover, usually found within easy reach of feed. Rusty saw his bay grazing alone, near the shed.

He hollered as the wagon rolled past the cabin, but no one answered. He put the vehicle under the shed. Quickly unhooking the team, he pitched the harness into the wagon instead of taking time to hang it up properly. He caught the bay and saddled him, then hurried up to the cabin to fetch his rifle. He had taken only his pistol to Tom's.

He found no fire in the kitchen. On the table he saw a sheet of paper weighted down by a tin cup half full of cold coffee. He held it so that reflected light from the open door made the penciled message readable. He grumbled under his breath as he read it.

Deer Rusty,

   I take pensil in hand to inform you that Me and Andy are gone off to the Rangers. We didnt wait becawz we knowd you would raiz Hell. Dont worry about Andy I will sea that he dont get in no trubbl. With best regards, your verry good frend,

Len Tanner

No trouble. Rusty declared aloud, "Damn that Len." If he was looking out for Andy, who would be looking out for Len? They both needed a guardian, one because he was still young and the other because he would never completely grow up.

Rusty sat down heavily in his chair and weighed the significance of this development. He could go to Andy's ranger captain and argue that Andy was underage. But he had no idea to what company the youngster might be assigned or where it would be stationed. As for age, Andy could pass for his early twenties on the basis of his looks. Rusty could not prove him younger.

This threw a bad kink into his rope.

Tom was not far behind him. He reined up from a hard trot as Rusty walked out to untie the bay. He asked, "Len and Andy goin' with us?"

"They're gone. Went off to join the rangers." As he slid his rifle into the scabbard and swung onto the bay's back he explained about the letter. "I could wring Len Tanner's scrawny neck like a chicken."

"You already told me *he* was goin'. But Andy is a surprise."

Rusty felt too disgruntled to talk about it. "Did you find the tracks?"

Tom nodded. "A couple of miles south of here. They're stayin' off of the roads. Don't want anybody seein' them."

Rusty had a bitter taste in his mouth. "Let's be goin' after them."

He had noted that the young man who brought the message had not stayed with Tom for the long pursuit. Tom explained, "I sent him back to town. The wrong kind of help can get you killed."

Tom led the way, angling southwestward. He cut the tracks in a short time. The fugitives were evidently depending upon fast horses rather than trying to cover their trail.

Tom said, "People noticed them camped outside of town last night but never gave them much thought. There's always folks passin' through. These were probably watchin' to see where business looked the best. Since we don't have a bank yet, the store must've seemed like the richest pickin's. Old man Bancroft was a gentle feller. He ought not to have reached for a gun."

"Maybe they'd have shot him anyway. There are men like that. Didn't get enough killin' in the war. Or didn't go, and now they're makin' up for it."

Tom's face twisted. "Which means we'd better be careful how we ride up on them. Bancroft's funeral is one too many."

"Another one or two would be all right, long as it's the right men gettin' buried."

Tom gave Rusty a long study. "You've got a hard look in your face. I don't know as I like it."

"Been some hard things happened to me. Andy goin' off like that doesn't make it any easier."

"He's not your son. He's not even your brother. Sure, he's still young, but he's shown that he can think and do for himself. I wouldn't mind havin' him with us right now."

"I'm glad he's not."

The trail presented little challenge. A recent shower had left the ground soft so that the hooves had made deeper than usual cuts in it. Tom stopped to study a place where one of the horses had paused to urinate. He said, "They ain't too far ahead of us. An hour or so, maybe two."

Farther on, Tom pointed to a spot where the ground had been scarred slightly. "Looks like one of the horses stepped in that hole yonder and went down."

Boot tracks showed that one man had walked around a little before remounting. Tom said, "Horse must not have broke its leg, but I'll bet it's limpin' some. That'll slow our boys up."

Presently Rusty saw a single rider ahead of them. At first he could not tell whether the person was coming or going, but soon it became clear that he was moving to meet them. He was on a bareback mule, with wagon harness instead of saddle. He carried the long reins looped like a lariat.

Tom said, "That looks like old man Gillis. What's he doin' ridin' a wagon mule?"

As Gillis approached, it was plain that he had been hurt. Blood had dried on the side of his face. A deep bruise had turned dark from his cheekbone up to the edge of his gray hair. Tom said to him, "You look like you'd been thrown off and drug."

"Two men stopped me. Swapped me a lame horse for my best mule. Taken it right out of the harness. When I tried to argue with them they hit me across the head with a six-shooter."

Rusty rode up close to examine the wound. Gillis said, "If I hadn't had this old wool hat on, it'd have broken my skull like an eggshell."

"Looks bad," Rusty said. "I hope you're not goin' far."

"Headin' for my son's place, over the rise yonder. Him and my daughter-in-law will fix me up. But it makes me madder than hell, losin' that good mule. How do they expect a man to farm without a good pair of mules?"

Tom said, "You're lucky you didn't lose more than a mule. They robbed a store and shot old man Bancroft."

The farmer's jaw dropped. "Old tightwad Bancroft? They must've found out he still had the first dollar he ever made. And most of the ones since." He seemed to regret his words. "I hope he ain't dead."

Tom shook his head. "Don't know. But I expect you'll be gettin' your mule back. I doubt your thief will want to ride him any farther than he has to. He'll be lookin' to steal another horse." He pointed his chin westward. "Who lives yonderway past your place?"

"Young folks named Plumley. Moved in last year and broke out new ground." Gillis's eyes widened as he pondered the possibilities. "I hate to think them young people are in danger. That boy's come and helped me several times. And he's got a mighty sweet little girl for a wife. I'd better come with you."

Tom gripped the farmer's thin shoulder. "No, you'd better go on to your son's place and get took care of. Me and Rusty, we'll see after them young people."

The farmer gave him a better description of the thieves than the town clerk had done. One was tall and lanky with a bushy black beard. The other was of heavier stock and had a brownish mustache with a couple of days' growth of whiskers. An instant before the heavier one had clubbed him, Gillis had seen a long, bluish scar on the back of his hand.

"They both had mean eyes," he warned. "I seen eyes like that in the war. A man with them eyes, there ain't much he won't do."

Tom nodded at Rusty. "Then we'd best not give them time for more than they've already done."

It would have been easy to have missed the Plumley farm had the tracks not led Rusty and Tom to it. The cabin was small, without a dog run, and had been built beneath a hill that hid it from the south. A modest field lay below the cabin. Corn plants stood inches high, for the growing season had barely begun.

Rusty pointed. "The corral yonder. I'd bet you that's Gillis's mule."

No horses were in sight. The thieves were probably gone, but Tom was taking no chances. "That cabin has got no window in the back. We'd better ride up on the blind side."

They dismounted fifty yards away and led their horses, pausing to tie them to a tree. They went the rest of the way with pistols in their hands. They paused to listen a minute before Tom pointed to the front door. Rusty noticed that it was ajar and that it opened to the inside. Oldtimers in the days of frequent Indian trouble usually made sure their doors swung outward so it would be more difficult for anyone to force his way in.

Rusty gave the door a hard shove with his shoulder and stepped quickly inside.

A woman cowered against a back wall. She brought her arms up defensively and screamed. "No more. Please, no more." She covered her face.

Rusty's eyes took a moment to adjust to the room's poor

light. The young woman was disheveled, her dress torn from shoulder to waist. As she lowered her arms he saw bruises on her face.

Rusty tried to say something to comfort her, but rage overtook him and left him unable to speak. Tom said gently, "We're here to help you, ma'am. We're not the ones who hurt you." He showed her the badge on his shirt.

She buckled at the knees. Rusty caught her before she went all the way to the floor. He carried her to a wooden chair at the table. Tom said, "There's a pint of whiskey in my saddlebags. You'd better fetch it."

Rusty went out and led the horses up to the house. He fumbled in the saddlebags, found the bottle, and took a long drink before he carried it inside. He lifted a coffee cup from an open shelf and poured whiskey into it. He held it to the woman's bruised lips. "Drink this. It'll do you good."

She choked but got the whiskey down. She began to calm. Tom asked her, "Where's your husband?"

She seemed unable to look him or Rusty in the eyes. Haltingly she explained that her husband had left early in the morning to look for some strayed cattle. He had not yet returned.

In one sense it might have been a good thing he was gone, Rusty thought. He would probably have resisted the thieves, and they would have killed him.

She said, "We just had one other horse. I heard them run it into the pen and shut the gate. When I went out to see what they were up to . . ." She dropped her head even lower.

Rusty walked to the door and stared out, trying to bring his rage under control. Tom comforted her the best he could.

She cried, "My husband . . . what's he goin' to say?"

Tom said, "If he's any kind of a man he'll know you couldn't help what they did. Wasn't none of it your fault. You got any neighbors, somebody we could send to be with you?"

She said she did, a couple of miles southwest. Tom promised, "We'll swing by and let them know. And don't you worry about them men comin' back. We'll stay on their trail 'til we catch them."

Rusty burned inside and knew it was not because of the whiskey. His hands trembled as he untied his horse. "I've seen some bad men in my time. I've known some that would murder a man without battin' an eye and steal anything that wasn't bolted to the floor. But I've never known any that would do a thing like this to a woman."

Tom grunted and climbed into the saddle. "It's a new world. I liked the old one a heap better."

They found the farm Mrs. Plumley had described and told a middle-aged farmer and his wife what had happened. The woman's eyes filled with tears. "That poor girl. Hitch up, Walter. Let's be gettin' over there."

Riding away, Tom said, "With all the new world's deviltry, there's a lot of the old world left. You can still find kindness when you look for it."

Rusty could not reply. He could not shake the image of terror he had seen in the young woman's face. As he reviewed the scene in his mind, her face became Josie Monahan's.

"We've lost time, Tom. Let's be makin' it up."

Dusk came too quickly. Rusty knew they would soon be unable to see the tracks. "They've got to stop sometime. They've got one fresh horse, but the other one has been pushed all day."

"Ours, too. We set off in such a hurry that we forgot about one thing."

"What's that?"

"We haven't got anything to eat."

Rusty patted the blanket roll tied behind the cantle of his saddle. "We're not plumb out of luck. I brought along some jerky left over from our trip down from the Monahans'."

"Jerky." Tom said the word with distaste.

"It's better than nothin'."

"Just barely."

Rusty said, "Indians can get by on it for days. And I ate a heap of it when I was with the rangers."

"Me, too. I always hoped I'd never have to again."

The tracks were hard to see as daylight faded. The fugitives had stopped to water themselves and their horses at a spring some early settler had rocked in but later abandoned. The remains of a picket cabin leaned precariously, threatening to fall over if given a fair push.

Tom asked, "Feel like sleepin' under a roof tonight?" He said it with a touch of humor, but Rusty was in no mood to appreciate it. Hatred simmered for the men they pursued. He said, "That roof would likely cave in on us. Anyway, I'll bet the place is full of snakes."

Reluctantly he conceded that they had no choice but to stop for the night. After watering the bay he staked it on a long rawhide rope so it could graze within a wide circle. Tom did the same, then said, "How about that jerky?"

Rusty unrolled his blanket and took out a bundle wrapped in oilskin. Jerky was strips of meat dried in the sun, usually tasting more of salt and pepper than of beef. Rangers had often carried it with them on long scouts because they had no guarantee of finding fresh game. Though far from sumptuous, it could sustain life until a man found better.

Tom chewed hard. "I've known of men losin' a tooth on this stuff, but I never saw anybody get fat on it."

Rusty realized Tom was trying to jolly him out of his dark mood, but he was not ready to give it up. There was justice to be done. From the description he tried to imagine the fugitives' faces. He could see only one. In his mind they both looked like Corey Bascom.

He said, "I don't understand men like that. What do you suppose gets into them?"

"Hard to say. War soured some of them. Then there's some raised that way by folks that had coyote blood in them. And some are just born with a deep streak of mean. Somethin' missin' out of their brain or their heart. They're hard to cure."

"There's one way. Kill them dead and bury them deep."

Tom frowned and pulled his saddle blanket around him.

Rusty awakened long before daylight. He rolled onto one side, then the other, trying to find a comfortable position. There was none. He felt as if he would willingly trade a good horse for a cup of strong coffee. He dared not light a fire that the fugitives might see. It irritated him to hear Tom snoring peacefully. He itched to be on the move but knew it would be futile to set out before he could see tracks.

At last Tom sat up, throwing back the blanket. Only the faintest hint of light showed in the east. The first thing Tom did was to look around for the horses. That instinct was deeply ingrained into men used to living along the frontier, where a good horse was always a temptation to the light-fingered breed, white or red.

Rusty said, "They're still where we staked them. I've been watchin' them for hours."

"You didn't sleep much?"

"Kept seein' that poor woman, and then I'd think of Josie. I kept thinkin' of her in that woman's place."

"At least that woman is still alive."

"And probably half wishin' she wasn't. There's not much worse a man can do to a woman short of leavin' her dead."

Tom threw his saddle onto his horse's back and tightened

the cinch. "Sooner or later you've got to come to grips with what happened to Josie. Otherwise it'll drive you crazy."

"I'll come to grips when I find Corey Bascom. But those two renegades will do for a start."

Rusty chewed on a strip of jerky as he set out impatiently in a stiff trot. It should have been Tom's place to pick up the tracks, but Rusty did not give him time. Once when they lost the trail, Tom was the one who picked it up. Rusty was adequate as a tracker, but he had never considered himself in a class with Tom and other frontiersmen of Tom's generation. Or even with Andy.

As the sun moved upward toward midday and the morning warmed, Rusty became uneasy. He could not put his finger on the cause. It was instinct, a feeling that all was not as it should be. "Tom," he said, "let's wait up a minute."

"You see somethin'?"

"I feel somethin', like cold wind on the back of my neck."

"You sure you haven't been listenin' to Andy too much? He's always got a hunch about somethin'. Hears voices talkin' to him. The Indian upbringin', I suppose."

"I don't hear any voices, and there's nothin' I can see. But I've been around Andy enough to know I'd better pay attention. Do you suppose those renegades could've doubled back? They could be comin' up behind us."

It was an old Indian trick. He had used it himself on the two younger Bascom brothers.

Tom's expression showed he took the possibility seriously. He drew the rifle from beneath his leg. "I should've thought of that. It's been done to me more than once."

Tom jerked in the saddle, dropping the rifle. Almost simultaneously Rusty heard a shot from behind. Whirling the bay around, he saw a puff of smoke behind a small clump of low-growing brush. Without taking time to consider, he drew his pistol and put the horse into a run toward the shooter's position. He fired three quick shots into the brush.

A heavyset man screamed and staggered out into the open. He stared with wide, unbelieving eyes before he buckled. He pressed both hands against his chest, trying to stop the flow of blood seeping between his fingers.

Rusty caught a movement from the corner of his eye. He swung down from the saddle, keeping the horse between him and a bearded man who raised up from behind another bush. Rusty dropped to one knee and knelt low, sighting his pistol under the bay's stomach. His shot and the fugitive's seemed to overlap.

Startled, the bay jerked the reins from Rusty's hands and trotted away, leaving Rusty exposed. He felt a searing along his ribs as he heard the man's second shot. He winced from the burn but leveled his pistol and squeezed the trigger. He caught the man squarely in the chest. The fugitive gasped and went down.

Rusty heard Tom's shout. "Look out."

The first man was up on his knees, both bloody hands gripping his pistol. Rusty shot him before he could fire. The man hunched, the pistol sagging in his weakening grip. His dying eyes were fixed on Rusty. His lips moved as if he tried to speak.

He could say nothing Rusty wanted to hear. Rusty stared into the contorted face, and somehow it became the face of Corey Bascom. Rage overwhelmed him. He had emptied the pistol. In his belt was the one he had taken from little Anse Bascom. He drew it and fired once, twice, three times.

Tom spoke behind him, his voice brittle. "For God's sake, how much deader do you think you can kill him?"

The fury that had swept over Rusty slowly receded. He stared at the dead man lying almost at his feet. "I must've gone crazy for a minute."

"I never saw you like this. You scared me."

"I've scared myself a little, I think."

"Have you sobered up now?"

"Sober enough to remember that you got hit by the first shot. How bad is it?"

Tom gripped his right arm below the shoulder. His sleeve was red, his hand bloodied. "Missed the bone. But I need to get this blood stopped or you'll be carryin' me home like a baby."

Tom squatted while Rusty cut the sleeve off at the shoulder and wrapped it tightly around the wound.

Rusty said, "I'd better get you back to that Plumley place where you can be tended to good and proper."

"And soon. I can feel sickness comin' on. Before long I may not be able to stay in the saddle." Tom jerked his head toward the nearest of the two fugitives. "Somethin' needs to be done about them."

"Let somebody else come bury them, or leave them for the varmints. They're kin to the coyotes anyway."

Rusty gave Tom a boost up onto his horse. The effort brought a sharp pain to his side and reminded him that a slug had grazed his ribs. The bay had trotted off a little way and stepped on the reins. There he had stopped. Rusty fetched him, then looked around for the horses the renegades had ridden. He found them tied to a bush, out of sight from the ambush spot. He checked the saddlebags and found a considerable amount of money. Loot from the store robbery, he assumed. He tied one horse's reins to the other's tail and led the pair back to where Tom waited, slumped in the saddle.

"Feel like you can make it?"

Tom looked pale, but he gritted his teeth. "I've had a wasp bite worse than this."

Setting out, Rusty reached inside his shirt to feel his ribs.

The slight blood flow had stopped. The wound was sore to the touch, but he doubted that a rib had been cracked. He would heal.

They had ridden perhaps a quarter of a mile when a horseman appeared. He approached them warily. He was young, a farmer by the look of him. He eased when he saw the badge on Tom's shirt. "I heard shootin'. You-all catch up to those bandits?"

Rusty said, "We caught them."

The young man nodded toward the two led horses. "One of them is mine. They stole him from my place."

Tom asked, "Your name Plumley?"

"Yes sir."

"How's your wife?"

His face darkened. "Fair, considerin' what they done to her. Some neighbors came to help. I thought I'd try to catch up with you-all and be there for the kill. Since you have their horses, I reckon you caught them already."

Rusty said, "If it's any satisfaction to you they're layin' back yonder a little ways. We didn't have time to bury them. The sheriff needs attention."

"I'll help you get him to our place. Later on I'll take a shovel and do the buryin'. It'll pleasure me to throw dirt on them." Riding along, he brooded in silence. Finally he said, "They don't deserve no Christian ceremony. I'll make sure they won't see Resurrection mornin', either. I'll bury them facedown."

Approaching a neat row of canvas tents lined beneath the protective branches of huge pecan trees fronting the San Saba River, Andy Pickard felt apprehensive. "We've come a long ways for me to get turned down. Are you sure the rangers aren't lookin' for somebody with more experience?"

Rusty had always said Len Tanner had the faith of the mustard seed, whatever that meant. Tanner declared, "They'll be tickled to have you. How many fellers your age can brag that they've been as far and seen as much as you have? Time I get through tellin' them about you they'll be rollin' out a red carpet and beggin' you to sign up."

That was one thing worrying Andy. Tanner never knew when enough was enough. He could take a good idea and talk it to a slow and painful death. "I oughtn't to've let you get me into this."

In truth, Tanner hadn't used much persuasion. Andy had toyed with the notion of becoming a ranger from the time he first heard they might be reorganized. But the closer he got, the less confidence he felt.

Tanner said, "Too late to turn back. They've seen us already."

Andy was aware that three men were watching them. He tried to brace up his nerve. "Which do you figure is the head-quarters tent?"

"The biggest one, naturally. Officers always get a little the best of it."

The best did not look much better than the others to Andy. Most of the tents were tepee shaped, lined evenly where the heavy foliage would provide partial shade in the afternoon. Beyond the tents and between the trees he could see sun reflected off the clear waters of the San Saba. An officer stood before the larger tent, talking to a couple of men. At least, Andy took him for an officer because his stance indicated authority.

The rangers had no official uniform. They wore what they would wear in civilian life as cowboys or farmers or town merchants. Tanner had told him they did not even have an official badge. Some men made their own out of Mexican silver pesos. Others did not believe they needed one. They expected boldness and a serious demeanor to cow most adversaries. The rest would be dealt with according to the demands of the moment.

Tanner said, "That'd be the captain, I imagine."

The officer turned his attention to the two horsemen. Tanner made a poor excuse of a salute. "Private Tanner reportin' for duty, sir. And I've fetched along a recruit you'll be glad to have in the company."

The officer frowned. "That is a determination I'll make for myself. As for you, Tanner, your enlistment started over a week ago. If you expect to be paid for time absent, . . ."

"Couldn't help it, sir. Things came up. But you don't owe me no more than you figure I got comin'." Money meant little to Tanner except in terms of what he could buy with it, usually as soon as he had the cash in hand.

The officer lowered his voice. "I've been notified of your

past service record, so I'll overlook your tardiness. This time."
He turned a critical gaze upon Andy. "You say I'll want this
young man as a recruit. Tell me why."

Tanner dismounted. "I could talk all day, tellin' you why
you want to sign up Andy Pickard."

"I had rather you didn't. Just the pertinent facts will be
enough."

"Well sir, in the first place he rides like an Indian. Truth
is, it was the Indians taught him. And shoot? He can knock
a flea off of a dog's ear at fifty yards and never singe a hair.
And he's got more nerve than a mouthful of bad teeth. Why,
he once slipped into a Comanche camp and—"

The officer raised his hand. "Let him speak for himself.
Tanner, you may put your blankets and gear into that farthest
tent yonder, then take your horse out and turn him into the
remuda. You'll find it on grass west of camp."

Tanner accepted the order with a nod. "Whatever you
say, Captain." He glanced at Andy. "Now, don't you be shy.
Tell him everything he ought to know about you. I'll see you
after you been sworn in."

The officer watched in silence until Tanner led his horse
beyond hearing. "Usually I am suspicious of a big talker, but
I am told Tanner was a good ranger in the old days."

"There's a lot more to him than just talk."

"But you are obviously too young to have been in ranger
service before. So come into the office and tell me why I
should accept you into that service now."

Andy tied Long Red to a rough hitching rack made of
live-oak branches. He followed the officer through the open
canvas door of the tent the captain called an office. He took
off his hat and twisted it in his hands. "First off, sir, Len
stretched the facts a little. I can ride, but just about everybody
I know can do that."

"How is your shooting eye?"

"Ain't braggin', sir, but I don't generally need two shots. Rusty Shannon taught me not to waste cartridges. They cost too much."

The officer's eyebrows went up. "Rusty Shannon, you say?"

"Yes sir, he's the one raised me, after the Indians. Used to be a ranger along with Len Tanner."

"I've met Shannon. Spotless reputation. I hope he is well."

"Healthy enough, but he lost the woman he was fixin' to marry. It tore him up a right smart."

"Sorry to hear that. But we're supposed to talk about you. What's this about an Indian raising?"

Andy explained that he had been carried off by raiding Comanches when he was small and lived with them until he was around twelve or thirteen. He decided not to go into the circumstances under which he had fallen into Rusty's hands. He doubted the captain would take kindly to the fact that he was trying to emulate his Comanche brothers on a horse-stealing foray. Most people did not like to hear that part of his story.

The captain said, "I'm glad you were rescued. A lot of young people remained prisoners. Grew up Comanche, ruined for life."

Rescued was not exactly the word for it. *Captured* would be a better description, for at first Andy had been an unwilling convert to the white man's road. He had tried to escape back to Comanchería. He judged that this was another aspect of his story best left out. Most white people did not understand how a boy could prefer living in a tepee and following the buffalo with a band of what they considered wild savages most akin to the wolves that also stalked the shaggy herds.

The captain frowned again. "How do you feel about the Comanches now?"

They were still his brothers, most of them, but this was something else the captain would not appreciate. "I've been away from them a long time."

"Part of our job will be to protect settlers from Indian raids. Mainly Comanches to the north, Apaches west and south. If it came to that, would you be able to fight them?" He stared at Andy with an intensity that would not permit evasion.

"I don't know, sir. I guess I could if I had to."

"I need a better answer than that. I can't afford to have men in my command that I could not depend on in an emergency."

"I'll do my duty, whatever that is."

"No matter how difficult it may be for you?"

"If it breaks my back, sir."

The captain chewed his lip in deep thought. "From what I know of Rusty Shannon he would have made you tough enough to do whatever has to be done, however unpleasant it may be."

"He tried awful hard."

"Very well, there are certain requirements to be met. First, you must furnish a horse."

"That's him, the sorrel I tied outside."

"It may be that the state will furnish weapons in the future, but for now you must arm yourself."

"There's a rifle on my saddle. Got a six-shooter and a skinnin' knife on my belt." Tanner had made sure he brought everything he needed.

"Then it would appear you meet the principal specifications. We need to fill out and sign some papers and administer the oath. Have you ever taken an oath?"

"I swore a time or two to tell the truth and nothin' else."

"The ranger oath is a solemn obligation between you and

the state of Texas, taken in the sight of God. I don't know what God's punishment is if you break it, but Texas's punishment can be severe."

"If I make you a promise, I won't back away from it."

"Spoken like a good Texan. Now let's see about this enlistment form. I assume you can read."

"Fair to middlin'." Andy's reading ability was about average, he thought, for most Texans aside from teachers, storekeepers, and lawyers. Schooling was sporadic. Many people living in the country and in small towns had no more than a smattering of formal education. Rusty had seen to it that Andy took schooling whenever it was available.

The captain filled out the forms. Andy ran his finger down the pages, lips moving as he slowly read to himself what was written. He signed where the officer pointed.

The captain said, "You understand that you are being accepted on a conditional basis? I have the right to dismiss you at any time you fail to obey orders or live up to expectations."

"Any time I feel like I'm not totin' my load you won't have to fire me. I'll quit."

"That's the proper attitude for a ranger of the Texas frontier batallion."

The captain administered the oath after calling up two rangers to stand witness. He said, "There is room for you in the farthest tent, where I sent your friend Tanner."

The two rangers shook Andy's hand and welcomed him into the company. One introduced himself as Sergeant Bill Holloway. He was a tall, broad-shouldered, flat-bellied man of roughly Rusty's age. His face was burnished brown. His pale blue turkey-tracked eyes had a permanent squint brought on by life in the Texas sun. He said, "I heard you mention Rusty Shannon. I rode with him under old Captain Whitfield 'til the war drawed me into the army. Southern, of course. How come he ain't joined up again?"

"He's had some bad luck lately. Got about all his plate will hold." Andy decided to say no more until he had time to size up the company. He had already told the captain more than he intended. Rusty might not want his personal troubles advertised all over the country.

Holloway said, "A couple more things the captain may not have mentioned. No drinkin' in camp."

"I don't drink."

"And no card playin'."

"Never learned no card games."

The sergeant shook his head as if he could not believe. "I guess you don't cuss, either."

"Yes sir, I do. Sometimes it's the only thing that helps."

The sergeant's squinty eyes laughed, and his mustache lifted at the edges. "That's all right. Just do it judiciously." He turned toward the tent but stopped. "Know any Comanche cusswords?"

"A few."

"I wish you'd teach them to me. Sometimes I use up all I know in English and Spanish and it's still not enough."

Andy untied his blankets and a small war bag of possessions from the saddle. He expected a row of cots inside the tent, but he saw only bedrolls spread on the ground.

Holloway said, "Find you an empty place anywhere. When you're tired enough, the grass will feel like a feather bed."

Andy had slept on the ground during his years with the Comanches and many times since when he was on the move. The Indians had considered it healthy to lie directly upon Mother Earth. A bed put distance between a man and nature, though Andy enjoyed the luxury when he had it.

Holloway said, "A bed just spoils you. Can't take one with you on scout, and the captain sees to it that the nights are short anyway. He'll have you up and goin' before day-light."

Andy said, "I've always heard that beds are dangerous. Lots of people die in them." He dropped his blankets on the ground near the back of the tent, beside the ones he recognized as Tanner's. "How's the food?"

"We have a good cook, blacker than the ace of spades. Old Bo's biscuits would make the angels want to give up their wings and come back to earth."

"Len Tanner will be tickled to know about that."

"I remember Tanner, too. He ever run out of conversation?"

"He hasn't yet."

"He's a man I'd want beside me in a fight, but I wouldn't want to have to listen to him talk about it afterwards."

Andy dropped his saddle on the ground and hopped up on Long Red's bare back. The sergeant pointed. "You'll find the horse herd out that way. One of the drawbacks of ranger service is standin' your day of horse guard every so often."

It stood to reason that the rangers would be careful of their horses. A ranger afoot was essentially useless. Though Indian raids had become less common, they still occurred from time to time. Comanches and Kiowas continued to steal south from the high plains and the reservations to add to their wealth, measured in horses. White horse thieves had increased even as Indian activity had declined. In a state still short of cash money, horses were a leading medium of exchange.

Glancing back once, Andy saw that Holloway still watched him. He decided serving under the sergeant should be pleasant enough, for in some ways he reminded Andy of Rusty. The captain seemed more businesslike and abrupt, but that was probably necessary for an officer. He could not be just one of the boys and still expect them to jump to his command.

Andy met Tanner walking back, carrying his bridle over his thin shoulder. Tanner said, "Looks like the captain taken you in."

"For forty dollars a month."

"Save it and you'll get rich. If you live for a hundred years." Tanner's face took on a worried twist. "You'll find one of your old friends on horse guard out yonder."

"An old friend?"

"Farley Brackett. He's always wanted your horse. He's liable to take him and ride off."

Resentment stung Andy. Of all the people he might run into, Farley Brackett would have been among his last choices. "If he lays a hand on Long Red, I'll . . ." He could not think of anything severe enough to say. "How'd he ever come to be a ranger? The state police rode some good horses to death tryin' to catch him."

"They weren't tryin' near as hard as they made out. They took care not to crowd him too close. The state police are long gone anyway, and good riddance."

"He shot a couple of them that I know of."

"Scallywags and scoundrels. Most folks didn't see it as a crime. Shootin' state police was looked on as a public improvement."

"Well, if he leaves me alone I'll leave him alone."

"I don't suppose the captain said what time they serve supper around here?"

"I didn't ask. Probably couldn't eat anything now." The thought of Farley Brackett being here had already begun to work on Andy's stomach.

He and Brackett saw each other at about the same time. Brackett and another ranger had the horses scattered loosely, giving them room to graze. Brackett rode over to meet him. His attention seemed more on the sorrel than on Andy.

"Howdy, Indian," he said. "You been takin' good care of my horse?"

Andy could think of no suitable answer, so he offered none. Once, under close pursuit by Union soldiers and state police, Brackett left his own tired horse and took one belonging to Rusty. In return, Brackett's father had given Rusty this sorrel, which Rusty turned over to Andy.

Andy demanded, "With your record, why did the rangers ever take you in?"

"They decided that anybody who had killed two carpet-bag state policemen must be all right."

A long scar ran down one side of Brackett's face, result of a wartime saber cut. Deeper internal scars had never healed. Andy had been a reluctant witness when state police cut down Jeremiah Brackett in his own home one dark night, mistaking the father for the son. He could sympathize with Farley's bitterness, but he could not excuse the man's unreasoning violence, or his coveting the sorrel horse.

Brackett's gaze was hard. Andy tried to match it. Brackett said, "I'm surprised the captain accepted you. Did you tell him about your Comanche upbringin'?"

"I did. It's no secret."

"Did you tell him that the first time we get into a scrap with the Comanches you're liable to run off and join them against us?"

"I promised him I'd do my duty. He took me at my word."

"The captain doesn't know you, but I do. If the day comes and you even act like you're fixin' to join your butcherin' brothers, I'll shoot you myself."

"Me and you won't get along. That's plain to see. Maybe one of us needs to ask for a transfer to a different company."

"I was here first. You goin' to turn that horse loose, or not?"

"That's what I came out here for. He'd better still be here in the mornin'." Andy slid from Long Red's back and pulled the bridle down over the ears, then slipped the bits from the horse's mouth. The sorrel hesitated just a moment before turning and joining the other horses. Andy suspected he would not get along with most of them. Long Red tried to dominate whatever company he was in. He would make a friend or two and buffalo the rest of the horses into staying beyond biting and kicking distance.

Andy gave Brackett a final glance but knew nothing more to say. Brackett would be a thorn in his side so long as both of them remained with this company. Andy resolved that he could be a thorn, too.

We'll see which of us hollers *quit* first, he thought.

He walked the three or four hundred yards back to camp. Tanner sat on a crude bench made of branches tied with rawhide strips. He was cleaning his rifle. "I didn't hear no shootin'."

"I didn't do any. But I might if he ever crowds me too hard."

Tanner used a ramrod to push a cloth patch down the rifle barrel. "Maybe it wasn't such a smart idee, me bringin' you along to join the rangers. It's too late to back out, but maybe if I told the captain you lied about your age, . . ."

"I didn't. I told him I don't know just how old I am. So maybe I'm guessin' a little on the high side. That's not the same as lyin'."

"Crowds the hell out of it, though." Tanner shrugged. "Always try to stay where I'll be between you and Farley Brackett. If it looks like trouble is fixin' to break out, I'll have a chance to step in."

Andy disliked the notion that he might not be able to take

care of himself. "The man who tries to break up a fight some-times gets hit from both sides."

"I dodge pretty good."

Andy did not doubt that Tanner would come to his de-fense no matter the cost. He would not want Tanner hurt on his account. "I'll try to keep my distance from him."

"I ain't the only friend you've got in camp. The Morris boys are in this company. Jim and Johnny are out on a scout."

"Scoutin' for what?"

"Indian sign, horse thieves, robbers, whatever there is. We're west of most settlements here. Good country for them bunch quitters who work in the moonlight so folks don't see what they're up to."

It had taken Andy and Tanner the better part of a week to ride here from the farm, taking their time. They had seen few people the last couple of days. Andy could remember the Comanches bringing their families down from the plains into these limestone, cedar, and live-oak hills to hunt. After white settlement began in earnest they came mainly to raid.

Tanner laid the rifle across his lap and glanced back over his shoulder. "They say there's good fishin' in the San Saba. Catfish so thick they'll crawl out onto the bank to nip at your bait."

Living with the Indians, Andy had spent most of his time in a high, dry country where fish were not plentiful. With Rusty down on the Colorado he had learned to throw a line in the river periodically to vary the menu from venison, pork, and beef. The catching had been all right, but he had not liked the cleaning. It seemed a lot of work for a little bit of eating.

The black cook walked out from the mess tent and struck an iron rod against a dangling piece of wagon tire, signaling time for supper. He gave a wordless holler as if he were call-ing hogs.

Tanner said, "Let's go see if the boys was lyin' about how good that cook is."

The rangers who lined up were all strangers to Andy, though Tanner knew a few of them by name. No one remained a stranger to Tanner for long. They were a mixed group, mostly young. He saw none who seemed to be nearing middle age. Two or three looked as if they did not have to shave often. That made Andy feel a little less concerned about his youth.

"Fellers," Tanner said, "I want you to meet my compadre, Andy Pickard. Weaned on buffalo milk, brought up by wolves, ripped the hide off of a live grizzly with his bare hands and made himself a bearskin coat. He'd be wearin' it today if the weather wasn't so warm."

Embarrassed, Andy could only stand quietly and look innocent. Sergeant Holloway grinned. "Was that a full-grown grizzly, or was it only half-grown, like that story?"

Andy saw that the rangers were going along with the joke. That eased his self-consciousness. He said, "It wasn't near as tall as Len's yarn. Next time he tells it it'll be two bears."

The grinning sergeant clapped a hand on Andy's shoulder. "Grab you a plate. You never want to miss a chance to eat. There'll be days when you won't get to." He pushed Andy ahead of himself in the line.

Andy decided he need not worry about being accepted. He warmed to the friendliness in the faces around him. He said, "I want to do a good job. Any time you-all see a way I can do better, tell me."

"You can bet on that. This outfit ain't up to strength, so every man has got to pull extra weight to make up the difference." Holloway paused, thinking. "Seems to me I remember some Pickards that used to farm down in the lower country, around Gonzales seems like. Any kin?"

Andy hesitated. "Might be. The only kin I ever met was an uncle. We didn't like each other much."

He did not want to disclose that the uncle had come to see him when he was recuperating from the broken leg that had caused him to fall back into Texan hands. The uncle had rejected him on the grounds that Andy's long exposure to Indian ways had made him unfit for life among white people. Andy had resisted any further attempts to be brought into contact with his blood family. He regarded his real family as a band of Comanches and Rusty Shannon. He also felt an emotional kinship with the Monahans, more than he could ever have with any Pickards who might condescend to accept him.

Holloway said, "You keep an eye on the captain. Watch what he does and learn from it. Sometimes he'll tell you what to do. Other times he'll let you think for yourself."

"Sounds a lot like Rusty Shannon."

"I wish we had Rusty in this outfit. Why didn't you bring him with you?"

"I wish I had." Rusty would be better off in this company than torturing his soul with grief and hatred and hunting for a man who by now might be a thousand miles away. "Right now he's got his own snakes to kill."

After supper Andy heard somebody tuning up a musical instrument. He was a little surprised to find Sergeant Holloway with a fiddle in his hand, adjusting the strings to conform with a banjo held by a young ranger. Holloway had not struck him as a lover of music. Soon the two were playing. Most of the other rangers gathered to listen. Even the captain emerged from his tent and sat on a canvas stool.

Andy found the music pleasant. He tapped his feet to the rhythm.

Farley Brackett ruined his good mood. He said, "I'd've thought a rawhide drum was more to your likin'."

Andy got up and walked to his tent.

· 10 ·

Rusty had never been to Fort Worth before. About the nearest place he had visited had been Jacksboro during his ranger days. He knew that the town had begun with a military post on the Trinity River before the war. It had grown as farming and ranching spread westward and northward toward the Cross Timbers country and the Red River. In recent times it had become an important stopping point for cattle drives coming up from the southern part of the state on their way to the new railheads in Kansas. It was a resupply center for cattle outfits and freighters, for military units on their way west. There was even talk that a railroad would be coming in soon to lessen the need for trailing herds farther north.

Fort Worth had gained a reputation as a wide-open town where a man could do just about anything he was big enough to get away with. If a little short in stature he could make up the deficit by carrying one of Mr. Colt's inventions on his hip or in his boot top.

This was one of several trips Rusty had made on the basis of tips that Corey Bascom had been seen in one place or another. It was said he had been observed playing poker in Fort Worth's red-light district, beginning to be known as Hell's

Half Acre. It was a name common to such districts in many frontier towns. Though previous searches had turned up empty, Rusty started each new one with strong hope. Now hope was about all he had left. The long ride had sapped his energy. Only the image of Corey Bascom kept him in the saddle mile after weary mile.

Each failure diminished his strength but increased his determination. To quit would mean that all his effort had been wasted. He had invested too much of himself in the search to give it up.

He rode through the thinly populated outskirts to a chorus of barking dogs and found a wagon yard a short distance from the courthouse. A young man of about Andy's age met him at the barn's open door. "Put up your horse, mister?"

"I'd be much obliged. And I'll spread my bedroll here tonight, too, if that's all right." He did not want to squander money on a hotel room.

"Sure. May not get a lot of sleep, though. There's two big cow outfits hit town today with herds on the way to the Indian nations. Apt to be a lot of whoopin' and hollerin'."

Rusty shrugged. "I'll just have to put up with it. Town looks a little quiet right now though."

"It's too early in the day. You lookin' for excitement?"

"Mainly lookin' for where the excitement takes place." If Corey was here, he would most likely be found where the action was.

"Wait 'til night. You'll hear it. All you have to do is follow the noise. Or follow a bunch of cowboys. They'll lead you to it."

This would be the drovers' last chance for relaxation and recreation before they hit the Red River and Indian territory. Leaving here they faced a month and more of toil and monotony on the long, dusty trail before they reached the railroad. It stood to reason they would want to let off some pent-up steam and have something to talk about on the tiresome miles ahead of them.

The hostler directed Rusty to a barbershop where he could bathe and have his red hair trimmed. He found a washerwoman to scrub the dirt and sweat out of the clothes he had worn all the way up here. Then he set out walking the dirt streets, locating the saloons and gambling houses where Corey might be. Those he entered appeared to have little business as yet.

A gambler playing solitaire looked up hopefully as Rusty entered. "Interested in a little game, friend?"

"Maybe later. I'm lookin' for a friend of mine. Maybe he's sat in on your game. Name of Corey Bascom?"

The gambler's eyes narrowed. "I know him, but I ain't seen him in a while. You say he's a friend of yours?"

"More like an acquaintance."

"Corey ain't the kind that makes many friends. Nice enough feller, after his fashion, but you got to watch him all the time. He'll cold deck you if you don't."

"That sounds like him. You're sure you haven't seen him lately?"

"No, and I ain't lookin' for him." Suspicion in the man's eyes indicated that he took a dim view of anyone who might be a friend of Corey's. "Even if he's in town he ain't likely to come in this place. He wore out his welcome at my table a long time ago."

Rusty was tempted to ask what Corey had done to earn the gambler's displeasure, but he had not come here to provoke a row, at least with anyone besides Corey.

The gambler said, "On the off chance that he shows up, do you want me to tell him you're lookin' for him?"

"I'd rather you didn't."

The gambler's attitude changed. He smiled thinly. "It's like that, hunh? What's your name, friend?"

"Shannon. Rusty Shannon."

"If I see or hear anything about Corey I'll try to get word to you. Goin' to be in town long?"

"That depends."

"Well, good huntin'."

Rusty returned to the wooden sidewalk and surveyed the street. The buildings were primarily modest one-story frame structures, most of them strangers to paint. A few log houses probably dated back to the town's earliest days. From where he stood he could not see a church anywhere.

A woman in a flimsy gown leaned out of an open window and smiled at him. She said, "Gettin' an early start?"

"Just killin' time."

"Me, too. Goin' to be lots of cowboys in town tonight. I'm apt to get awful busy. But right now I've got lots of time."

He knew an invitation when he heard it. He said, "Thanks, but you'd better get your rest while you can."

Walking away, he heard her call after him, "Later on you'll get to thinkin' about what you missed, and you'll hate yourself."

He passed a uniformed policeman twirling a nightstick. The officer gave him a nod. Then Rusty heard him address the woman by name. He told her, "Them cow outfits'll be in after a while. You better get ready for a busy night."

"I'm always ready. If you find any of them lookin' for a place to light, steer them my way. It'll be worth your while."

"It always is."

Rusty grunted disapprovingly to himself. He had heard that many city policemen shared in the proceeds from illegal activities in return for looking the other way or even, as in this case, participating. It was against all the principles he had learned in his years as a ranger. But that was Fort Worth's misfortune and none of his own.

He walked into a false-fronted building whose sign proclaimed that it offered the finest in spiritous liquors, beer, and hot lunch. It also offered a billiard table. He heard the crack of billiard balls and looked toward the rear of the room where two young men who ought to be at work this time of the day were engaged in a heated game.

A middle-aged man of ample girth and broader smile approached him. "Howdy, friend. If you're lookin' for the best drinks in Fort Worth you've come to the right place."

Something about him struck Rusty as being familiar. The man gave Rusty a moment's intense scrutiny and said, "Seems to me I ought to know you. Sure as hell I do. You're Rusty Shannon. Used to serve under old Captain Burmeister in the rangers."

Rusty remembered. "Right. And so did you." He struggled to remember the name.

"Simon Newfield." The man extended his hand and almost broke Rusty's fingers. "Scouted some with you and old Len Tanner. Reckon he's still alive?"

"Still alive and still talkin'." Rusty grinned, old memories coming back in a rush. He looked around the saloon. It was the fanciest he had seen here, or just about anywhere else he had been. "It's a cinch you didn't buy this place from your ranger savin's."

"No, I came into a windfall." Newfield looked around to see if anyone could hear. "Right at the end of the war I captured me a Yankee army paymaster. Took the money in the name of the Confederacy. But the Confederacy folded, so there wasn't anybody I could legally give it to that needed it worse than I did."

"They're probably still lookin' for it."

"I figured it like a loan. I'll pay it back to them someday when I feel like I've got rich enough. Ain't there yet. What brings you to Fort Worth? I never seen you here before."

Rusty lost his grin. "Lookin' for a man."

"Are you a ranger again? Maybe I oughtn't to've told you about that paymaster."

"No, I'm not a ranger. This is a personal matter. Do you know Corey Bascom?"

Newfield sobered. "Lots of people around here know Corey. Some to their profit and some to their regret. I take it that in your case it's regret."

"He killed the woman I was about to marry."

"That's tough. It doesn't sound much like Corey. Robbery and cheatin' at cards are more his style. But I suppose anything is possible when a man has been listenin' to the owls hoot long enough."

"Seen him lately?"

"He was in here two, maybe three, weeks ago. Never saw him lookin' so sour. Got in a game with a man that was better at cards than he was, and better with a gun, too. Seemed like a stupid thing to do, but Corey tried to egg him into a gunfight. The other feller wasn't lookin' to bloody himself, though. He hit Corey across the head with the barrel of his six-shooter and laid him out cold. Said there wasn't any profit in killin' fools and drunks. Corey left town the next day with a knot so big he couldn't put his hat on. I ain't seen him since."

"Any idea where he went?"

"None at all. Never saw Corey act like that before. It was almost like he was tryin' to get himself killed. Doesn't make any sense."

"It doesn't make sense that he'd come here in the open like that. He's bound to know he's been posted for murder."

"That wouldn't make any difference in the Acre. Jesse James himself could come here and not be bothered. The police keep their hands off of this district. It's a sanctuary, sort of, like church."

"Not like any church I ever saw."

"Poor choice of words. The point is, even if you're not the law anymore, it wouldn't be a good idea to let everybody know you're lookin' for Corey. There's some that would kill you on general principles whether they like Corey or not."

"I'll try not to make a show of it."

"Good. Now let's have that drink. We'll toast old times, and better ones."

While he waited for nightfall Rusty killed time talking with Newfield about long-ago days. Though he did not feel hungry, he partook of the lunch on one end of the bar, boiled eggs, loaf bread, and sliced ham. He washed it down with a beer that would not leave him impaired in the way that whiskey might.

With dusk the crowds began milling. A dozen or so cowboys lined up at the bar. Some moved to the billiard table. Rusty watched them a while, listening to their laughter and loud talk. Most were young, not of an age to be in a place like this. He envied them their youth but wished they were spending it and their money more wisely.

He told Newfield, "I'd better get started if I'm goin' to find Corey."

"Chances are he's not in town. If he was I might've heard. But you won't know 'til you look."

Rusty visited every saloon he could locate, down to a couple of dark dives that made the hair bristle on the back of his neck. Now and then he saw someone who at first glance in dim light looked like Corey but proved not to be. His hopes rose, then fell. Each time they fell they sank lower than before.

He finally returned to Newfield's. The ex-ranger did not have to ask. Rusty knew his face betrayed his disappointment.

Newfield said, "You could hunt every night for two or three months and never find him. You got that much time?"

"No. I ought to be home tendin' the farm. But I've got to look."

"There's no guarantee that he ever will come back here. Gettin' his hair combed with a gun barrel may have turned him away from Fort Worth forever. He could've gone down to San Antonio or maybe over to Fort Smith, even up the trail to Kansas, wherever he might find a card game. If there's paper out on him for murder he might even have sailed to South America like some of them die-hard old Confederates did. You'd just as well try and chase a cloud."

Rusty sighed. "I'll give it another day or two. If I don't find any sign of him, I'll go home."

"I don't like to mess in other people's business, but I'll keep my ear to the ground. If I hear anything I'll let you know."

"I'd be obliged."

"Just don't kill him in here if you can help it, or get killed in here yourself. It's hell to get the blood cleaned up after it's soaked into the wood floor."

Rusty went to the wagon yard and rolled out his blanket on the ground. As the young hostler had said, the place became noisy as cowboys began showing up, full of fun and Fort Worth whiskey. By the time the last of them dropped off to sleep, Rusty had lost the urge. He sat up staring into the darkness and thinking of Josie.

He made up the next day by napping much of the morning after the cowboys departed. At dark he began repeating the rounds he had made the night before. By midnight he had visited every potential place twice. He did not find Corey. He had a strong feeling that Newfield was right. Corey might never come back here.

He decided to give it one more night.

In the late afternoon he returned to Newfield's place. The former ranger came out from behind the bar to meet him, wiping a glass with a white cloth. "Did my boy find you?"

"I haven't seen any boy."

"I sent him out huntin' for you. I got word that somebody named Bascom is in town. Don't know if it's Corey or not."

Rusty's heart jumped. "Where's he at?

"One of the girls from Fat Beulah's house was in here to buy a case of whiskey. She said a man named Bascom is bedded down with a girl over there. Corey used to take a fancy to the women. He knew every sportin' house in town."

"Thanks, Simon. I'll remember you in my will."

"You better write one before you tangle with Corey. He's tricky."

Rusty was out the door and a couple of houses down the street before he realized he did not know where Fat Beulah's was. He stopped a cowboy and asked. The cowboy pointed. "It's that house yonder. But they got a prettier class of girls over at Miss Flo's place."

Rusty examined his pistol before walking up to the house. The low porch was ornate, with freshly painted gingerbread trim. Three lanterns hung from the edge, but they had not yet been lighted for the evening. He peered through the oval glass in the front door before he entered.

A very large woman sat in an oversized rocking chair, darning a black stocking large enough for two normal legs. Flame in a kerosene lamp gave her light to see her work. She looked up at Rusty but did not stand. "Come in. Come in. It's a little early, but what the hell? Never too early for pleasure or business."

"I'm lookin' for somebody."

"We've got lots of somebodys here. Dark, light, one for any preference. What's yours?"

"It's a man I'm lookin' for, name of Bascom."

Her expression quickly changed from welcome to near hostility. "Don't know no Bascom. Most of our customers go by the name of Smith. Now, as long as you're not interested in my girls I want you to get out of here. If you got troubles, take them someplace else."

"Not 'til I find Bascom."

"All I got to do is blow this whistle and half a dozen policemen will come runnin'." She showed him a whistle on a string, half hidden by the pearls around her thick neck.

He grabbed the whistle and pulled. The string broke, but not before biting into her neck a little. He drew his pistol.

She looked at it fearfully but summoned courage to say, "You wouldn't shoot a lady."

"No, but I'd shoot that lamp on the table beside you. Probably start the damndest fire you ever saw." He thumbed back the hammer.

She slumped deeper into her chair. "All right. The man you're lookin' for is upstairs with Cindy Lou, second door on your right. Only don't kill him here, please. It'll give this place a bad reputation."

Rusty hurried up the stairs, knowing it would not take long for Fat Beulah to work up nerve to fetch the police. The pistol still in his hand, he paused at the door, then kicked it open.

A woman screamed. A man sat up in bed, flinging a blanket aside and reaching for a gunbelt hanging across a high-backed chair. Rusty grabbed it first and flung it out the broken door. "Now, Corey . . ."

His finger tightened on the trigger.

He saw then that this was not Corey Bascom. A strong resemblance was there, but the face was not Corey's. He could not stop his finger from tightening, but he tipped the muzzle up in time. The pistol cracked, and a bullet smashed into the ceiling. The woman screamed again and covered her face with the blanket.

Newley Bascom blanched, his body shaking. "My God, Shannon, don't kill me."

Rusty recognized him as Corey's brother, the one who along with younger brother Anse had tried to ambush him. He found himself trembling a little, too. "I came awful close. I thought you were Corey."

"I'm not. I'm Newley."

"Where is Corey?"

Newley fought to bring his voice under control. "I don't know. I came here lookin' for him. Ain't seen him in weeks."

"I don't know if I ought to believe you or not. I think I ought to just shoot you on general principles."

Newley began to cry.

Rusty felt pity, then disgust. He sensed that Newley was telling him the truth, badly as he wanted not to believe.

But he had to believe. He backed up a step and said, "If you ever do see Corey, tell him he can't go so far that Rusty Shannon won't find him. And when I find him, I'm goin' to kill him." He waved the muzzle at Newley for emphasis. Newley whimpered.

Rusty told the girl, "You ought to give him child's rates. He's not but half a man."

He started out the door. He saw Fat Beulah and a policeman coming up the stairs. He turned back and shouted at Newley and the girl. "Now go on with what you were doin'."

He knew Newley couldn't, not now.

He gave Fat Beulah five dollars for the broken door and the policeman a like amount for his trouble. He did not have the heart to make all the saloons and gambling houses again tonight. He sensed that it would be futile.

Frustration was like acid foaming in his stomach. He just wanted to put Fort Worth behind him. He wondered how far he could ride before dark.

· 11 ·

The captain gave Andy a little time to settle in and begin to feel at home before he sent him out of camp on any special duties. Unlike military service, the rangers did not require marching and close-order drill, but they did encourage target practice. The state offered a supply of ammunition to help make up for the fact that the men so far had to provide their own weaponry. Targets were marked on scrap bits of board and nailed to the heavy trunk of a pecan tree. A bank of earth behind would stop stray bullets, though any shot that missed hitting the board threw the shooter's marksmanship into question.

Andy watched several rangers take their turns. The first board was soon splintered so badly it had to be replaced. Tanner missed centering the target by only about an inch.

Andy said, "Good shot."

Tanner waved off the compliment. "Sun got in my eyes or I'd've hit it plumb center."

Farley Brackett's turn came before Andy's. He hit the target almost squarely in the middle. Turning away, he ejected the spent cartridge from his rifle. "All right, Indian boy, let's see if you can even hit the board."

Riled, Andy resolved to do better. He took a deep breath, sighted down the barrel, and squeezed the trigger. The bullet cut into the edge of the hole left by Brackett's shot. By a tiny fraction it was nearest to the center. Andy noticed the captain watching him with interest.

Brackett looked surprised. Then he frowned. "A target don't shoot back. The trick is to do the same thing when you're lookin' down the muzzle of somebody's gun."

Andy let malice creep into his voice. "Somebody like the state police?"

"I seldom shot at one but what I hit him."

Andy could not argue with that. Burning with bitterness acquired on the battlefields, Brackett had become a terror to occupation officers who attempted to enforce reconstruction laws.

Tanner edged in between the two. He said, "Andy, you stick your right elbow out too far. Let's go over yonder away from the crowd and practice holdin' that rifle."

Andy knew his stance was all right. It was the one Rusty had taught him. But he realized Tanner was trying to get him away before an argument started. "I'd be much obliged for anything you can show me."

When they had moved apart from the other men Tanner looked back over his shoulder. "Ain't really nothin' wrong with the way you hold your elbow if it feels right to you. It don't matter how you do it as long as you hit what you shoot at."

"I usually do."

"I'm just tryin' to keep you from havin' to aim at Farley Brackett, and him at you. One of you is just as good a shot as the other. You'd probably both go down."

"I don't want any trouble with him. But he keeps pokin' at me every chance he gets."

"A smart fish don't grab at bait that's got a hook in it."

*   *   *

While Andy was taking the measure of the company, the captain had been taking the measure of him. One evening he assigned Andy to night horse guard. "Private Pickard, you will take first watch tonight."

Andy was pleased. He had begun to wonder when or even if he would be given any real responsibility. "Yes, sir. I'll be glad to."

The captain gave him a quizzical look. "You don't have to be glad around here. You just have to do what you're told to, glad or not. And always be ready for the unexpected."

After supper Andy saddled Long Red and checked his rifle.

Brackett leaned against a pecan tree, watching. "Where's your bow and arrow?"

Andy tried not to let Brackett see that his tone stung a little. He pretended he did not hear.

Brackett turned to Jim Morris, just back from a lengthy and uneventful scout. "You know that boy was raised by the Indians? He's a Comanche at heart."

Jim retorted, "I know his heart has got a lot of fight in it. He helped me and Johnny and Len spike a Yankee cannon, with them Yankees shootin' at us the whole time."

That seemed to be news to Brackett. "When was that?"

"Last January, when the carpetbaggers tried to hold onto the state capitol."

"How many of them did he scalp?"

"Not more than five or six. He had to share with the rest of us."

Andy decided Jim could hold his own in a lying contest with Tanner.

Jim said, "They tell me the Comanches called him Badger Boy. He fights like a cornered badger when he's riled."

Brackett appeared impressed, but that did not last long. As Andy started to ride away, Brackett said, "If any of your red brothers come callin', don't you let them get my sorrel horse, Badger Boy." He spoke the name with derision.

Andy said, "Not them, and not you."

Allowed to spread out and graze during the day, the horses had been brought close to camp and pushed into a fairly compact group that could be watched more easily during the night. Though Indians could strike a horse herd at any time, they favored darkness, when they were hard to see and hard to hit.

Andy had come to rely heavily upon his instincts. Sometimes, though by no means always, he had premonitions about future events. He supposed this resulted from hearing about visions that often came to the People like his foster brother, Steals the Ponies. On several occasions he had sought after visions himself, but they never came. Or if they came, they were so vague that he did not recognize them for what they were. Perhaps he had to be a real Comanche, not an adopted one, for visions to work.

He had no premonition tonight. Nevertheless he was determined to remain alert. He listened to night birds settling in the trees. Indians often imitated the sounds of birds and other creatures in signaling to each other. He did not intend to be fooled. The horses quieted down and began going to sleep, some lying down, others remaining on their feet. Now and then one would snort or stamp the ground or nip at a neighbor that crowded too closely. The one bitten would usually squeal and kick at its tormentor. These were all natural sounds. He catalogued them in his mind so he might recognize any that were not natural.

He had no watch, but Rusty had shown him how to tell time in a general way by the movement of the stars.

The camp routine had kept him busy enough during the

days that he had not thought much about the farm. Now, in the long solitude of the night, he thought back on the place where he had spent the years since his return from life with the Comanches. He thought of Rusty and wondered where he was, what he was doing. He wondered if he had made headway in his search for Corey Bascom.

After getting past his initial reticence, Andy had told the captain about Josie Monahan's death. The officer had written down Andy's description of Bascom. "I'll have every man add this to his fugitive list, and I'll send it to the other companies," he said.

Andy had been shown what was called a fugitive book, containing hand-written descriptions of wanted men. The offenses were many and varied: theft of livestock and personal property, burglary, fraud, robbery at gunpoint, assault with intent to do bodily injury, rape, murder. . . . The book was only partially filled, leaving room to add more miscreants to the list. That these pages would eventually be used up was a foregone conclusion. Texas was not a comfortable place for the timid.

No Indians were listed. Few of their names were known. Any found roaming freely within the state's boundaries were automatically considered hostile and in open season, so a listing would have no purpose.

Andy had been instructed to read the book over and over, to memorize the descriptions in as much detail as possible so he might more easily recognize any fugitives he came across. It was considered likely that many were hiding in this thinly settled western country where law was scarce. Local lawmen varied in their diligence, some relentless in pursuit, others tolerant so long as the offenses had been committed elsewhere and were not repeated within their own jurisdiction. In these cases, rangers were the only peace officers likely to bring the offenders to hand.

Andy rode a slow circle around the horses, pausing to listen for any sound he considered alien. He thought the most effective solution would be to build a corral large enough to contain the herd at night. But this campsite was considered temporary. The company might be moved at any time, so nothing of a permanent nature had been constructed.

Even corraled, the horses would have to be watched. Accomplished horse thieves, red or white, could quietly dismantle a section of the enclosure and put the whole bunch on the move before the rangers could muster an adequate defense.

Eventually Andy's relief rode out to take his place.

He called, "Where you at, Badger Boy?"

Andy recognized Farley Brackett's gruff voice. He replied, "Here." Choking down his dislike for the man, he moved over to meet him.

Brackett said, "Anything stirrin' out yonder?"

"I haven't seen or heard a thing."

"You sure you ain't been asleep? Nothin' gets a man fired out of this outfit quicker than bein' caught asleep on guard."

"My eyes are wide open. They have been all night."

"Glad to hear that. Been worried about my horse."

"Long Red is fine. You worry about the rest of the horses."

Andy turned away. He looked forward to a few hours of sleep before daylight.

He heard a movement of horses behind him, then a shouted challenge. The voice was Brackett's. "Who goes yonder?" He heard the jingle of Brackett's spurs as the man put his mount into a run. Andy turned back, trying to see in the dim light of a half moon. Sound more than sight told him the horse herd was moving. A pistol shot echoed through the trees. He assumed it was Brackett's.

He set Long Red into a lope, trying to circle around and

head off the running horses. He heard the thieves holler, pushing for more speed. Andy overtook the moving herd and cut in front of it. He shouted, trying to turn the horses back. He fired his pistol into the air. Some of the animals slid to a stop, then ducked aside, frightened by the shot.

For a moment Andy saw the dark outline of a horseman. He brought his pistol up into line but hesitated. What if these were Comanches? What if his foster brother might be among them? Steals the Ponies had been given his name for good reason: he had earned it.

In a moment the question was moot, for the rider was lost in the darkness and the dust.

He saw a blur as another horseman came at him. He thought this was Brackett but he was mistaken. The man rammed his horse into Long Red. The impact knocked the sorrel off its feet and jarred Andy loose from the saddle. He grabbed at the horn but missed. He hit the ground hard on his left shoulder.

The rider loomed over him, his horse almost on top of Andy. Andy felt around desperately for the pistol lost in the fall. He had time for one terrible thought: that a Comanche brother was about to kill him. He saw the rider's hand come down, steadying the pistol.

He heard a shot, but it did not come from the gun that had been leveled at him. The rider pitched forward over the horse's neck. His body fell across Andy's legs.

Brackett's voice shouted, "Get up from there, Badger Boy. We got horse thieves to catch." Brackett turned and disappeared again, his horse in a dead run.

Long Red had regained his feet. Andy pushed the heavy body off his legs. The Comanche side of him regretted the thought of an Indian being shot, though the white side rejoiced that it had not been him instead. Andy remounted and set out in a run after the horses. He heard a few more shots.

He fired at a shadowy figure which crossed his path but knew he had missed. In a way he was relieved.

He found himself in front of the horses again. They were slowing. He shouted until he was hoarse. Gradually they began to mill. Somewhere beyond sight he heard a few more shots, then the night fell quiet except for the nervous stamping of hooves against limestone rocks, the nervous nickering of horses.

He saw a rider coming toward him from the west and brought up his pistol. He lowered it when he recognized Brackett's voice. "Holler out, Badger Boy." The man and his horse were both breathing hard. Brackett struggled for breath. "Got them stopped did you? I hope we didn't lose any."

Andy said, "I never knew Comanches to give up so easy."

"Comanches? Didn't you get a look at any of them?"

"It was too dark, and things moved too fast."

"If they was Comanches, I'm an Apache squaw. They were as white as me and you. Me, anyway."

Several rangers came up, riding hard. They had had mounts staked in or near camp. The captain was among them. "What happened here, men?"

Brackett said, "Just had a little company. They didn't stay long."

"Did we lose any horses?"

"We can't take a good count 'til daylight. Looks like most of them are still here."

"Indians, I suppose?"

"Not this time. I'm sorry to say it, but there's some white men near as bad as Comanches."

The captain accepted the report with a satisfied grunt. "You did good work, Brackett. You too, Pickard."

Andy said, "Captain, one of them went down back yonder. Private Brackett shot him."

"Dead?"

"I didn't wait to see, sir. Seemed more important to catch the horses."

"We'll pick him up as we drive the remuda back."

Andy gritted his teeth. He had rather take a whipping with a wet rope than acknowledge that Brackett had saved his bacon, but he owed it to the man to tell the truth. "My horse got knocked down. That outlaw was fixin' to kill me. Private Brackett shot him first."

The captain was pleased. "I'll put that on your record, Brackett. It might help make you a sergeant one day."

Brackett said, "I'd've done the same thing for the camp cook. Quicker, maybe. He makes good biscuits."

Tanner and the Morris brothers rode ahead of the horses, looking for the raider Brackett had shot. By the time Andy reached them, they had him. Tanner said, "Looky what we found, Captain, tryin' to sneak off into the timber. He's leakin' some, but he's breathin'."

The man was hunched over, holding one arm tightly against his ribs. Andy did not think he had ever seen him before, though a ragged beard covered most of his face except for his frightened eyes.

Tanner said, "We got no jail to put him in."

Johnny Morris said, "We got plenty of trees to hang him from. What do you say, Captain?"

The man cried out, "Somebody help me. Can't you see I'm shot?"

The captain's voice was grave. "You present us with a problem. As Private Morris said, we have no jail to put you in and no doctor to see to your wound. There seems to be but one answer."

Brackett waved a pistol. "It's my fault, Captain. I was movin' fast and in the dark. Couldn't aim straight. I'll make up for it right now if you want me to."

Andy hoped Brackett was just trying to intimidate the prisoner, but he sounded as if he meant it.

The outlaw sank to his knees. "For God's sake, give me a chance."

The captain made a show of struggling with his decision. "My better judgment tells me to put an end to it. But I might consider an alternative if you'd cooperate."

"Anything. Leave me go and I won't stop 'til I get to California. Maybe even further."

"I'll want you to identify your confederates and tell me where we might be most likely to find them."

"I'll tell you all I know. They run off and left me. I don't owe them nothin'."

The captain pointed his chin at the herd. "Pickard, catch him a horse. He can ride to camp bareback."

The outlaw cried, "I can't ride. I been shot. I think my ribs are busted."

"A little hurting will help you repent your wayward life."

Andy doubted that. The only thing this renegade would regret was getting caught. A while earlier he had been willing to murder Andy. Despite his pleas, he was unlikely to reform. He would travel a crooked road until a better-aimed bullet or a strong rope stopped him for good.

The prisoner grunted in pain with almost every step. Andy mustered no sympathy. Leading the horse, he maneuvered it across the roughest ground he could find.

He wouldn't have lost a minute's sleep over killing me, he thought. What's more, he made me beholden to Farley Brackett.

That might have been the worst offense of all.

Brackett eased over beside Andy. "I been mullin' this thing over. You thought it was Indians, didn't you?"

Andy wondered what he was driving at. "Thought it might be. I couldn't see much."

"Occurs to me you had a chance to shoot this man before he ran into your horse. Why didn't you?"

"I didn't see him soon enough."

"Or maybe you didn't want to shoot a fellow Comanche."

Andy's face warmed. He was glad the darkness kept Brackett from seeing it. He had told the truth about not having time to fire at this raider, but moments earlier he had seen another. He had a few seconds in which he might have fired, but he had hesitated. Brackett was partially right.

He managed a defiant tone. "Believe what you want to."

"I try to give a man the benefit of the doubt, the first time. And I've damned sure got some doubts about you, Badger Boy."

"I suppose you'll tell the captain about them?"

"I'll keep them to myself for now. But I'll be watchin' you."

The prisoner's horse stumbled on a rock outcrop and almost went down. The man grabbed his side and screeched, "Damn you, can't you watch where you lead this horse?"

Brackett said, "You're lucky we ain't leadin' him out from under a tree limb and leavin' you attached to it."

Andy was grateful that Brackett transfered his malice to the prisoner. He settled into quiet meditation over his own situation. Would he have reacted differently had he known from the first that the horse thieves were white? He was not sure. He feared he might have.

The captain had left a strong guard on the horse herd. At daylight they brought the horses into a clearing at the edge of camp for an accurate count. He and Holloway agreed that they were short only three horses. The thieves might have gotten away with them, or they might simply have strayed away from the main bunch during the excitement. He sent part of the company out on a search for the missing three. Then he watched the cook clean the prisoner's wound.

The renegade protested over the fact that the cook was black. "I ain't never let no dirty nigger touch me."

The captain retorted, "That black won't rub off on you. Keep at it, Bo."

The prisoner squalled as the cook poured alcohol into the wound. Bo grinned and poured more. By the time the bandage had been applied and the ribs tightly wrapped, the prisoner had regained some of his lost courage. When the captain began to question him, he refused to answer. "I changed my mind. I ain't tellin' you a damned thing."

"Regrettable. I hope you realize that if you won't talk, you're of no use to us."

"Never meant to be."

The captain nodded gravely at Holloway. "Sergeant, I have a report to write. Would you take charge of the prisoner? See if you can bring him around to our way of thinking." He retired to his headquarters tent.

Holloway said, "Brackett, bring your rope. We're takin' a little walk down to the river."

The prisoner's eyes widened. "What're you fixin' to do?"

"Like the captain said, you're of no use to us, and we've got no jail." He tied the man's hands behind his back with a rawhide string, then took a firm grip on one arm. Brackett grabbed the other. Though the prisoner dragged his feet, they hustled him along. Andy followed at a short distance, curious.

Holloway pointed at a sturdy pecan limb about ten feet off of the ground. "That one ought to do. Throw your rope over it."

The prisoner blustered. "You're tryin' to bluff me. You wouldn't do this to a man. It's against the law."

Neither Holloway nor Brackett replied. Brackett slipped the loop over the prisoner's head and tightened it around his neck. He pulled the other end of the rope and took up the slack.

The renegade was sweating but tried to show a brave face. "You won't really do this. You ain't allowed."

Holloway nodded, and Brackett pulled the rope. It drew taut. The prisoner choked as his legs straightened. He bent his toes, trying to keep them touching the ground. Brackett pulled until the prisoner's feet were clear by a full six inches. Brackett held him there for a bit, then let him down.

"Got a kink in the rope," he explained. "Need to straighten it out."

The prisoner went to his knees, gasping, his face turning purple. Holloway bent over him. "We forgot to ask if you have any last words for the Lord."

The man coughed but could not speak. Holloway pulled him to his feet. "We'll get it done right this time. Go ahead, Brackett."

As the rope tightened the prisoner found voice. "No! No! For God's sake . . ."

Holloway seemed unmoved. "Tell me why not."

"Get the captain. Ask me anything."

Holloway appeared disappointed, but he turned and winked at Andy. "Don't put your rope away, Brackett. We'll need it if he changes his mind again."

The prisoner was so limp from terror that it took both men's support to get him back to the headquarters tent. A heavy smell indicated he had soiled himself. Holloway said, "Captain, I believe he's come to Jesus."

The captain emerged from the tent, smiling thinly. "He just needed time to consider the error of his ways."

When he quit coughing and regained his breath the culprit became a fountain of information. He said four including himself had been involved. They had planned in the excitement to cut off twelve or fifteen horses and get away with them in the darkness while the rangers chased after the main herd. They had hoped the raid would be blamed on Indians.

He rattled off his accomplices' names without hesitation: Arliss Wilkes, Brewster Pardo, and a boy called Scooter. He didn't know the boy's last name.

Holloway flipped through the pages of his fugitive book. "I find everybody in here except the boy."

The prisoner wailed as the cook rubbed salty bacon grease on his neck, burned red and raw by the rope. The captain told a nearby ranger, "Handcuff him to a chain and lock the chain around a tree. By the time he gets to a real jail he'll think it's the Menger Hotel in San Antonio."

Andy asked Holloway, "Can you do this? Is it legal?"

"Anything is legal if it works, and if you don't let the wrong people see it."

"Somebody is bound to ask about the mark around his neck."

"I'll just say he wears his collars too tight."

The captain chose five men to follow after and attempt to apprehend the thieves. They were Andy, Brackett, Tanner, Johnny Morris, and Sergeant Holloway. "Stay on their trail as long as you feel there's a chance it will be fruitful. Take them alive if it can be done without undue risk to yourselves. Otherwise, shoot to kill. If the rangers are to be respected we must show the outlaw class that we will exact a price for every offense."

Brackett jerked his head at Andy. "Captain, don't you think this boy is a little green?" Andy had not once heard him say *sir*.

"If so, he will ripen with experience."

By the time the five were prepared to leave, the rangers who had sought the three missing horses returned. One reported, "We found them, Captain. Looks like the thieves didn't get anything except experience."

"With a little luck we'll give them more of that."

It took some circling and searching before Andy found that the three remaining raiders had rejoined one another a couple of miles west from where they had first jumped the remuda. He waved his hat over his head to draw the attention of the other four rangers. Len Tanner had to be sent out to find Johnny Morris, off on a tangent of his own.

Sergeant Holloway said, "Since you found the trail, Andy, we'll let you track for a while. If you run up a stump, somebody else'll take it."

Tanner said, "I'll bet there ain't a better tracker in the company than Andy, unless it's me."

Holloway said, "You may get your chance. We'll see first what Andy can do."

Andy had not expected so much responsibility so soon. He felt a glow of pride, though he knew Holloway was testing him.

Brackett did not allow the glow to last. "Don't you mess up them tracks, Badger Boy. Remember, we ain't trailin' your Indians."

Andy could not think of an adequate retort.

He had left Long Red behind. The sorrel had had a hard

run last night and might tire out before this search was finished. The gray he had been lent had a rougher trot than Long Red's, pounding Andy's innards. This was going to be a long, tiresome ride. But at least he was doing something other than following a plow.

The frustrated horse thieves were not experienced at covering their trail. It seemed to Andy that they did not even try. Perhaps it never occurred to them that the rangers would be vengeful enough to follow them inasmuch as they had failed to get away with any horses.

Tanner observed, "They don't seem very smart."

Holloway said, "Most crooks aren't. Very few make much of a livin'. If they'd work as hard at honest labor as they do at mischief they could make somethin' of themselves. They live like coyotes and die like dogs, most of them, dead broke and bleedin' to death in the dirt."

Andy found where the fugitives had camped for the night on a creek. They had built a fire on a flat rock just above the waterline. A couple of drying rabbit skins, covered with flies, remained as evidence of their meager supper.

Tanner said, "Jackrabbit. That's about as far from prosperity as you can get."

Holloway said, "There's misguided kids back East wishin' they could run away and become outlaws. I wish every one of them could see this."

Andy remembered famine times with the People when he had eaten jackrabbit, even rattlesnakes. The thought almost made him feel sorry for the outlaws. But not quite. They had chosen this path. He doubted that anyone had forced them to it at gunpoint. He would reserve his sympathy for people upon whom hard times had fallen without fault of their own.

At midday he approached a small cedar picket cabin, the first dwelling he had seen. Holloway called, "Better hold up,

Andy. We'll ride in slow and careful. Tanner, you and Johnny circle way around and come in from the back side."

Andy, Holloway, and Brackett dismounted to present less of a target. They gave the other two time enough to reach their position. Andy said, "Looks like somebody has chopped down an awful lot of cedar." A large area had been cleared around and beyond the cabin. Brush was stacked in piles, probably to be burned when it dried enough.

Holloway said, "I'd figure they're clearin' a field, only this ground has more rocks than soil. I'd hate to try and put a plow in it."

Andy saw a movement and squinted to bring it into focus. "I see a man afoot out yonder. Looks like he's drivin' stakes into the ground. Why would anybody do that in a place like this?"

Holloway shook his head. "Damned if I know. Every time I think I've got people figured out, somebody throws a new puzzle at me."

While the three rode toward the man with the stakes, Andy saw Tanner and Johnny approach the cabin from the rear. Cautiously the pair dismounted and entered, then came back out. Obviously the fugitives were not here. Tracks showed they had passed this way, however.

The man carried a sledgehammer and a long cedar stake, sharpened at one end. Andy saw that he had made a line of stakes stretching to the cabin and beyond.

Holloway raised his hand. "Howdy. We're rangers, on the trail of three riders that came by here. Did you see them?"

The man wiped his sleeve across a gray-stubbled face to clear away a heavy sweat. His manner was jovial, his blue eyes bright though given a wild look by thick, bristly eyebrows. Andy saw that he wore a heavy boot on one foot and a loosely laced shoe on the other. Perhaps that was the only footwear he owned, or perhaps he had not noticed the difference. "They came by early this mornin' and traded me a couple of tired-out horses for two old skates I had. I sure got the best end of that deal."

"Maybe you did and maybe you didn't. Those men are horse thieves. They may have traded you stolen property."

The man's face fell. "You mean you're goin' to take them away from me?"

"We won't, but if the real owners should happen to turn up, you'll lose them."

The eyes brightened again. "By that time maybe I'll be rich enough to buy plenty more horses. I've got me a gold mine here."

"Gold mine?"

"A town. Don't you see it? A town all my own." He waved his hand toward the line of stakes. "I'll be sellin' lots as soon as I finish layin' out the townsite. Pretty soon there'll be houses all over this place. I'll put in a store and later on a bank."

"But a town has to have people. I don't see anybody except you."

"There's thousands of people back East lookin' for a new home. I've got the place for them right here. How about you gentlemen? Any of you want to be the first to settle in Hanleyville?"

"I take it your name is Hanley?"

"Yes sir, Joshua B. Hanley. *Mayor* Hanley."

Andy looked around but saw nothing to attract people to a site like this, certainly not in any numbers. The ground was unsuitable for farming except in narrow little valleys where rains had deposited soil washed down from the rocky hillsides. It might do for grazing cattle or sheep, but cedar was so thick the grass was sparse. He did not see a spring or creek.

Hanley said, "My daddy fought with Sam Houston at San

Jacinto. The Republic of Texas gave him this land grant. He never could claim it because the Indians was too thick out here. They're pretty well gone now. I decided it was time to plant a garden in the desert and build a town where there wasn't nothin' but a cedarbrake."

Holloway did a poor job of concealing his misgivings. "Mind if we water our horses before we go on?"

"There's a well up by the cabin. Dug it myself. Take all the water you want."

The town builder resumed stepping off the lots and driving his stakes. Holloway looked back on him with pity. "I've seen many a 'town' like this, somebody's wild dream. Poor devil'll sit out here waitin' by himself 'til he goes crazy. Maybe he already is."

Brackett asked, "What about those horses?"

"They're not ours. Whoever they were stolen from, there's not much chance they'll ever come this far huntin' them. Leave the poor fool somethin'."

Hanley's description of the fugitives, two men and a boy, had matched the one extracted from the prisoner after his early-morning rope dance.

At midafternoon the searchers came across a limping horse, its head down in fatigue. Nearby lay an abandoned saddle, blanket, and bridle.

Holloway said, "The two horses they've got left are probably the ones they traded from Hanley. One of those'll wear down fast, too, carryin' double. We'll have them pretty soon."

Shortly before sundown Andy caught a whiff of woodsmoke on a warm breeze from the west. He had not seen sign of a human since after they had left Hanley's townsite. It stood to reason that the fugitives had found what they considered a good place to camp. He waited for the others to come up even with him.

Holloway sniffed. "I smell it, too. They can't be far."

Andy flinched at a shot, followed quickly by another. By instinct he was half out of the saddle before he realized the sound came from far away. The shots had not been aimed at the rangers.

Holloway said, "Probably tryin' to get a deer or somethin' for supper. They need it, judgin' by the jackrabbits they ate last night."

The rangers moved into the edge of a cedarbrake and waited, listening. Andy heard nothing else. Either they hit their game with the first shots or it got away and they hadn't found anything else.

Brackett said, "I could stand a chunk of venison myself. Bo's cold biscuits are startin' to taste like horse sweat."

Holloway said, "They'll have to do for now. We'll wait here 'til dark, then close in on them. Maybe they'll have their bellies full and drop off to sleep." He glanced at Andy. "Nervous?"

"Am I supposed to be?"

"Most people are the first time they come up on a situation like this."

"This isn't my first time."

Tanner said, "Andy could tell you lots of stories."

Holloway said, "Another time. I'm fixin' to catch a little nap while I can."

Andy wondered aloud how the sergeant could drop off so quickly and easily.

Brackett said, "I was with him several times in the war. He could go to sleep twenty minutes before a battle or after one. Ain't much that scares him, aside from gettin' old. Bein' a ranger, he may not ever *get* old."

Andy realized that Brackett respected the sergeant. That surprised him. He had not seen Brackett show much respect for anybody.

What'll it take for him to respect me? he wondered.

Holloway awakened at good dark, as if he had planned it that way. He dug one of the cook's leftover biscuits from a canvas bag tied with his blanket roll. He watched Brackett while he ate it. "Horse sweat don't taste too bad," he said. "You just hold your breath and swallow, like it was gyppy water."

He checked his weapons, a silent indication that the others should do the same. He said, "We'll take them alive if we can. If we can't, it's their hard luck. Johnny, you and Tanner circle around. We'll come in on them from this side. Just be careful you don't shoot one another in the dark. I don't want to bury anybody but those horse thieves, and not even them if we don't have to."

The three thieves were either supremely overconfident or not very good at their calling. The rangers took them by complete surprise. They looked at their captors with disbelief for the few seconds the rangers required to take charge of their weapons. One made a grab for a rifle just as Brackett picked it up. Brackett swung it and struck him across the head. The outlaw went down like a sack of potatoes.

Holloway said, "You-all just sit right still and don't twitch an eyebrow. Brackett, you and Johnny put the handcuffs on them."

Two of the thieves were grown men. One snarled at the other, "You said they wouldn't come after us because we didn't get none of their horses. I told you we oughtn't to've built a fire like that."

The other was the one Brackett had struck. Blood trickled down his forehead. "It was you that kept hollerin' about bein' hungry and wantin' to stop and eat."

The third sat quietly and looked frightened. He was a boy of perhaps fourteen or fifteen years. His wrists were so thin that Brackett could not make the cuffs fit tightly.

Holloway asked, "What's your name, son?"

The lad would not look at him, nor would he answer. Holloway tried again without result. He asked, "Son, is one of these men your daddy?"

That seemed to irritate the boy. He exploded, "Hell no they ain't." Then, in a subdued voice, he added, "They're friends of mine."

Holloway asked the men their names, though he already knew from their confederate's confession back at the ranger camp. One said he was John Smith. The other was John Jones. Holloway made a wry smile. "Smith and Jones. I've arrested a lot of your kinfolks in my time."

"We're from big families," the oldest man retorted.

"Of all the victims you could've picked, what made you think you could get away with a raid on ranger horses?"

"We don't know nothin' about no ranger horses. We're just honest settlers mindin' our own business, lookin' for a place to make our homes."

"I don't think you'll need to worry about a home for the next few years. The state of Texas is fixin' to give you one. Maybe I can help get your terms shortened if you'll talk to me straight."

"Straight about what?"

"Whatever I decide to ask you." Holloway turned to the boy, who by now seemed to have lost most of his fear. "I'm askin' you again, son, what is your name?"

The answer was curt. "Brown. Bobby Brown."

"Jones, Smith, and Brown. You got yourself tied in with some real gallows bait, son. They'll get you nothin' except a hard life and an early death."

"I already had the hard life. Maybe death ain't so bad."

"Don't you believe in hell?"

"Hell can't be no worse than what I've already had. And the devil can't be no meaner than some people I know."

Andy felt a swelling of pity. It was clear that this boy had been badly treated for a long time.

The outlaw who called himself Smith quickly put in, "It wasn't us. We been good to him. Treated him like a kid brother almost."

Holloway's voice had acid in it. "Teachin' him to be like you?"

"Teachin' him how to get along in a hard world. Every boy needs to learn a trade."

"Some trade, stealin' horses."

"We ain't stole no horses. You see any of your horses in this camp?"

"It's not because you didn't try." Holloway studied the boy a minute. "We ought to hang the two of you right here for leadin' this kid astray."

The boy came to their defense. "Wasn't nobody around to take care of me after my mama died. My daddy's in jail. Goin' to be there for a long time. Arliss and Brewster, they picked me up and let me come along with them. Didn't nobody else care if I lived or died."

Holloway almost smiled. "Arliss and Brewster. Not John." He had known that all along.

Smith growled, "Them's our middle names."

Part of a deer carcass was hanging from a cedar limb, a butcher knife stuck in it. Holloway said, "Well, Arliss and Brewster, I'm grateful to you-all for providin' that venison. We've made do on cold biscuits and air all day." He jerked his head toward the deer. Tanner moved quickly to the task.

After eating his fill, Holloway fetched the fugitive book from his saddlebag. "Arliss Wilkes and Brewster Pardo. Both of your names are on the list. You're wanted for several things besides horse stealin'."

Arliss said, "We get blamed for things we didn't do."

"Accordin' to our information the boy's name is Scooter. But Scooter's not a Christian name." He looked at the youngster. The boy said nothing.

Arliss was the one who had called himself John Smith. He said, "Ain't heard no other given name but Scooter. His last name's Tennyson."

Holloway smiled. "That's more like it. See, it's not hard to talk to the rangers."

"We don't have much choice when you got guns on us."

Brackett growled, "At least we know what names to put on your headboards if you-all give us any trouble. Every man ought to have his right name on his headboard."

Later, chewing on a half-broiled strip of meat, Andy studied Scooter Tennyson. He looked as if he had been brought up in a brush thicket. His hair was a-tangle. Someone had made a bad effort at cutting it, leaving a ragged job that looked more like the work of a butcher knife than of scissors. His shirt was too large for his thin frame. It hung on him like a partially collapsed tent. His trousers, also too big, had patches on both knees and holes in both patches.

Andy let his imagination run free. He could have been in the same situation at almost the same age had it not been for Rusty Shannon. Fate had been kind to him. It appeared that nobody had been kind to this boy.

In a quiet voice he asked Holloway, "What'll happen to the kid when we take him in?"

"The state has got a home for boys like this."

"It's like a junior penitentiary, isn't it?"

"Pretty much, I guess. I've never seen it."

"Doesn't seem right. He's never had much of a chance."

"He's old enough to know right from wrong. Some people set out on a crooked trail earlier than others. He said his daddy's in jail. It's probably in the blood."

"I don't believe that. I'll bet if he was among decent folks a while he'd straighten out."

· Holloway's face showed his doubt. "Maybe. You want the job?"

"I don't know that I'm the one to do it. I'm not but a few years older than him. And I've got a job as a ranger."

"I'll talk to the captain when we get back to camp. Maybe he'll see his way clear to do somethin' for the boy. What's your interest in him?"

"Maybe it's because when I look at him I see what could've become of me."

Talking to Scooter was like talking to a post. The boy turned away and made a show of ignoring Andy. His patience strained, Andy said, "I'm just tryin' to help you, kid."

"Don't need your help. Don't need nothin' but a good leavin' alone."

"You won't get much leavin' alone if they put you behind the bars."

"Maybe that's what I was born for."

"Nobody's born for a life like that. They choose it or get pushed into it. Looks to me like you've been pushed. I'd like to see you get a decent chance."

"You a preacher or somethin'?"

"No, I'm just a ranger, and a new one at that. Mostly I guess you'd say I've been a farmer."

"Then go back to your plow and leave me alone."

Andy caught a look from Holloway that said for him to ease off. The boy pulled away from Andy and closer to his outlaw friends. Holloway beckoned Andy away from the campfire, out into the darkness.

He said, "You're wastin' your breath."

"Maybe he hasn't had time to understand the trouble he's in. Once he does, he might be easier to talk to. It took me a while when I was where he's at."

"I tried once to raise an orphaned coyote pup. Thought since I'd caught him young he'd train like a dog, but he never did. He never was anything but a wild chicken-killin' coyote. I finally caught him killin' a baby calf. Bad as I hated to, I had to shoot him."

"There were folks who thought the same thing of me, comin' out of a Comanche camp."

"From what Tanner has told me, some good folks took an interest and set you right."

"Maybe that's all Scooter needs."

"I think you're puttin' yourself in for disappointment, but I'll talk to the captain."

Andy went back and sat down near Scooter, trying to think of an approach that might work. It was Scooter who made the approach. The boy said, "I heard some of what you were sayin' out there. What's this about you and the Comanches?"

Andy took the boy's interest as a hopeful sign. "They killed my folks and carried me off when I was little. Raised me for several years. I was luckier than you. Some good people cared enough to take me in and give me a home."

"I never found no good people except Arliss and Brewster. Arliss was in jail a while with my daddy. He got a notion Daddy had buried money someplace and I might know where it was. But my daddy never had enough money that he could afford to bury any."

"Arliss and Brewster aren't the kind you ought to be travelin' with."

"They're all I got." The boy went pensive. "We come across another feller a few days ago. He was nice to me. Him and Arliss and Brewster robbed a little bank over at a burg called Brownwood. But he didn't cotton to the notion of stealin' ranger horses, nor of goin' farther west. Said there wasn't no banks out there, so he left us. I kind of wished he'd stayed. Seemed smarter than Arliss and Brewster. Maybe we wouldn't have got ourselves caught."

"You were bound to get caught sooner or later."

"I felt kind of sorry for him. Said his wife got shot a while back. He was still takin' it hard."

Andy felt a tingling along his spine. "Who was he? Did he give a name?"

The boy thought for a moment. "Bascom, it was. Yeah, Bascom. At least that's what he told us."

"Corey Bascom?"

"I believe so."

Andy's excitement built. "Did he say where he was goin'?"

The boy looked at him as if he did not believe the question. "I don't never ask a thing like that. Anybody wants you to know, they'll tell you."

So Bascom had been with these two-bit badmen as recently as the last day or two. It was a starting place, at least. Andy could hardly wait to write Rusty a letter. He would do it as soon as he got back to camp.

Sometime during the night he awakened to the sound of a running horse. Brackett shouted, "That damned kid has gotten away."

Andy flung his blanket aside and pulled on the boots he had put beneath it to protect them from dew. He saw Brackett pick up a pair of handcuffs.

Brackett said, "Those cuffs were too loose on him. He slipped them off."

Holloway declared, "Andy, you're so interested in givin' the boy a chance, go see if you can catch him and bring him back. Brackett, you'd better follow along."

Wilkes and Pardo were handcuffed to the trunks of young

trees. Scooter had been, too. Wilkes said, "Good for the boy. I hope he gets plumb to Mexico."

Holloway took a quick inventory of the horses. "At least the kid has an eye for horseflesh. He took mine. You'll have to ride hard to catch him."

Andy could not see far in the darkness, but the hoofbeats had told him the boy was headed west. He wished he had Long Red with him. The sorrel had outrun almost everything Andy had ever pitted him against. He had not tested the gray for speed, but he gave it the spurs. He felt the rush of wind in his eyes and ears. Limbs whipped him across the face and shoulders.

Brackett shouted, "You'd better slow down. That horse is liable to fall and bust his leg."

The horse had better night vision than Andy, for it leaped over fallen limbs and cut around trees Andy had not seen. He leaned low in the saddle and gave the animal its head.

He saw the dark shape of the fugitive ahead of him, making a crooked trail through the cedar brush and live oaks. "Scooter," he shouted. "Stop."

Scooter shouted a reply. Andy could not discern the words, but the tone left no doubt about their meaning. The boy was outlining Andy's ancestry in scathing detail.

The chase came to a sudden stop as a low limb caught Scooter across the chest and held him while the sergeant's horse ran on without him. By the time Andy reached him the boy lay curled up on the ground like a wounded caterpillar, gasping for lost breath. Andy demanded, "What the hell were you tryin' to do? You've just added another horse-stealin' charge to your record."

Scooter tried a sharp answer, but he could only wheeze. Brackett went after the runaway horse. It stopped when it realized it had lost its rider.

Andy gave way to anger. "There I was, beggin' the sergeant to give you a chance. Then you pull a stunt like this."

The boy was not as helpless as he had appeared. He jumped to his feet, pushed Andy aside and made a grab for the gray horse. Andy caught his shirt and pulled him away just as the boy's left foot hit the stirrup. He gave Scooter a hard shove that put the boy on the ground again.

Brackett came back, leading the sergeant's horse. He seemed to be enjoying himself. "Looks like that kid's got some badger in him, too, Badger Boy."

Andy's anger subsided. He remembered that he had tried to fight back when he was first recaptured from the Comanches. The difference was that a broken leg gave him no chance of winning. He had tried once to run away, but the weak leg had betrayed him.

"I guess we can't blame him too much for tryin'." He nodded at Scooter. "Get back on the sergeant's horse." He cut a long leather string from his saddle and tied Scooter's hands to the pommel. "I'll bet you don't slip out of that."

The boy tugged at the bonds, then began crying softly.

The last of his anger drained, Andy wanted to comfort him. "Maybe the worst thing you've done is fall in with bad company. They can't do much to you for that."

Brackett said, "He's a horse thief."

"He's just a little reckless about his borrowin'. Seems I remember you takin' one of Rusty Shannon's horses once."

"But I left another one in his place."

"One you'd 'borrowed' from the U.S. Army. Got Rusty into a lot of trouble."

"That was a whole other time. Things are different now. And this boy ain't you. He's somethin' else entirely. Pretty soon you'll be wishin' you'd never seen him."

Andy already wished that. But he *had* seen him, and he could not give up on him, any more than Rusty Shannon had given up on a half-wild kid named Badger Boy.

· 13 ·

Rusty Shannon leaned on the hoe and looked across the field at the weeds still to be chopped out of his growing corn. It was a job without an end, for before he could get the last row finished, the first would need hoeing again. He missed Andy and Tanner. Andy had always been a diligent worker. Tanner could be, too, when the mood was upon him and he wasn't fidgeting to go somewhere.

Old Shanty had ridden over here yesterday on his mule and offered to help, but Rusty had politely declined. Shanty had work enough of his own. A man of his age and frail constitution needed a lot of rocking-chair time.

"Your eyes show the miseries," Shanty had said. "This old place just keeps you studyin' about the girl you was fixin' to bring here."

"I stay busy, but it doesn't help much."

"Swingin' a hoe don't tie up your mind. Leaves you free to think too much. You need to get away a while."

"I'd be thinkin' about her no matter where I went."

He had left here twice following false rumors that he had hoped would lead him to Corey Bascom. He had ridden for days, only to be left frustrated and sick at heart. So far as he knew he had never been anywhere close to Corey.

Shanty had suggested, "Everybody says you was a good ranger once. The man you been lookin' for could be way down in Mexico by now or plumb out to the California ocean. But there's a-plenty other sinners runnin' loose. They need catchin'. Maybe you'd ought to be a ranger again."

"It wouldn't be the same."

"Sometimes the Lord don't hand us a full bucket. We give Him thanks for what we do get, even if it's just half a bucket."

Rusty recognized Sheriff Tom Blessing's big horse coming in on the trail from town. He gratefully carried the hoe to the turn row and laid it down. Tom usually opened his conversations with either the weather or the state of the crops. He hollered, "Your corn's lookin' good."

"Not as good as the weeds."

Tom dismounted, and Rusty shook hands with him. Tom took another look across the field. "You need to go to town and hire a boy or two to help you."

"I wouldn't want to take anybody away from school."

"School's out. And workin' in the fields will teach them more practical stuff than studyin' about the history of England and all them other places a long ways off from here."

"I'll think about it. How's Mrs. Blessing?"

"Better every day, thanks to Alice." Tom frowned, waiting. "Ain't you goin' to ask me about Alice?"

Rusty thought he probably should. "How's Alice?"

"She's a good-hearted girl. Homesick, of course. And she's still afraid you resent her because she's alive and her sister's not."

At a conscious level Rusty had tried to put such feelings aside, but they still rose to the surface at unexpected times when he was not prepared to confront them. "I know it wasn't her fault. Except for her bad judgment in marryin' Corey Bascom."

"Speakin' of Corey Bascom, ..." Tom reached into his shirt pocket. "While I was at the post office gettin' my mail I found you had a letter, too. It's from Andy. He thinks he's got a line on your man."

The envelope had been opened. Tom had read the letter. Rusty did not mind. He had far too much privacy out here anyway, living by himself. He hurried to unfold the letter, running his finger along the lines as he read.

Tom said, "They sent Andy and Len to a frontier ranger company camped way out on the San Saba River. That's where he heard about Corey Bascom."

Rusty hurried ahead to the part of the letter that told about a kid who had ridden a short time with Bascom. His hands shook so that it was difficult to read the lines. "Reckon how many days it'll take me to get to that camp?"

"A bunch. It's liable to be a cold trail anyway."

"No colder than others I've tried. At least we know Bascom has been there, or close by." He turned his eyes to the west. "I've never been that far out yonderway." He started walking toward the barn.

Tom rode along beside him. "Me and my boys will keep an eye on the place while you're gone. Can't guarantee to cut all the weeds down, though. If a man could get his crops to grow as good as his weeds ..."

"To hell with the weeds."

"What about that hoe you left layin' out there?"

"To hell with the hoe, too. I've got some country to cover."

Together he and Tom sketched out a rough map. Tom said, "You've been to Austin, so you know the road that far. From there you'll head west into the hills. I'm a little hazy

about the towns, but you'll pass through some German settlements like Friederichsburg. From what Andy says in the
letter the camp is west of Fort Mason, close to a settlement
called Menardville. Feller told me he saw ruins of an old
Spanish mission there. Jim Bowie's name was carved over the
gate."

"I'll ask directions as I go along," Rusty said.

"I wouldn't be tellin' everybody my business was I you.
There's some wild old boys out yonder. They may get hostile
if they find out you're after one of their own kind."

"I take pretty good care of myself."

"You haven't always. I've seen a couple of your scars."
Tom thrust his hand forward. "Don't worry about your farm.
And don't worry about Alice. Me and the missus never had
a daughter before. It's nice havin' one for a while."

Rusty packed a smokehouse ham and a slab of bacon as
well as flour and salt and coffee. There had been a time he
could usually sustain himself on wild game for days on end.
But wherever settlers moved in, the game tended to thin out.
He saddled the bay horse and tied his pack onto a fancy-
stepping Spanish mule he had acquired at a trade day in
town.

Tom warned, "I never trusted them little mules. They can
kick so fast you can't see it comin'. They'll break your leg
before you can spit."

"I'll be careful."

Tom watched as Rusty rode away. He hollered, "Anything you want me to tell Alice?"

"Just don't let any strangers see her."

In his eagerness he rode far into the first night and had
to search in the darkness for a grassy spot to stake the horse
and mule and for wood to build a fire. He resolved not to do
that again. The road was familiar as far as Austin. He wasted
no time there reminiscing about last January's confrontation

over possession of the state capitol. He sought directions and nothing else.

He found the topography changed abruptly west of Austin. The road led into rocky cedar-covered hills and scattered live-oak mottes. The land was drier. He wondered at the feasibility of cultivating it. Settlers so far had restricted the plow to valley flats. A scattering of cattle, sheep, and Mexican goats made use of the hillsides, grazing the short grass, browsing whatever parts of the brushy plants were edible.

Looks like a hard place to make a living, he thought.

Yet the first settlement he encountered had a more prosperous look than he would have expected, given the land's meager prospects. The buildings were mostly of native stone, the individual pieces carefully chiseled to fit closely together. The roofs were shingled with cypress, which some artisan had trimmed to just the proper dimensions.

His second night out of Austin he reached the German town Tom had told him about, Friederichsburg. The streets were wide and generous. Most of the signs were in words he did not know, though he could figure out some that bore a passing resemblance to English, such as "Bäckerei" and "Drogerie." He found a tall wooden building with an odd steamboat-looking front. The sign proclaimed it the Nimitz Hotel.

He would not spend money on a hotel room, but he decided to treat himself to the luxury of a dining-room meal. The staff spoke English with an accent that reminded him of the way old Captain—now Judge—August Burmeister talked. After a pleasant supper of venison, gravy, and hot bread, he rode up the Hauptstrasse to look at the rest of the town. Evidently these people had wrung a living from the land despite its less than impressive appearance.

He tipped his hat to a middle-aged woman of generous proportions who was watering a flower bed from a metal

bucket that had holes punched in its bottom. Her husband
pulled weeds by hand from a vegetable garden beside the
stone house. A young girl carried a bucket of milk up from a
cow pen in back.

Rusty could see how they prospered against the odds.
Everybody worked.

He received directions to the Fort Mason road and left at
daylight. The little mule seemed to like Friederichsburg and
resisted leaving it until Rusty applied the quirt across its
hindquarters. It kicked at him and missed, then gave him a
resentful look that said it would exact revenge sometime
when he was not looking.

A friendly storekeeper had told him Fort Mason was forty
miles away. He also hinted that trouble was brewing between
some of the German settlers and a segment of the English-
speaking citizens for no good reason that met the eye except
that they came out of two different cultures. "Might be a good
idea if you take roundance on that town," he said.

Rusty had traveled forty miles and more in a single day
when the occasion demanded it, but it was hard on the animals. He decided not to push them. Chances were that Bascom's trail would be cold, as Tom had said. But if it wasn't,
he would not want to take it up with a worn-out horse and
mule.

He camped on the bank of the James River. A German
family came along in a wagon, heading in the opposite direction. They said they had found the atmosphere uncom-
fortable in Mason. "It is for the children that we go," the
father explained, his words labored. "It is not good that they
see men fight."

Rusty was aware that during the Civil War many German
settlers in the hill country had remained loyal to the Union.
They had suffered severely for it. Whatever the current trou-

ble was, he suspected it had its roots in the war years and the distrust created between neighbors, even within families.

These people were short of provisions. Rusty gave them most of his flour and coffee, knowing he could replenish his supply in Mason.

He reached the town toward mid-morning. Riding in, he noticed that people watched him with suspicion. It was much like the reception he had received in Austin some months ago when that place was threatened with violence over possession of the governor's office.

The proprietor of the store where he chose to stop spoke with a German accent. He offered no pleasantries but simply sacked up some flour and coffee beans and laid them on the counter. His mistrust was palpable though his manner was civil. Rusty asked, "Where do I find the road to Menardville?"

The storekeeper seemed a little friendlier. "You do not stay here?"

"Just passin' through. Got business at a ranger camp over there."

"You are not here for the trouble?"

"Whatever your troubles may be, they're none of mine."

Leaving the store, Rusty found three men standing in the dirt street, watching him. Their grim faces indicated that their intentions were not benign. Rusty tied his provisions on the little Spanish pack mule, then turned to face the men. "You-all got business with me?"

One appointed himself spokesman. He took a step forward. "We got business with any stranger that drifts into town. How come you to stop at that Dutchman's store?"

"It was the first one I saw."

"Around here these days a man has got to know which side of the fence he stands on. There's them, and there's us. Which are you?"

"Neither. I'm a passin' stranger, and I'm fixin' to pass."
He swung into the saddle, feeling angry.

Damn it, he thought, I didn't come all this way to get
tangled up in somebody else's fight.

Looking back, he saw that they had caught up horses and
trailed behind him. He suspected they would follow him out
of town, then challenge him or perhaps even waylay him. He
decided to meet their challenge here and now. Reaching
down, he brought up his rifle. He turned abruptly and faced
them. "I can find my own way. I'm not lookin' for any escort."

The spokesman said, "Just because you talk good English
don't mean you're all right. There's some Americans around
here sidin' with the Dutchmen. I'm goin' to see what you got
on that pack mule and make sure you ain't smugglin' guns."

Dismounting, the man walked up to the pack mule and
reached for the rope that held the pack in place. The little
mule whirled half around and kicked him on the leg. The
impact sounded like a small-caliber gunshot. Grabbing his
knee, the man gave a cry of pain and crumpled. The other
two got down to see about him while he howled that his leg
was broken.

Rusty spurred the bay into a fast trot toward the Menardville road. The little mule had to trot extra fast to keep up.

He could not remember exactly what he had paid for the
animal, but he decided it had been cheap at the price.

He met a horseman wearing a badge and found him to
be a deputy sheriff. The lawman asked, "What was the argument down yonder?"

"No argument. Some feller got a little too close to a mule."

He could tell that he had not fooled the deputy. The man
said, "Stranger, ain't you?"

"First time I was ever here. Nice lookin' town, but it's got
some testy citizens."

"Was I you, I wouldn't linger. Them boys yonder belong

to one side. They probably suspicion that you've come to throw in with the other." He narrowed his eyes. "Or maybe that's why you're here."

"I'm just tryin' to find my way to a ranger camp over on the San Saba."

"You a ranger?"

"Used to be."

"You're in luck. Been some rangers in town tryin' to stop trouble. A couple of them are fixin' to report back to camp. If you was to ride along with them, nobody'd bother you none."

"Just point me to where they're at."

"This used to be a pretty good town. Will be again when we get rid of a few rotten apples."

Rusty was pleased to find Jim and Johnny Morris preparing to leave Mason. He had a feeling the deputy did not fully trust him until he saw the welcome the brothers gave him, pumping his hand, slapping him about the shoulders.

The three men who had accosted him made no attempt to follow. He mentioned that to the Morris brothers.

Jim said, "You're in West Texas. A lot of frisky old boys come here when they've wore out their welcome everywhere else. Mason's not the only place that's got a two-bit local feud goin' on."

Johnny put in, "If you think there's some hard *hombres* here, you ought to see Junction City."

"Right now I'm just lookin' for Andy."

Jim said, "I hope you ain't come to take him home. Andy's took to rangerin' like a duck takes to water."

"No, I felt that way myself once. I won't try to get him to quit."

Johnny asked, "Why don't you join up with us? Captain's still got some openin's left, and you can see how bad the rangers are needed out here."

"I have my farm to worry about. And other things."

"We know about the other things. Len Tanner told us."

That was no surprise. Len had never recognized a secret in his life. Rusty explained about Andy's letter.

Jim said, "Yeah, that boy Scooter's still in camp. Rougher than a corncob. Andy's tryin' to work the rough edges off of him, but the kid has got a coyote eye. I wouldn't want him sneakin' up behind me."

Rusty could understand Andy's sympathy for a boy like that. Andy had been in much the same position a few years earlier. "He thinks the boy might give me a lead on Corey Bascom, the man I've been lookin' for."

"The captain's already made inquiries about that bank robbery. Andy talked to them three horse thieves 'til he was blue in the face, but he didn't find out much about Bascom. It's been so long now that I'm afraid you won't be able to pick up the trail."

"I'd like to talk to the boy, anyhow."

"Gettin' him to talk to *you* will be the hard part. He can cuss like a muleskinner, but he don't put out much information."

Sight of the ranger encampment brought back memories, most pleasant, a few painful. It looked much like the wartime camp he remembered far to the north near Fort Belknap. This one appeared better equipped, for the state's Confederate government had always teetered on the edge of bankruptcy. Necessities had been scarce, luxuries not even considered. Postwar Texas was hardly wealthy, but it was better off than ten years ago.

Jim said, "I'll introduce you to the captain."

"I'm much obliged."

Rusty remembered meeting the captain a long time back. The officer said, "Welcome to camp, Mr. Shannon. I hope you have come to enlist."

"No sir, I have other business here."

Sergeant Holloway walked into the headquarters tent. Recognition was immediate, and he grasped Rusty's hand. He said, "Captain, me and Rusty rode together up at Fort Belknap. Chased outlaws and Indians. Even caught a few now and then."

The captain said, "If you have not come to join us, what brings you so far west?"

Rusty explained about his mission and showed Andy's letter. The captain nodded grimly. "I'm afraid you've come a long way for nothing. We interrogated the three prisoners at considerable length before we sent them away to jail. All we got out of them was that a man named Bascom was with them in the bank robbery. He left them before they made a try at our horses. I sent men out to try to pick up a trail, but evidently your man traveled a public road long enough to mix his tracks with a hundred others."

"What about the boy?"

"He is still here in camp, to everybody's regret. Private Pickard thinks he can redeem him. I had about as leave try to redeem a wildcat cub."

"Andy's got a good heart."

"One that outweighs his judgment, I am sad to say. I'd have already sent that young heathen back east to the dubious mercy of the court if Pickard hadn't put up such an argument for him. But the boy has pushed me almost to the end of my tether." The captain glanced at Holloway. "Where *is* Pickard?"

"Out on horse guard."

"Send someone to replace him and tell him he has com-

pany." The captain gave Rusty a quiet and calculating study.
"This company could use a man of your experience. Are you
sure you would not like to enlist?"

"It wouldn't be fair to you. The first time I heard something new about Corey Bascom I'd be up and gone."

Andy arrived at the headquarters tent, riding his sorrel.
Rusty imagined he looked older and more mature, but only
a few weeks had passed since they had last seen one another.
After the howdies Rusty said, "I got your letter."

Andy appeared troubled. "I didn't realize how long it
would take you to get it and how long it'd take you to reach
here. I'm afraid you've wasted the trip."

"I'd still like to talk to that boy."

"Don't judge Scooter too quick. He looks rough and talks
rough, but he's never had much chance to be otherwise. I'd
like him to get that chance."

Andy's eyes looked so earnest that Rusty could only go
along with him. "All I want to do is talk. Maybe there's somethin' he's forgotten to tell."

Andy led Rusty toward the cook tent. He said, "I hope
you weren't mad at me, leavin' sudden like I did. Len was
goin' to report to the rangers, and it seemed like a good idea
to ride along with him."

"You're old enough to know your own mind. I wasn't
any older the first time I joined."

Andy showed him a boy he took to be twelve or thirteen,
peeling potatoes for the black cook. A dark scowl showed his
opinion of the job.

"Boy," the cook said, "there's too much tater goin' out
with them peels."

The youngster flourished the knife as if threatening to use
it for a weapon. "There'll be an old darkey throwed out with
them if you don't leave me the hell alone."

"Captain says you've got to work if you're goin' to eat.

Otherwise he's fixin' to send you where he sent them friends of yours. Be a long time before they see freedom."

"I'd be in better company than what I got here."

"I swear, youngun, I don't know what to do with you."

"You don't have to do nothin', just let me be."

Rusty gave Andy a quizzical look. "You really think you can reform that?"

"You reformed me."

"I don't remember you ever sassed me that bad."

"I'd about forgotten how to talk English. By the time I learned it again I'd smartened up." Andy moved into the cook tent. "Bo, can I borrow your helper a little while?"

"Borry him? You can *keep* him. He ain't much help to me."

Andy introduced Rusty. "Scooter, this is the man who raised me after I came back from the Indians."

Scooter gave no sign that he was impressed. To Rusty he was a freckle-faced ragamuffin in donated ranger clothes so large they swallowed him up. His hair was badly in need of barbering. His eyes were his only outstanding feature. Brown and dark as coffee beans, they seemed to be searching for a fight.

Rusty said, "I want to ask you about Corey Bascom."

Scooter's voice was full of resentment. "I already told them all I know. They've asked me twenty times."

"Didn't he give you any idea where he was goin' when he left you?"

"Didn't even say he was leavin'. Just pulled out. Told Arliss and them it was a fool idea tryin' to steal horses from the rangers. He wasn't havin' no part of it."

"What direction did he go?"

"I didn't watch." The boy stuck out his chin in a challenging gesture. "For all I know, he went straight up."

Andy gave Rusty a quiet look that said it was no use. Corey Bascom was too cagey to tell his plans to a kid he had just met. Even if the boy knew more, which was unlikely, he had no intention of sharing it.

Rusty sent him back to his potato peeling. In a show of rebellion, Scooter cut the first skin even thicker than before and flipped it at the cook.

Bo said, "Youngun, I'd like to get a preacher ahold of you. A fire-and-brimstone Baptist."

Rusty and Andy looked at one another. Andy said, "Preacher Webb."

After reflection, Rusty rejected the idea. "Preacher's gettin' too old to take on a wildcat like this."

Andy said, "But you're not."

"Don't try to push that job off onto me. I've already been down that road once, with you."

"I turned out pretty good, didn't I?"

"This boy isn't you. Like as not he'd run off the first chance he got. And if he didn't, he'd make me wish he had."

"Think about it at least. Don't be quick to say no."

"I've already said it."

Andy accepted defeat, if only for the time being. He said, "I'd better go out and finish my turn on horse guard. See you about supper." He untied the sorrel horse.

Rusty said, "I see that Farley Brackett hasn't talked you out of Long Red."

Andy leaned forward and patted the sorrel on the shoulder. "He knows he'd be wastin' his breath."

Rusty watched Andy ride out to where the rangers' extra horses were loose-herded on grass.

The captain said, "I understand you raised Private Pickard."

"Mostly he raised himself, after the Comanches. I just tried to point him in the right direction from time to time and keep him from gettin' killed."

"Now he has a notion he can do the same for that vagabond kid. I'm afraid he is letting himself in for a terrible disappointment. A tree grows as the sapling is bent. This boy has been bent the wrong way too long."

"I guess Andy feels that he owes me, and the way to pay the debt is to do for somebody else what I did for him."

"That speaks well for his intentions, if not his judgment. You'll stay the night with us, won't you, Shannon?"

"So you can keep tryin' to recruit me?"

"You've already said no. I'll not make a nuisance of myself."

"Then I'll be glad to stay. Reminds me of old times."

The cook rang the supper bell. The rangers gathered around, filling their plates from pots and Dutch ovens. The captain glanced about, then asked, "Bo, where's your young helper?"

"He ain't no helper of mine. Sneaks off every chance he gets. Didn't finish half the spuds I gave him to peel. You ever looked at his neck?"

The captain seemed puzzled. "Can't say that I have."

"He's got a ring around it. Born for a hangman's noose, if you ask me."

"That's just dirt."

After supper Len Tanner and two other rangers rode out to bring the horses up close to camp and relieve Andy of guard duty. The horses came in, and the rangers, but Rusty saw nothing of Andy. He walked up to Tanner.

"Where's Andy?"

"Didn't see him. The horses was scattered more than they ought to've been. It ain't like Andy to've rode off and left them."

Rusty felt stirrings of concern. "No, it's not. Wait 'til I get my horse. We'll go out and look for him."

Jim and Johnny Morris joined them without having to be asked. When they reached the area where the horses had grazed, Jim said, "Me and Johnny will split off and go around this way."

Rusty jerked his head at Tanner. "We'll take the other side."

He had ridden about two hundred yards when he saw Andy rise up out of the grass and stagger to his feet. Rusty whistled to Tanner, who had ridden a wider outside circle. Tanner came in a run.

Rusty saw a bloody streak down Andy's forehead, all the way to his jaw. Andy swayed as if about to fall. Rusty stepped down quickly from the saddle and caught him.

"Did Long Red fall with you?" he asked. So far as he had ever seen, the horse was surefooted.

Andy turned and caught hold of Rusty's saddle to steady himself. "Wasn't Long Red. It was Scooter."

"That kid?"

Tanner and the Morris brothers rode up. Tanner dismounted and took a critical look at Andy's head. "Looks like somebody gave him a six-shooter shampoo."

Andy started to nod but raised his hand to his head and grimaced. "Twice. You wouldn't think a boy that small could hit so hard."

Jim Morris said, "I been warnin' you about him. A little rattlesnake can bite you as bad as a big one."

Rusty said, "Let's get him back to camp. He can tell us about it there."

Jim pointed northward. "We found tracks of a horse headed off yonderway."

Andy said, "He took Long Red."

Tanner spat. "Thievin' little coyote." He mounted his horse, then freed his left foot from the stirrup. "You-all boost Andy up here."

Riding toward camp, Andy explained that Scooter had walked out around the horse herd. "Said the captain wanted to see me right away. He had stolen a pistol somewhere. Soon as I let him swing up behind me, he hit me over the head with it and shoved me out of the saddle. Then he hit me again for good measure. Next thing I remember was Rusty ridin' toward me."

"Ungrateful little whelp," Jim said. "He'd already be in jail if it wasn't for you."

Rusty said, "Not much chance of catchin' him now. It'll be dark pretty quick. By mornin' there's no tellin' how far he'll be gone."

"And on my horse," Andy lamented.

· 14 ·

Andy's head throbbed so painfully that there were moments when he thought he might die. There were other moments when he feared he might not. He expected the captain to lecture him on his misspent sympathy for a wayward boy, but evidently the officer decided the experience was lesson enough in itself. At daylight the captain detailed the Morris brothers and another ranger to find Long Red's tracks and determine if they could be followed. By late afternoon the men were back. They had lost the trail.

Andy had expected Rusty to start home, but instead he remained in camp. For the time being, at least, he was more concerned about Andy than about trying to find Corey Bascom.

Andy was sick at heart, partly from loss of the sorrel horse but more from the realization that his good intentions toward Scooter had gone for nothing. He felt betrayed. He kept wondering if he might have done more, or done better. In a way he could not analyze, he even felt that he had let Rusty down. Rusty had taken a chance on Andy against long odds a long time ago. What Andy had tried to do for Scooter had been meant as an oblique thank-you to Rusty.

Rusty seated himself on the ground near the spread-out blankets on which Andy lay, a wet cloth across his forehead. He said, "If it's any consolation to you, Farley Brackett is mad as hell. He says if anybody deserved to steal that sorrel horse, it was him."

Andy was too miserable to appreciate Rusty's dark humor. He said, "Everybody kept tellin' me. I thought I could change Scooter the way you changed me."

"Maybe it was in his blood. More likely it's because he's been mistreated all his life. Beat a young horse every day and he'll outlaw on you. He'll reach a point where there's nothin' much you can do except shoot him. Else he's liable to kill you. That boy was ruined before you ever saw him."

"I guess. I just hoped for better."

"Look at the fugitive list the captain has. Most of the men on it had mothers and daddies who did the best they could to make somethin' out of them. Somewhere, every one of them came to a fork in the road and took the wrong direction. Most of them will never turn around. They'll stay on the devil's road 'til it leads them to the cemetery."

"You figure that's the case with Scooter?"

"He'll end up on the fugitive list, if he lives that long."

After two days Andy felt much better. He expected Rusty to start home, but Rusty showed no inclination to leave. He said he was hanging on a few days longer, hoping some word might come about Corey Bascom. Andy suspected one strong reason was that he enjoyed the rangers' company and the camp life that reminded him of other times.

Whatever the cause, Andy was comforted by Rusty's presence.

The third day after Scooter ran away, Andy saw a horse gallop into the edge of camp, lathered with sweat. The rider pulled up in front of the headquarters tent and dismounted, so exhausted he almost went to his knees. In a weak voice he called for the captain.

The officer came out before the rider could yell a second time.

The man struggled for breath. "Indians, Captain. We got Indian trouble."

Andy turned toward Rusty. He felt a cold dread. "I hoped I'd never have to face this."

Rusty said, "You had to know it was bound to come."

The captain called the company together. He asked Sergeant Holloway, "How many men could be ready to go right away?"

"We have four out on detail. Leaving a few to guard the camp, we have a dozen available men at best, sir, including ourselves."

"Very well, send a detail to bring up the horses."

Farley Brackett had not spoken directly to Andy since Scooter had absconded with the sorrel horse. Andy was conscious now of Farley watching him. He imagined the thought behind the critical eyes: that in a showdown Andy would not be able to go against his Comanche friends.

Rusty gave Andy a gentle nudge. "Somebody's got to help guard the camp. If you don't feel right about this, why don't you stay? Tell the captain you're still not up to a hard ride."

Andy wished he could. "I took an oath. Whatever the captain gives me to do, I'll do it."

"Would you feel better if I went along?"

Andy was not certain what his reaction should be. Rusty's presence always gave him a feeling of security. But in this case it might indicate doubt about Andy. "You're not a ranger anymore. It ain't your fight."

"If there's people bein' killed, it's everybody's fight."

Grim faced, the captain approached Rusty. "Shannon, we are shorthanded, as you can see. You have no obligation to us, and I would not be so bold as to ask you. But if you should decide to ride with us of your own free will, I would happily accept your company. I cannot promise that the state will pay you for your services."

"Half the time I *was* a ranger I didn't get paid for it. I'm not askin' for anything now."

"Spoken like a true Texan." The captain looked at Andy. "Perhaps you should remain here."

Andy said, "I heal fast. I'll go."

He knew the chances of Indians hitting this camp were remote. The report had them many miles to the north, where they had hit a group of cowboys on roundup and had driven off a substantial number of cattle as well as horses.

Farley said, "I can't figure what the Comanches would want with cattle. Their preference runs to buffalo."

Andy replied, "The cattle are for tradin', not eatin'. They drive them north to the canyon country and swap them to Comanchero traders for white-man goods. They don't know much about money, but they know how to trade. They've been doin' it a long time."

Farley grunted, malice in his eyes. "You'd be the one to know."

Andy clenched a fist. One of these days, he thought, me and you are going to knock heads. I'm betting that mine is harder.

The rangers pushed their horses as much as they dared, stopping to camp at dusk. Andy was tired, his head aching. Rusty, on the other hand, seemed rejuvenated. He said, "I feel like I never left the rangers. It's like I've stepped back into old days at Fort Belknap."

Andy said, "The captain would be tickled to have you sign on permanent."

"I might if it wasn't for Corey Bascom. And the farm."

"People like Bascom generally come to a bad end. Sooner or later he'll try to rob the wrong outfit and somebody'll blow his light out. It doesn't have to be you." He realized that what he said about Bascom sounded more than a little like Rusty's comment about Scooter.

Rusty frowned. "If it happens that way, well and good. But if it fell to me to be the one, well, . . . I owe him for Josie."

"Do you think you have to kill him before she can be at rest?"

"No. Before *I* can be at rest."

The ranch was little more than a rough cow camp, its few structures having picket walls and dirt-covered roofs. Its owners clearly intended it to be temporary. None of the cowboys had been killed, but the outfit had been shot up and had lost most of its horses, including several with saddles on.

The wagon boss walked out to meet the rangers. His left arm rested in a sling made of tarpaulin torn from a wagon sheet. His face reddened as he described the incident. "Caught us flat-footed, the boys all scattered around the herd. Took cattle, horses . . . even the camp dog followed and never came back."

The captain said, "I'm sorry we don't have a doctor."

"We taken care of ourselves." The boss raised his wounded arm a little and winced. "This don't hurt near as much as losin' the outfit. I am madder than hell. At them, at us. I'm even a little mad at you for not bein' here when it happened."

The captain nodded. "I suppose you're entitled. Would any of you like to ride with us?"

"We ain't got but two men still on horseback, but they're rarin' to go. It's been all I could do to keep them from chasin' off after the Indians alone." He cursed. "A cowboy with no horse is a sorry sight to behold."

The rangers tarried only long enough to water their mounts and for the two hands to saddle up and join them.

The wagon boss shouted as the riders moved away, "Give them hell, rangers."

The cowboys led the way to where the attack had taken place. "Lucky none of us got killed," one said. "They seemed more interested in gettin' away with the horses and cattle than in takin' scalps."

Holloway told the captain, "If they'd just taken horses they'd be hard to catch up with. But the cattle will slow them down a right smart."

The captain said, "That is our main hope. Otherwise they would probably be out of our reach already."

Andy knew from experience that the raiders would abandon stolen horses only under heavy pressure, for these quickly became regarded as personal property. They would more readily abandon the cattle if they discovered close pursuit. Those, after all, had value to them only for trading.

He hoped they would give up the cattle and push on at a fast enough pace that the rangers would not catch them. Long ago he had been forced to a reluctant choice between white people and red. But his stomach churned with a dread that he might have to fire upon those he had for years regarded as his own.

He felt Rusty's speculative gaze. Rusty, more than anyone here, should understand Andy's conflicting emotions. Farley Brackett studied him with open distrust.

Andy might stretch the facts about his age, but he had given a man's word. He would not back down from it.

A trail left by stolen horses could sometimes be difficult to follow, but to hide the tracks of a cattle herd was impossible. Andy could have followed it with one eye shut. The Indians must have been confident that the cowboys would not be able to follow and chastise them. It was possible they were unaware so far of the rangers' reinstatement. In the past they had feared rangers more than the army or civilian volunteers. They had regarded rangers as a warrior society of unyielding determination and fearsome power.

The trail became fresher, the tracks cleanly cut, the droppings soft and still warm enough that Andy could smell them. For a while now the rangers had been coming across young calves the Indians had left behind because they could not keep up the pace. Andy heard cows bawling. His nerves tightened. He saw Rusty quietly slip the rifle from beneath his leg and bring it up to the pommel of his saddle.

The captain gave an order for the men to stop and tighten their cinches. A slipping saddle could be fatal in a running fight. He said, "If anybody feels like communing with his maker, this would be the proper time."

Andy had a dark feeling it was too late to pray for what he had hoped most, that the Indians would slip away without confrontation.

Holloway asked, "Any orders, Captain?"

"Just one, Sergeant. When we see that they've spotted us, charge. Don't give them time to take count."

Rusty said, "Sounds like old Captain Whitfield. Bible in one saddlebag, whiskey in the other. He was hell on horseback."

The Comanches had three men trailing the herd as a rear guard. They appeared surprised by sight of the rangers riding up over a stretch of rising ground. They hesitated for a moment, seemingly undecided whether to stand and give fight or to run and give warning. One carried a rifle. He threw a quick shot in the rangers' direction and wheeled about, riding away at a high lope. His partners struggled not to be left behind.

The captain said, "We've caught them asleep. Let's wake them up." He motioned with his hand and spurred his horse into a run.

The rangers split around the herd. The cattle spooked at first, splitting off in various directions. Andy thought there might be a hundred or more. The animals stopped their forward movement once the rangers pulled back together beyond the herd.

Ahead, Andy saw dust kicked up by the remuda. The Indians were whipping them into a run. The two cowboys, eagerly responding to sight of their quarry, pulled ahead of the rangers. The captain tried to call them back, but they did not hear. Or perhaps they chose not to.

Rusty spurred his bay horse. He shouted at Andy, "Let's try and catch up to those cowboys. They're liable to get themselves into a fix."

Farley Brackett pushed his horse into a run that put him a little ahead of Andy and Rusty.

The Indians stopped running. Having stampeded the stolen horses, they pulled together into a defensive line. Rough-counting by twos, Andy guessed they numbered twenty or so. They looked like a solid wall.

The captain shouted, "Don't hit them head-on. Cut around the end."

The flanking maneuver momentarily confused the Comanches, but the surprise did not last long. They broke out of the line and made for a stand of timber. Several hung back, fighting a rear-guard action. Rifles and pistols cracked, raising clouds of white smoke. Arrows whispered like wind in a stovepipe. Andy saw a couple of warriors on the ground. He heard a ranger cry out as he was hit. The vanguard of the Indians reached the timber and turned to mount a defense.

The captain shouted, "Smite them hip and thigh."

The rangers lost any semblance of a line. They plunged into the timber by ones and twos. The combat was almost hand-to-hand. Gunfire racketed in Andy's ears. He saw several Comanches who offered good targets, but he could not bring his pistol to bear on them.

He became aware that Farley had gotten himself isolated out to one side and had the full attention of three warriors. His horse was down. The ranger dodged among the trees, afoot. Andy wanted to laugh over his antagonist's precarious situation, but he sobered quickly. Farley stood a strong chance of being killed. He forced down his resentment and spurred in that direction.

Andy wanted to give the Indians a chance to escape. In Comanche he shouted, "Get away! Run!"

One paused long enough to snap a shot at him with an old muzzle-loading rifle much too cumbersome to be effective from horseback. Two warriors disappeared into the heavier growth.

The third appeared determined to bring Farley down. Farley tripped over a deadfall limb. The Indian rushed his horse toward him, drawing back an arrow in his bow. Farley turned over onto his back, eyes desperate. His hands searched for a pistol that had fallen out of his reach.

Again Andy shouted in Comanche, "Get away!"

The Indian turned, swinging the point of the arrow toward Andy. Andy saw the face and recognized it. Holding his breath, his skin afire, he aimed his pistol, then let it drift to the warrior's left. His shot missed. So did the arrow. The Indian turned his horse away and followed the others into the trees.

Andy trembled. His pounding heart seemed about to burst. The man he had almost killed was a friend to Steals the Ponies.

Ashen faced, Farley struggled to his feet. He picked up the weapon he had dropped and quickly glanced around. "Let's get out of here before they decide to come back."

Andy extended his arm. Farley grabbed it and swung up behind the saddle. He almost jerked Andy from the horse. Andy felt as if his arm had been wrenched from the shoulder.

Farley's voice trembled in the aftermath of fear. "Where's the rest of the rangers?"

Andy found it difficult to speak. "I lost sight of them in the trees. Whichever way we go, we're liable to run into Indians."

"Let's go someplace, even if it's wrong. I don't like it here atall."

Andy could understand that. "Which way?"

"Back out of this timber to where we can see somethin'."

Andy pointed his horse south, where open country showed through the trees.

Farley said, "I felt the devil's breath on my neck. It had the smell of brimstone."

Andy waited for Farley to thank him but soon concluded it was going to be a long wait. Instead Farley said, "You've got a reputation as a good shot. Wasn't no reason for you to've missed that Indian."

Andy would not admit that he had done so on purpose. He wondered if the Comanche might have missed for the same reason. "It's hard to hit a target when you're whippin' through the timber."

"Especially when it's a Comanche. Friend of yours?"

Andy did not reply. He reined up at the edge of the trees, hoping to see the other rangers. He heard continued firing at some distance and wondered how Rusty was doing. He wished they had not become separated in the excitement of the skirmish.

He heard a running horse and whirled around. A Comanche warrior was almost upon him, arrow drawn back. His mouth was open, making a war cry meant to chill the blood of an enemy. By instinct more than calculation, Andy fired. The arrow drove into his shoulder, knocking him back against Farley. He would have fallen had Farley not held him. Shock was instant. Andy's head reeled. His stomach turned over.

He was aware that the Indian had fallen from his horse and lay in a twisted heap. His face was turned upward, his dying eyes open. Andy recognized him. He was from Steals the Ponies' band.

Andy's meager breakfast came up. He felt himself slipping from the saddle. Farley pulled him back. "Don't you fall, boy. You're liable to drive that arrow plumb through. I don't want two dead Indians on my hands."

Through a red haze Andy saw several rangers ride out of the timber, driving some of the reclaimed horses. Half a dozen Indians came out in an effort to head them off. They quickly spotted Andy and Farley and moved toward them. More Indians appeared behind, blocking escape.

Farley reloaded his pistol. "Hang on. We're fixin' to ride like hell." He put the horse into a hard run straight toward the half dozen warriors. He fired one shot after another, as rapidly as he could pull the trigger. He shouted at the top of his lungs.

"Out of the way, you dog-eatin' sons of bitches!"

Andy felt consciousness slipping away, yet he found enough resentment to murmur, "Comanches don't eat dog."

He was aware that the Indians were surprised by Farley's audacity. They pulled apart, letting him pass between them, then shooting at him in vain. Incongruously Farley laughed aloud. He fired once more and brought a man down.

Farley pulled up. The rangers circled protectively around him and Andy. Andy heard Rusty's worried voice. "Lift him down. We've got to get that arrow out."

Someone said, "The horses are gettin' away."

"To hell with the horses."

Several hands eased Andy from the saddle and lowered him onto his back in the grass. Andy could see swirling images of the men through a reddish haze. He felt his shirt being ripped open.

Rusty said, "A couple of you hold him down. I sure hope that arrowhead ain't barbed."

Andy felt a sharp pain as Rusty tested the shaft, trying to determine how deeply the arrow had penetrated. Rusty said, "Grit your teeth, Andy. This won't be any fun."

Andy started to say, "I'm grittin'," but the words never quite made their way out. Instead he gave a sharp cry as Rusty gripped the shaft and jerked it free. Andy felt as if he were spinning backward, sinking into a bottomless well that blazed with flame, then went dark. The hurting diminished, and he was briefly at peace.

Rusty examined the arrow. He said, "The point is broken off. I'm afraid it may still be in there, too deep to dig for."

Andy's sense of peace was shattered by searing pain as Rusty cauterized the wound with a red-hot knife blade. Andy was aware of a sharp smell of burning flesh. He knew it was his own.

Rusty said, "Sorry. I had it done to me once, and I know it hurts like hell. But out in the field there's no other choice."

Consciousness slipped away again. Andy could hear, but he was not sure what he heard was real. It might be a dream. He thought he heard someone say, "Maybe we can fix up some sort of drag, like the Indians do."

Rusty said, "Too bumpy a ride. Liable to kill him. Let's

cut down a couple of those small trees. We'll make a stretcher."

Andy had a sense of floating on air. It took some time for him to realize that the rangers had rigged a makeshift stretcher with blankets and poles. He was being carried between two horses. The ends of the poles were tied into stirrups on each side.

He hoped the horses were gentle enough not to spill him. He had a feeling he would break like an eggshell. The wound in his shoulder felt as if a fire were burning in it. His mouth was so dry that when he ran his tongue over his lips he felt no moistening.

Rusty rode alongside him. Seeing that Andy had awakened he said, "Lay still. Else you're liable to get the blood started again. We like to've not got it stopped in the first place."

Andy had no intention of moving. It hurt too much. He was being jostled enough by the horses that carried him.

Andy found voice, though it was weak. He felt choked. "I killed a Comanche."

"You didn't have a choice. He was set on killin' you."

"But I knew him. He was one of my people."

"Maybe he knew you, too. That didn't stop him from comin' after you. Farley said—"

"Farley." Speaking the name came hard. "If I hadn't gone to pull him out of a tight spot I wouldn't have had to kill anybody."

"That's one way of lookin' at it. Another way is to realize that Farley saved your life, too. He held onto you and got you out of there."

"Where *is* Farley?"

"Helpin' drive the cattle. We got them back. Some of the horses, too."

"Anybody killed?"

"Not on our side. Couple of boys were wounded a little but not as bad as you. Can't say about the Indians."

Andy closed his eyes. He kept seeing the man he had killed. It was a face he knew. He did not want to remember the name, but it came nevertheless. The warrior had been known as Bugling Elk. He had had a piercing voice that could reach far across the prairie. Andy recalled hearing his war cry just before the warrior loosed the arrow. That cry would echo in his mind again and again, perhaps for the rest of his life.

He turned his head to one side.

Rusty said, "Hang on. I know it hurts."

It was not the wound that hurt most.

After long hesitation Rusty said, "There's somethin' else. It's good news in a way. It's also bad."

"How can it be both?"

"We found a sorrel horse amongst those we got back from the Indians. He's your Long Red."

It took a moment for Andy to grasp the ramifications. "What about Scooter?"

"We'd have to figure that the Indians got him."

Andy wanted to cry, but he was too old for it.

· 15 ·

———————————

Corey Bascom studied the cards he had dealt himself, then looked across the table into his adversary's eyes. He searched for a flicker of emotion that might betray the quality of the cowboy's poker hand. He saw a fleeting disappointment, quickly covered. He bet and the cowboy folded, as had two other players before him.

Corey had smiled little since learning of Alice's death. He did not smile now, smothering a momentary elation over winning. The penny-ante bank out at Brownwood had not been as flush as expected, and a four-way split had left him only a few days' traveling money. Since coming to Fort Worth he had more than doubled his stake, however. The lamp-lighted poker tables in Hell's Half Acre had been good to him. They usually were.

In recent years Fort Worth had become his favorite place to go for liquor, women, and some rewarding poker. Here trail outfits on their way to Kansas resupplied for the long trip that still faced them. Their cowboys grabbed a last chance to see the elephant and buck the tiger before beginning the last long leg of their trip north. They often stopped again on their way home.

For a man better than average at manipulating the paste-boards, it was a good place to pad out his roll so long as he did not pit himself against the real professionals from places like Chicago and Kansas City. The district's rowdy action had long offered temporary relief from his family's stifling influence. Though Bessie Bascom was his mother, and he had the affection for her a dutiful son should, she often rubbed him raw like burrs in his underwear. An occasional visit to Hell's Half Acre was akin to a safety valve on a steam boiler.

It had been several weeks since he had left the family, bitter that Lacey had shot Alice on his mother's orders. He had to leave, for had he stayed he might have killed Lacey. The temptation had been strong. His bitterness had only deepened since. For a time he had lost his grip to a point of feeling suicidal. He had provoked a fight with a gambler whose skill with a gun he knew was superior to his own. The son of a bitch had clubbed him to the floor with the heavy barrel of a Colt Navy revolver but had left him alive. Perhaps he had recognized Corey's brief madness for what it was and chose not to take advantage of it.

The close encounter with death had been shock enough to revive Corey's desire for life. He had wandered without purpose, always aware that local law enforcement might be on the lookout for him because of past offenses. Here in this raucous section of Fort Worth he felt relatively secure. Its peace officers were not inclined to be foolhardy. Some had a financial stake in the prosperity of Hell's Half Acre, exacting a percentage of the take as protection money. Several were known to own a substantial interest in some of the district's illicit enterprises. They were selective in their diligence as keepers of the law. Others who had no financial ax to grind were nevertheless aware of their own mortality and did not arbitrarily poke at hornets' nests.

Before he met Alice, Corey had invested enough in commercial female companionship to have bought a small ranch. Since her death the notion had repelled him. Odd, he thought. He had never expected one woman to take such a hold on him that he lost interest in all others. He had tried a couple of nights ago to break Alice's spell by going upstairs with a dark-eyed raven-haired beauty who affected a French accent and claimed to be from New Orleans. To his dismay he had not been able to get past her doorway.

He had never thought about ghosts enough to believe or disbelieve. Now he wondered if Alice's ghost might be riding on his shoulders.

Well, that New Orleans queen was probably just from Arkansas, anyway. Fort Smith, more than likely.

A rough voice demanded, "You goin' to play or just daydream about it?" The other players had shoved back from the table, but the cowboy evidently had not yet lost all of his money. Corey felt honor-bound to oblige him and see that he did not leave here overburdened. He ordered the cowboy a fresh drink and resumed the game.

As his pile grew and the cowboy's shrank, Corey became aware that a couple of men were watching him with more than casual interest. Their clothes were threadbare and dirty, as if they had been sleeping beneath a porch or in a haystack. He knew the breed on sight: two-bit footpads and pickpockets, feeding on the fringes of the real action like dogs prowling under a table in search of scraps fallen to the floor.

He sensed also that they had picked him as a target. Unless he stayed and played until dawn, he eventually had to leave the lamplight and venture out into the darkness. There they would pounce on him like coyotes on a rabbit.

Well, boys, he thought, you may be coyotes, but I ain't no rabbit.

The cowboy threw in his final hand with a gesture of disgust. "You just cleaned my plow."

Corey gave him back five dollars. "Never like to see a man leave the table dead broke." The cowboy hesitated. Pride told him to refuse. Practicality told him to take it. He took it.

Corey cast a quick glance at the two thugs. They were still watching him. He said, "Cowboy, step over to the bar and I'll buy you a drink."

Once there he said in little more than a whisper, "How would you like to earn some of your money back?"

"How? There ain't much I know to do except on horseback. I just proved I ain't no poker player."

"This won't take any skill. All you have to do is go out that door and start walkin'."

Suspicious, the cowboy said, "I was fixin' to do that, anyway. What's the catch?"

"Don't look behind you. Look in the mirror back of the bar. See those two ginks yonder in the corner? One's got a black wool hat. The other one's wearin' a cap he probably stole off of a railroad conductor."

"I see them."

"I think they've got it in mind to lift my roll. I'd like to see them disappointed."

"Then you'd ought to get you a policeman. I'm a trail hand, is all."

"Any policeman I'd find around here may be a friend of theirs. I want you to walk out ahead of me, then wait for me just out of the lamplight."

"You fixin' to use me for a decoy?"

"They won't hurt you. I won't give them the chance."

The cowboy thought it over for a minute. "I wouldn't do this if it wasn't for the money. If you let them kill me I'll be mad as hell."

"Don't worry. I'll be right behind you."

"So will they." The cowboy finished his drink. "Oh well,

I'll probably get drowned anyway when we reach the Red River."

Corey watched the drover walk to the door, then pause to look back at the would-be robbers. He feared that might arouse their suspicion, but the thugs were paying no attention to the cowboy. Their gaze was fixed on Corey. He nodded a silent good night to the bartender, then strode at a leisurely pace across the room and out onto the wooden sidewalk.

The cowboy awaited him, just beyond the lamplight that fell upon the dirt street. Corey said, "Here, swap hats with me. Now start walkin' yonderway. Walk slow and stay out of the light."

He ducked into a dark passageway between the saloon and a mercantile store. In a moment he heard footsteps on the boards. A man's low voice said, "There he goes. Let's catch him before he gets to that next streetlamp."

The two footpads passed Corey's hiding place but did not glance in his direction. He stepped out behind them. Without a word he swung his pistol and slammed it against the woolen hat. The thug went to his knees. His hat rolled across the boards and out into the dirt. Corey clubbed him again for good measure.

The second robber spun around, a small derringer in his hand. Corey struck the pistol barrel down across the man's hairy knuckles, causing him to drop the tiny weapon. He jammed the muzzle of his six-shooter into the man's wide-open mouth.

"If you don't want me to blow all your teeth out, you'll raise those hands," he declared.

The thug's hands shot into the air.

Corey called, "Cowboy, you can come back now."

The cowboy stopped but took a moment to size up the situation before he risked returning. He looked down at the robber crumpled on the sidewalk. "You must've scared him to death. I didn't hear you shoot."

"Just gave him a Sam Colt massage. He'll come around directly. Search this one. Be sure he doesn't have another gun on him."

The cowboy found no weapon. Corey poked the muzzle into the thug's stomach. "Are you a fast runner?"

The robber tried to answer but could not summon voice.

Corey said, "Let's find out. I'll let you start runnin'. I'll count to five, then shoot. Now go."

The cap fell off halfway across the street, but the thug did not stop to retrieve it. Corey counted to five, then put a bullet into a wall just behind the running man. It seemed to encourage him in his speed.

He knelt and went through the fallen robber's pockets. He found a watch and some folding money. He said, "I'll bet you don't even have a pocket watch, cowboy. Here, take this one." He picked up the derringer. It was an over-and-under model that allowed two shots. "How would you like an extra gun?"

"I wouldn't even shoot a rabbit with that little thing. It'd probably make him mad enough to come after me with his teeth bared."

"Well, I'll keep it. Never know when somethin' like this might come in handy." It was small enough that a lawman might overlook it. He stuck it in his pocket. Corey also kept the money. That seemed just inasmuch as the thug had intended to take *his.*

He was a little surprised that the shot did not attract curious onlookers. It took more than a single shot to excite the citizens of Hell's Half Acre. He counted off roughly half the money he had won from the drover. "Much obliged for the help, cowboy. Like a little advice?"

"As long as it don't cost me nothin'."

"Maybe it'll save you somethin'. Stick to playin' mumblety-peg. Poker ain't your game."

He was staying in a little ten-by-twelve room above a whiskey mill. He had used it several times during his visits here and knew he did not have to worry about the management giving him away to any policeman who had more curiosity than judgment. The room key had long since been lost, but a door key would only lead to overconfidence. Any burglar worth his salt could pick a lock as easily as he could pick his teeth. A pistol beneath the pillow was much more reliable for protection.

He climbed the outside stairs and started down the short hall toward his door. Instinct told him to pause. He had left the door closed, but now it was slightly ajar. A thin streak of lamplight showed around its edges. Holding his breath, he drew his pistol. He hit the door hard and rushed into the room, then jumped to one side in case someone was waiting for him with a gun.

He almost shot his brother Newley.

The surprise left him speechless, his heart pounding hard. "I like to've killed you," he said when his breath came back. "What the hell are you doin' here?"

Newley was his next to youngest brother and his favorite of the three. Lacey had always been an irritant to him, cruel and a little dangerous when left to his own devices. Little Anse had always been headstrong and impervious to advice from anyone except Ma and Lacey. Newley was his mother's obedient lackey to the best of his limited abilities, but he showed occasional signs of thinking for himself when he was not under her shadow.

Newley was in deeper shock than Corey had been. He was still looking down the muzzle of Corey's pistol. Shakily he said, "For God's sake put that six-shooter away."

Corey did. Newley swallowed hard. The color began coming back into his face. He said, "That's the second time lately I've come near gettin' shot on your account."

"You oughtn't to surprise me like this."

"I've been huntin' you from Fort Griffin to kingdom come. This is the third time I've been to Fort Worth. I figured you'd show up here sooner or later."

"What do you want with me? I told Ma when I left that I wasn't comin' back, after she had Lacey kill Alice."

"That's one thing I came to tell you. Alice ain't dead."

Corey went stiff, his body tingling. He stared at his brother, not sure he had heard correctly. "Not dead?"

"Lacey got the shakes and picked the wrong target. It was Alice's sister he shot, not Alice."

"Her sister?" Corey's head seemed to spin.

"The one called Josie. It was a natural mistake. Ma was awful put out about it, though. She's still bound and determined to get Alice."

A chill passed through Corey. "Not if I can stop her, and I'll stop her if I have to kill her." He sat down heavily on the edge of the bed. Hell of a thing to say about one's own mother, he thought, but there weren't many mothers like Ma Bascom. "I'm glad you found me. That's good news about Alice."

"It ain't all good. You know Josie was fixin' to marry a farmer named Shannon."

"I remember some talk."

"Shannon thinks you're the one that shot Josie. He's huntin' for you with blood in his eyes. He mistook me for you. Came within an inch of killin' me." He explained about Shannon breaking into the room at Fat Beulah's.

Corey demanded, "Didn't you tell him it wasn't me that shot Josie?"

"I never got the chance."

"You were probably too scared to think about it."

This was a new experience for Corey, being sought for something he *didn't* do. Up to now he had always been guilty as charged. "If he finds me he'll wish he hadn't. There ain't no clodhopper goin' to get the best of me."

"This one might. He used to be a ranger. And he killed little Anse."

Corey was jarred again. "Little Anse?"

"You know he always thought he could do anything but walk on water. He thought he could draw and shoot faster than Shannon. But he couldn't." Newley explained that Ma had sent him and little Anse out to search for Shannon, to try to kill him before he could find Corey. Shannon had outsmarted them.

Corey's sense of loss over his youngest brother was tempered by his learning that Alice was still alive. He said, "I saw Shannon once at the Monahan place, so I'll know him on sight. But first I've got to think about Alice. If Ma has her mind set on seein' her dead, . . ."

"You know Ma. She says it has to be done. If Alice ever testified in court she could send us all to the penitentiary. Maybe worse."

"I'll worry about Shannon later. First thing I'll do is go to the Monahan place and steal Alice away. I'll take her so far that Ma and Lacey will never find her."

Newley seemed to approve. Like Corey, he had sometimes questioned Ma's opinions, though seldom to her face. That took more courage than he could usually muster. "I'll help you any way I can."

Corey was aware that Newley had had feelings for Alice. During the time she had been with the Bascom family he had seen Newley watching her with sad hound-dog eyes, wishing. Corey had no intention of sharing her, but he knew Newley would help him get her away. Once Corey and Alice were safe from Ma and Lacey he would cut Newley loose on his own. The boy was weak, but maybe he could find some backbone if he were free from Ma's poisonous influence.

"We'll leave come daylight," Corey said.

Ma always kept a dog or two. They were essentially worthless except that they alerted anybody within hearing when someone approached the cabin. Corey had heard her say she never expected much of a dog, so no dog had ever disappointed her. She had often been disappointed in her sons.

Corey remembered a number of occasions when she had also been disappointed in her husband, the late Ansel Bascom. She would chase him away with orders never to come back. He would return, however, and she would grudgingly accept him. After all, he usually brought money with him. She had carried on at the top of her lungs when the state police killed him, but Corey had suspected a lot of it was for show. At least she would never have to wonder anymore where he was.

Right now Ma was down to one dog. It barked long and loud until Corey dismounted and chunked a rock at it. It retreated behind the saddle shed and resumed the alarm. Ma stepped out of the picket house, a shotgun in her hands. She lowered it when she recognized the arrivals, but her stern face offered no warm greeting for the prodigal son.

She said, "I'd about decided you never was comin' back."

"I hadn't figured on it 'til Newley told me Alice is still alive."

Her face took on an ugly twist. "Only because Lacey ain't been able to get close enough to the Monahan house for a clean shot. She don't let herself be seen. I don't reckon you've worked up spine enough to do the job yourself?" She studied him a moment. "No, I didn't figure you would."

"I came here hopin' I might talk you into leavin' Alice alone. I'll take her far away, to where the law never heard of us."

"Sooner or later she'd get dissatisfied and want to come home. She's like a dagger hangin' over this family."

"Not if I take her plumb out of the country."

"You'll have to kill a bunch of Monahans to get her, and she wouldn't have anything to do with you after that. If she wanted you she'd have come back here already."

"Knowin' you intended to kill her? She's not a fool."

"Maybe not, but you are. If she ever got on a witness stand she'd talk like a revival preacher. Whatever me and Lacey done, we done to protect this family."

"Shootin' the wrong woman and settin' a ranger on my trail? The best protection I can think of is distance. Once I get Alice, you won't see any more of me or her."

"You ain't got her yet. We don't even know for sure if she's still at the Monahans'. Lacey thinks they might've spirited her away someplace."

"If so, they can't take her so far that I can't find her."

"Then you'd better be sure you find her before me and Lacey do. Otherwise..." She shook her head sadly. "I thought I'd raised you better than to let a pretty face turn you against your own. Your poor old pa would be mightily ashamed."

"My poor old pa never felt ashamed for anything in his life except gettin' caught. Where *is* Lacey, anyway?"

Ma jerked her head toward the cabin. "Catchin' him some rest. He's laid up many a night watchin' the Monahan place, hopin' for another chance at Alice."

"You tell him that if he tries again I'll kill him."

"You'd kill your own brother?"

"Dead as a gut-shot mule." Corey could not remember a completely happy day he and Lacey had ever spent together. He glanced at Newley. "You comin' or stayin' here?"

Newley shrugged as if neither choice offered any pleasure. "I reckon I'll go along with you."

Newley showed him where they had buried little Anse beneath a tree a couple of hundred yards from the house. The marker was a cross made from two pieces of pine lumber. Painted on it in crude letters was *Ansl Bascom.*

Couldn't even spell his name right, Corey thought. It didn't matter much. Nobody was likely to see it except family. The paint would weather away, the cross would fall over and rot, and the grave would be forgotten. It would be as if little Anse had never lived. Other than immediate family and the Bascoms' victims, no one had ever cared.

Poor kid never had much chance. He let Ma run his life, and obeying her had caused his death. Corey felt more resentment toward his mother than toward the man who had shot little Anse.

He asked Newley, "Are you set for a few more days' ride? I figure on goin' to the Monahan farm."

"Why not? All I've done lately is travel."

Corey and Newley sat on their horses in the edge of the timber and studied the Monahan farm three hundred yards away. It looked no different than the last time Corey had seen it. He knew things had changed drastically within the family, however. He could only imagine what a shock Josie's death must have been, coming on top of Clemmie's illness. He had developed a grudging liking for the Monahan family, though he knew his elopement with Alice had created a hostility he would never be able to overcome. It would be useless to ride in boldly and assert his claim to his wife, even if he argued that it was the only way to save her. James Monahan would probably shoot him on sight. If he didn't, and Clemmie had recovered enough to hold a gun, she would probably do it.

No, the only way would be to slip in there in the dark hours of early morning and rush her away before the family could react. That would be no easy matter. If it were, Lacey would already have sneaked in and killed her. Lacey had a streak of cowardice that limited the risk he was willing to take. Corey told himself he had no such shortcoming. Being brave did not have to include being foolish, however. He would study the situation and plan his move carefully.

The time he had worked for the Monahans had made Corey familiar with the layout of the farm, where its buildings stood in relation to one another, where he could hide horses as near as possible and the route he could take to get into the main house. He remembered the configuration of the rooms and where Alice would be sleeping. This was knowledge Lacey did not have.

It was almost certain that someone would stand watch at night. Corey was confident he could find and take care of the guard. He felt he could get into the house and into Alice's room. The real trick would be getting her out and to the horses, especially if she resisted and put up a holler. The quickest way would be out the window. The Monahans probably would not risk shooting at him for fear of hitting her in the dark.

Newley asked, "What if she ain't there? What if they've snuck her away like Ma said? You might get in the house, but you're liable to have hell gettin' out."

That question had nagged Corey, too. "I wish there was some way to be sure she's there before I go dancin' around a bear trap."

"It's a cinch you can't just ride in there and ask them."

A horse left the barn and moved in their general direction. A small boy sat on its back.

Corey motioned for Newley to pull a little farther into the trees. "Yonder may be the answer. That's Clemmie's grandson Billy. I used to saddle his pony for him so he could ride. Him and me got along real good."

"Things may be different with him now. He's old enough to know that they don't speak your name anymore without addin' a cussword to it. And if he tells his folks he saw you, they'll figure out what you've got in mind."

"We'll keep him with us a while. When he doesn't come in for supper the menfolks'll start out huntin' for him. That'll make it easier for me to grab Alice and go."

Newley shrugged. "We've been charged with everything else. Kidnappin' a kid will be somethin' new."

"Not kidnappin'. Just borrowin' for a little while."

He waited until the boy had skirted around the edge of the timber and was out of sight should anybody be looking in his direction from the houses or barn. "You stay back," he told Newley. "He doesn't know you. You might scare him."

Corey rode out to intercept the youngster. Billy reined up, surprised.

"Howdy, Billy. How's my boy?"

Billy said nothing. He lifted the reins as if he were about to turn and run away.

Corey said, "Don't be scared. I'm not fixin' to hurt you. Just want to talk. What're you doin' out here by yourself?"

Billy swallowed hard. "Lookin' for a milk cow. She ain't come in for a couple of days. Daddy says she's probably had her calf and she's hidin' it out."

"Cows do that."

"Everybody's mad at you. They wouldn't want me talkin' to you."

"I know. They think I killed your Aunt Josie, but I didn't. I wasn't even here."

Billy seemed to want to believe. "You wasn't?"

"No. If I'd known it was goin' to happen I'd have stopped it. How's your Aunt Alice?"

"I don't know."

"But she's livin' right there in your grandmother's house. How come you don't know?"

"Because she's not there. Rusty Shannon took her away, him and Andy."

Somehow Corey was not especially surprised. They had smuggled Alice out under his brother Lacey's nose. He even began to see a little humor in it. "Where did they take her, Billy?"

"Down to Rusty's farm, I guess."

"Where is his farm?"

"I've never been there. They say it's a long ways. I've heard them talk about the Colorado River."

That did not tell him much. The Colorado River cut across most of Texas, starting somewhere up in Comanche country and flowing generally southeastward all the way down to the Gulf of Mexico. During the time Corey had worked for the Monahans he had heard them mention Shannon's farm a few times. He reasoned that it must be somewhere downriver, probably around Austin or farther east, where the settlements were no longer new.

He asked, "Are you sure they haven't mentioned the name of a town?"

Billy thought a moment. "Alice has written Granny a couple of letters. Postmark had the name of a place called Columbus."

Corey knew in a general way where Columbus was. He also knew that the letter had probably been posted miles from

where Alice was staying. That was a logical precaution in case
the wrong people saw it.

But Columbus was a starting place. It narrowed the
search.

"Billy, it might be a good idea if you don't tell your folks
you talked to me. I wouldn't want you to get a spankin' on
my account."

"I wouldn't want one, either."

"And believe me, I didn't kill your aunt." He had developed a soft spot for the boy while he had lived here. Billy's
approval meant something to him.

Billy said, "You were always nice to me. I never wanted
to think you done what they said."

"You're a good boy. You'll be a good man someday. Now,
you go find your cow. And remember, don't tell anybody
about me."

The boy went on. Corey watched him a while, glad there
was no reason to hold him, after all.

Newley rode closer. "You just lettin' him ride off?"

"There's no point in keepin' him. Alice is gone."

"I heard some of what he said. Where is this Columbus
town?"

"Down on the Colorado River."

"What'll I tell Ma?"

"Don't tell her a damned thing. I'm goin' down there and
hunt 'til I find Alice."

"And then what?"

"I'll cross that river when I get there."

· 16 ·

Bessie Bascom was churning butter when she heard the dog start to bark. She muttered under her breath, for she hated to be interrupted in her work. She picked up her shotgun and checked to be sure shells were in the chambers, then she stepped outside. She could not remember the last time a stranger had brought good tidings to her door. Her tensed-up shoulders relaxed when she saw that the incoming rider was her son Newley. He was alone.

"Where's your brother Corey?" she demanded as soon as Newley came within hearing distance.

"Gone."

Drawing a reluctant answer out of her sons could be almost as difficult as pulling their teeth. It always irritated her. When the boys became evasive it was a sign things were not going just right. In trying to avoid touching off her volatile temper they often carried her to the brink of violence and sometimes pushed her over. Every one of them bore marks left by her quirt, testimony to past outbursts.

"I ain't blind," she replied, "but where did he go?"

"Off huntin' for Alice. She's not at the Monahan place."

She had suspected that. "Has he got any notion where she's gone to?"

Her son's hangdog manner told her he was holding back. Dismounting, he did not look directly into her eyes. "Didn't tell me nothin'. Just rode off."

"Whichaway?"

"South."

"He must've had some notion, then. You sure you're tellin' me all of it?"

"As much as I can."

Now she was certain he knew more than he was admitting. She heard footsteps and saw her son Lacey walking up from the barn. She said, "Lacey, you've always had a knack for keepin' your younger brothers in line." He was half a head taller and thirty pounds heavier than Newley. "Corey has gone off after that Monahan wench. I think Newley knows where, but he ain't tellin'. See if you can persuade him."

Newley backed away. "I've done told you all that Corey told me. Ain't no use in us fightin'."

There was not much fight to it. Lacey got an arm under Newley's and around the back of his neck. He applied pressure until Newley cried out, "Enough."

Ma asked, "How's your memory now?"

She thought for a moment Newley was going to cry. Damned poor conduct for a grown man, in her opinion. He took after his old pa in some ways she could not abide. Ansel Bascom had always had more mouth than guts despite the glowing image of him she held up to her sons. She had wanted to make them better than their father had been, but she was often disappointed.

Newley regained his composure, to a degree. "He's just tryin' to save Alice. He knows you and Lacey want to kill her."

"Damned right we do. She's bad medicine for all of us,

you included, if you had the sense to see it. Now, where's he gone?"

"He didn't tell me hisself, but I heard that little boy of the Monahans's say somethin' about a town called Columbus. It's way down on the Colorado River, the other side of Austin. Seems like that ranger Shannon has got a farm down there someplace."

"The one that killed little Anse?"

"That's him."

"So Corey figures if he can find Shannon he can find Alice."

Newley's voice took on a pleading tone. "He still loves her, Ma. Says if he finds her he'll take her a long ways off. She won't be talkin' to no court, nor testifyin' to nothin'."

"She sure won't if we can find her. And if Corey can, we can, too. You boys catch us some fresh horses to ride. And a pack horse. I'll go rustle up grub for the trip."

Newley protested, "I don't want no part of this."

"You'll go if I have to whip you like a chicken-stealin' hound. I swear I don't know what it'll take to put some manhood into you."

Lacey grabbed Newley by the collar and pushed him toward his horse. "Get goin'. I expect Corey has got a good start on us. We have a lot of country to cover."

Rusty and Tanner lifted Andy from the improvised stretcher and placed him upon a blanket on the ground. Fully conscious, Andy was aware that they had reached the cow camp. His shoulder burned all the way through. He imagined he could still feel the searing of the cauterizing blade.

Rusty asked, "You feelin' all right?"

Damn fool question, Andy thought, but he chose not to be sarcastic. He lied, "I'm makin' it fine."

The wagon boss was exuberant over recovery of the cattle. He counted the horses and accepted the losses with good grace. "You got back more than half of them," he said. "I'd already said good-bye to the whole bunch."

Though Andy knew the feeling was disloyal, he was glad the Comanches had held onto some of the horses. They had paid a considerable price. At least they would not have to return to their encampment empty-handed.

He was gratified to have Long Red again, but he grieved over the cost. He could only guess what had happened. He did not want to think about it, but the image refused to leave him. The kid probably had but one thought, to get away, and had ridden blindly into the Indian raiding party. Had he been only five or six years old they might have kept him as they had once kept Andy. But he was old enough that they would regard him as a man, a potential warrior against them. They would have made short and bloody work of him.

Perhaps everybody had been right, that Scooter was fated to a violent end, if not this way, some other. But Andy thought he had deserved at least one more chance to compensate for suffering through a life of abuse and deprivation.

Rusty had tried to ease Andy's distress. "Been many a boy even younger killed for no fault of his own. He brought this on himself."

The wagon boss gave Andy a minute's brief sympathy for his wound before turning to other matters. He told the captain, "The least I can do is make you the loan of a wagon so you can carry your wounded back to camp. And we'll whup you-all up some dinner so nobody goes away from here hungry. I hope you like beans."

The captain said, "When men are hungry, a pot of red beans is like ambrosia."

The thought of food made Andy nauseous. He knew he was running some fever.

Farley had given Andy little attention since the skirmish. Now he walked up to the blanket where Andy lay and stared down at him with accusing eyes. He said, "We're even now. You ran off the Comanche that wanted my scalp. I toted you out of there before some other heathen could snuff you out. We don't owe one another nothin', do we?"

His tone of voice rubbed Andy like coarse sand. He muttered, "Not a damned thing."

"Good, because the captain needs to know what happened out there."

Rusty butted in. "And what *did* happen?"

"This boy had a clean shot at that first Comanche. Wasn't no way he could've missed unless he wanted to. I'm thinkin' he wanted to. If that Indian hadn't got scared off he'd have killed me deader than hell."

"But he shot the next one."

"It was *his* life on the line that time. If he hadn't fired, that arrow might've gone into his heart."

"You're makin' a serious charge. You'd better think about it twice before you talk to the captain."

"I'm tellin' it the way I saw it."

"You saw it the way you wanted to see it. You've carried a grudge against Andy for a long time. Now, if you're lookin' for a fight, . . ."

Andy raised his good hand. "Rusty, don't. There's no use you and him bloodyin' one another. The truth is, he's right."

Rusty did not show as much surprise as Andy would have expected. He had probably sensed it all along but was willing to fight for Andy's sake.

Andy said, "I recognized the one that was after Farley. He used to teach me how to track game. I hoped I could scare him off without killin' him."

Farley said, "So you left him alive to raid again."

Rusty retorted, "Killin' or not killin' one Indian ain't goin' to make much difference. There's still aplenty more."

Farley said, "The point is that when it came to makin' a choice, he chose the Comanches over his friends."

Rusty argued, "You never was his friend. A friend wouldn't carry a story like this to the captain."

Their voices were becoming strident. Andy tried to shout to get their attention, but he could not muster the strength. He waved his hand. "You-all back off. I'll tell the captain myself."

Farley continued to glare at Rusty. "All right, but I want to be there to see that you tell it straight."

Rusty said, "Andy doesn't lie."

The captain came around when one of the cowboys brought up a wagon. "Pickard, you and Private Mitchell will ride in this the rest of the way back to camp. It should be more comfortable than that makeshift stretcher."

Andy said, "Captain, you may want to leave me behind after you hear what I have to say."

"That you hesitated about shooting an Indian?"

Andy had not anticipated that the captain might already know. "Somebody told you?"

"No, I guessed. I halfway expected it, under the circumstances."

"And you still let me come along?"

"I doubted it would make a life-or-death difference."

"It almost did. Maybe I'd have made the second shot good if Farley's life had depended on it. Maybe not. I can't be sure."

The captain frowned. "You're hurting, and you look feverish. This discussion can wait until we get back to camp and you are better fixed to know your mind." He motioned for a couple of rangers to lift Andy into the waiting wagon. They stretched him out on a folded blanket.

Rusty leaned worriedly over the sideboard. "If the ride gets too rough, be sure to holler. The point of that arrowhead may start workin' around in your shoulder."

Andy felt it would be fitting if a little of the arrow *was* still imbedded. It would afford a punishment of sorts for his having killed one of those he had considered his own people. It would be his penance.

Andy caught the welcome smell of wood smoke and knew the trip was almost over. By any standard the ranger camp was Spartan, but the line of tents looked like home. Reaching it meant an end to the wagon's jolting and jerking. The black cook came out to meet the arriving rangers. Andy saw him pointing with his forefinger, silently counting them one by one, smiling when he saw that none were missing. He turned his attention to Andy and Private Mitchell, the only two other than the wagon driver who did not come in on horseback. Mitchell had taken a bullet in his thigh, but it had passed through without striking a bone.

Bo clucked in sympathy. "Looks like you-all found the Indians you was lookin' for."

Tanner rode up and said, "We whupped up on them pretty good." He described the fight in more detail than the cook probably wanted to hear. Andy cringed, especially at the account of his killing an Indian.

Rusty noticed his discomfort. He said, "Len, I think I heard the captain call your name."

Tanner left. He was back in a while. "All that shootin' must've done somethin' to your hearin', Rusty. Captain wasn't lookin' for me, after all."

By then the cook was busy in the mess tent, preparing supper. Tanner went in to finish his story, but Andy did not have to listen to it.

The captain came around to check on his wounded.

Andy said, "Captain . . ."

The captain waved him off. "Get some rest, Pickard. We'll talk about it tomorrow. Or maybe the next day."

Rusty waited until the captain was out of earshot. He said, "Leave well enough alone. The captain isn't blamin' you for anything, and you shouldn't be blamin' yourself."

"I can't help it. I didn't do right by the rangers when I pulled my aim off of that first warrior. And I didn't do right by the People when I shot the other one."

"You did right by yourself. If you hadn't you'd be dead and I wouldn't be standin' here tryin' to pound some sense into you."

"When do you figure on goin' home, Rusty?"

"I haven't decided. I was kind of enjoyin' the camp. Took me back to the old days. For a little while it even made me think maybe I'd like to join up. But that skirmish took me back to a part I never did like. The farm gets to lookin' pretty good."

"Will you take me with you when you go?"

"Thought you was tired of the farm."

"Like you said, that fight has made the farm look pretty good."

"You ain't been a ranger long enough to draw your first pay, hardly."

"It'd be blood money if I did."

"That's the fever talkin'. Wait a couple of days before you jump off into a ditch you might not be able to climb out of."

The next day Andy felt like leaving the blanket and walking around the camp a little. The cook waylaid him at the mess tent. "What you need for healin' is lots of meat, wild meat. Ain't nothin' better for you than venison. Come, let me fry you up a piece of backstrap."

"You gave me more at breakfast than I could eat."

"That was a while ago. This'll put strength in your legs, let you run like a deer."

"I don't care about runnin'. I just want to get to where I can ride so I can go home."

"What's this about goin' home? Mr. Tanner been tellin' me what you done out there. You're too good a ranger to be quittin' on us now."

"Don't take what Len tells you as gospel. If hell has a place for liars, he's due a good scorchin'."

"Just don't be in no hurry. My old master was bad to make fast judgments. Most generally they was wrong, like the time he seen somethin' in the brush, movin' toward his hog pen. Figured it was a mongrel dog. He went chargin' in there throwin' rocks. Turned out it was a bear. You never seen a fat old man run so fast."

The next day Andy asked Rusty to saddle Long Red for him. He rode him around the outside of the camp. His shoulder ached a bit but not as much as he expected. Rusty waited for him at the corral, silently asking with his eyes.

Andy said, "It's not so bad."

"You just made a little circle. It's several days' ride back to the farm."

"Give me a couple more days. I can do it."

"That Indian still weighs heavy on your mind. Do you think a couple hundred miles will make him go away?"

"It'll put me where I'll never have to do that again."

By the third day Andy was convinced he was ready. Rusty followed him to the captain's tent but remained outside. Andy asked, "You got time to talk to me, Captain?"

The captain studied him, then shrugged in resignation. "Your face betrays your decision. You are not a good poker player."

"I've decided to resign. I'm goin' home with Rusty."

"I believe you have it in you to become an exceptional ranger. Perhaps even an officer someday. May I suggest an alternative course?"

"Won't hurt to listen to it."

"In view of your wound and the healing time it will require, you are due a leave of absence. Without pay, of course. At the end of that time, if you are still of the same mind, I will accept your resignation with regret."

Andy considered. This was a way of leaving the door ajar without firmly committing himself. "Sounds fair to me, sir. I'll write you if I decide not to come back."

The captain extended his hand. "Don't push yourself too hard. You may be hurt more than you realize."

More than *you* realize, Andy thought. The pain was not all physical.

Andy hesitated at the front opening. He turned back. "If you ever find out just what happened to Scooter, . . ." Someone, sometime, might come across the boy's body.

"It's not likely we'll ever know."

Rusty frowned. "Looks to me like you're carryin' a double load, that boy and that Indian. You couldn't help either one of them."

Like you couldn't help Josie, Andy thought. Me and you are both saddled with ghosts.

They prepared to leave the ranger camp after breakfast. Rusty made one last attempt to postpone the trip. "A couple more days would make you stronger."

"In a couple of days we'll be closer to home."

Rusty took the pack mule's lead rope. After a mile or so he could turn the mule loose and trust it to follow the horses. "If that shoulder really gets to hurtin', let me know. We'll stop and rest."

"I'll holler." Andy had no thought of doing so unless the hurting became more than he could handle. He had made strong talk and intended to back it up. By mid-afternoon he was gritting his teeth in an effort not to give in to the pain. Rusty must have sensed it. He dismounted beside a narrow creek.

"We've come twenty-five miles or so. My bay is commencin' to slow down."

Andy was grateful but felt obliged to put up a good front. "Me and Long Red are doin' fine."

"We've got to consider the stock." Rusty unsaddled and caught the mule. He lifted the pack of provisions from its back. "Bo gave us enough vittles to get us to Friedrichsburg or maybe Austin. We can swing around and miss the troubles in Mason town."

"You know about them?"

"I didn't get a very warm welcome there. It's a local feud. No point in us gettin' mixed up in it."

"The rangers *are* mixed up in it, a little. The captain's been sendin' men over to try and hold the lid down."

"It's a good thing Texas has rangers again."

"It is. But there's no law says I have to be one of them."

They reached Friedrichsburg on the third day of a slow trip. Rusty said, "Bo was right good for a camp cook, but you're fixin' to get one of the best meals this side of Clemmie Monahan's table." He took Andy into the Nimitz Hotel for supper. Andy felt out of place with the white tablecloths and fine tableware.

Rusty said, "I could get spoiled in a hurry with fixin's like this."

Andy realized Rusty was trying to lift his spirits, to relieve for even a while the darkness that had come over him since the fight. He made up his mind to smile and enjoy it whether he wanted to or not.

At the easy pace Rusty set, they were more than a week in getting back to the farm. At a glance Andy knew someone had been taking care of the place in Rusty's absence. Tom

Blessing and his sons, he guessed, and perhaps old Shanty. The corn was near shoulder-high. In the garden, cut and shriveled weeds showed the mark of a hoe.

Rusty said, "Maybe your shoulder will be a lot better by the time the garden needs much work again."

"It feels better this mornin' just by us gettin' here. I don't aim to lay around doin' nothin'."

"I don't want you takin' on very much for a while. You might ruin that shoulder. I'd have a cripple on my hands from now on."

"The place won't be the same without Len Tanner comin' around every so often."

"Ranger or not, he'll find a way. You go in and get a fire started so we can fix dinner. I'll unsaddle the horses and unpack the mule."

Tom Blessing came by in the early afternoon. He shouted, "Hello the house" before riding all the way in. Rusty and Andy walked out on the dog run to meet him. Tom dismounted and led his horse up to the hitching post.

"Saw smoke from your chimney, but I couldn't be sure if it was you or some passin' stranger stopped to fix him a meal. Glad to see you home." He looked at Andy. "Thought you joined the rangers." He noticed Andy's bandaged shoulder. "What did you get in the way of?"

Rusty answered for Andy. "A Comanche arrow. Andy hasn't made up his mind if he wants to be a ranger anymore. How's Mrs. Blessing?"

"That Alice girl has been like a tonic to her. She's startin' to act like she's thirty again. Forty, anyway." Tom's smile gave way to an expression of concern. "I'm glad you've made it home. We've got to do somethin' about Alice."

Rusty turned apprehensive. "Somethin' happened to her?"

"Not yet, but she's awful homesick. Wants to go see her

mother. Every time I leave the house, I worry that she may not be there when I get back."

"You think she'd go all by herself?"

Tom nodded. "I wouldn't be surprised. She's got nerve."

"Nerve runs in the Monahan family. But she can't take care of herself against the likes of Corey Bascom. He already tried once to kill her. He might get it done the next time."

"I wish you'd go talk to her. My wife tends to take Alice's side. Neither one of them seems to realize the danger she'd put herself in, strikin' out alone."

Rusty did not study long. He said, "I'll ride over there with you."

"You'll have to go by yourself. I'm on my way to town. Got to be in court for a couple of days."

"I'll try to talk her into stayin' a while longer."

"Stayin' may not be a good idea, either. I heard a feller was in town askin' how to find your farm."

"Corey Bascom?"

"Might be. The description fits what you've told me."

Rusty smiled coldly. "Maybe I won't have to hunt him anymore. Maybe he'll come huntin' me."

Tom said, "The only reason he'd be lookin' for you would be to locate Alice. If he can find out where you are, it's only a matter of time 'til he learns where Alice is. We need to move that girl to a safer place."

"I could bring her here. And when he comes for her, I'll have him."

Tom gave him a look of disbelief. "Use that girl for bait? It's not like you, Rusty. What if somethin' went wrong?"

Rusty reconsidered. "You're right. It was a fool notion that just popped into my head."

"The reason you brought her to my place was so her husband couldn't find her. Now I'm afraid he's fixin' to. She's been wantin' to go home, and I'd say that's the best place for

her, amongst her own folks. They can protect her better than
I can."

Andy had listened without saying anything. Now he told
Rusty, "You snuck her away from home in the dead of night.
You could do the same thing again."

Rusty nodded. "Looks like that's what I've got to do.
Think you can take care of yourself 'til I get back?"

"You're talkin' to a ranger. Used-to-be ranger, anyway.
Go and do what has to be done."

· 17 ·

Rusty had just finished unpacking the mule. Now he packed again with provisions for the several days' ride to the Monahan farm. Andy helped where he could, though he had but one hand to work with. He said, "There's liable to be gossip, you and Alice goin' all the way up there by yourselves. It'll take several days . . . and nights."

"I've got no interest in Alice, not in that way. I'm just tryin' to save her life."

"And maybe playin' hell with her reputation."

"Reputation doesn't plow a field or put money in the bank, and gossip doesn't draw blood. Everybody knows it was Josie I wanted. Alice is too young for me."

"Not that much younger than Josie was. Looks a lot like her, too. All three of them Monahan girls favored one another."

Rusty felt a rising irritation. In an oblique way Andy was reminding him that he had lost Geneva, then had first been attracted to Josie because she resembled her older sister. True, Alice looked a bit like Josie, but that was different. Besides, she was married, or would be until justice overtook Corey

Bascom. It wasn't in Rusty to trifle with a married woman even if she did remind him a little of Josie and Geneva.

Riding toward Tom's place, he considered the long trip ahead. He did not expect pursuit if they got away in the dark of the moon. They would strike out across country instead of following the usual trails, so interception would be unlikely even if Corey outguessed them.

He had an uneasy feeling that he was being followed. Looking back, he saw no one.

Getting Indian notions like Andy, he thought.

After a time he came to a dry creekbed and took advantage of its cover to double back on his trail. Still he saw no one. He decided Tom's report had cut the reins on his imagination.

Alice stood on the dog run, watching his approach. For a moment the sight of her was unnerving. He could easily have mistaken her for Josie. Andy's words came back to him. By the time Rusty reached the double cabin, Mrs. Blessing stood at Alice's side. She looked stronger than he had seen her in the past year.

Rusty took off his hat and spoke first to Mrs. Blessing because she was the oldest and due the deference. Then he told Alice, "I was talkin' to Tom. He said you're itchin' to go home."

"Don't try to talk me out of it. I've been away too long."

"Hear anything from your mother?"

"Her letters say she's a lot better. Walkin' on her own, doin' most of the things she wants to. But she still needs my help."

She sounds like Josie, too, he thought.

Mrs. Blessing said, "I hate to lose Alice, but she's right. It's time you took her home. She'll be a godsend to her mother like she's been to me."

Rusty had argued with himself on the way over here. Should he tell Alice that Corey might be about to track her down? He had decided she was entitled to know about the danger she faced. He said, "Somebody's been askin' questions about my farm. Tom thinks it was probably Corey. Once he finds me it won't take him long to find you."

The news did not disturb her as much as he had thought it might. "All the more reason I ought to go home."

"That's what I brought the pack mule for. Soon as it's good and dark we'll leave. You'd best pack whatever you want to take."

Alice smiled the way Josie used to smile, and Geneva. "*Home.* The prettiest word I know."

Mrs. Blessing said, "I'll miss you, but it's for the best if you're in danger here."

Rusty led the bay horse and the mule down to the barn. He took off the saddle and pack and poured some dry oats into a wooden trough. "Eat good, boys. You've come a long ways, and you've hardly got started yet."

The two women cooked supper, the best meal Rusty had eaten since the hotel in Friedrichsburg. Afterward he stood on the dog run or walked around the outside of the cabin, looking for anyone who might be out there watching. Dusk seemed to last for hours. He tingled with anxiety to be on his way.

At last, when he thought it was dark enough, he went out to the barn and packed the mule, then saddled the two horses. He was about to lead them from the corral when the mule snorted and poked its long ears forward. Rusty turned quickly, but not quickly enough. He caught a glimpse of a dark figure just before a gun barrel came down on his head. It knocked him to his knees and elbows.

A rough voice said, "I always found that the best way to

win a fight is to get in the first lick. That one was for little Anse. Try to get up and I'll hit you again. That one will be for me."

Rusty felt paralyzed, unable to move. He knew this was Corey Bascom. He wanted to shout to Alice to stay away, but he could not summon voice.

He sensed that she was on her way to the barn. He could hear her footsteps. She opened the gate and said, "I'm ready, Rusty."

Corey said, "Rusty ain't ready, but I am."

She made a sharp, involuntary cry before he grabbed her and clapped a hand over her mouth. "Don't holler. I wouldn't want somebody else to come out here and get hurt."

He removed the hand from her face. She gasped. "Corey! What're you fixin' to do?"

"Same as he was, gettin' you away from here before Ma and Lacey find you. I know they're lookin' because I've felt their breath on the back of my neck."

"What makes you think I'd go with you?"

"Because I ain't givin' you any choice. Listen, woman, I'm tryin' to keep you from bein' killed."

"Like you killed Josie?"

"I didn't kill Josie. That's the God's truth. Lacey done it. He thought she was you. Next time he may not miss."

She took a moment to consider that. "I'm inclined to believe you. But Rusty was fixin' to take me back to my people."

"That's too close to *my* people. I'm takin' you someplace where they'll never find you."

Rusty reached for the corral fence, trying to pull himself up. Corey raised the pistol. Alice caught his arm. "Don't, Corey, please. He was just tryin' to help me."

"From now on that's my job. You're still my wife. What's this man to you, anyway?"

"A family friend, that's all. Josie and him was plannin' on gettin' married."

"There ain't nothin' goin' on between the two of you?"

"Of course not. But please don't hurt him any more. He's already been hurt a way too much."

"I won't hurt him if you'll get on that horse and behave yourself. We're leavin' here." He threw Rusty's pistol over the fence. He unsaddled Rusty's horse and ran it out of the corral. He remounted his own and grabbed the reins of Alice's horse. He said, "I don't know what all is packed on that mule, but it'll come in handy on the trip. Let's go."

As the two rode by the cabin, Mrs. Blessing stood on the dog run, a silhouette against lamplight from the kitchen. She shouted, "Alice, I thought you-all were headed north."

Corey said, "Don't answer her."

Alice shouted back anyway. "Rusty's hurt. Out at the barn. Go help him."

"Then who's that you're with?"

Alice tried to answer, but Corey gave her horse's reins a rough jerk. She swallowed the words.

Though the rising moon was little more than a sliver and yielded faint light, she knew they were traveling south. She kept looking back in the darkness, half hoping Rusty was coming, yet afraid of what might happen if he was. She believed what Corey had said about Lacey having killed Josie. Though Corey was capable of violence, she had found it difficult to believe he could have shot her sister. Lacey, on the other hand, . . .

They rode in frosty silence a long time. Finally he demanded, "Ain't you goin' to say somethin'?"

"There's nothin' to say. You've said it all."

"You might cry a little then, so I'll know you're still breathin'."

"I got over cryin' a long time ago, after Josie died."

"I told you I had nothin' to do with that. I came near killin' Lacey for what he done. I never intended for you to be hurt, nor none of your family. Damn it, Alice, I love you."

"Is this the way you show it, by kidnappin' me?"

"I'm not kidnappin' you. You're my wife. I'm takin' you where you'll be safe."

"And where is that?"

"Mexico. I figure we can lose ourselves down there. Nobody'll find us."

"What can we do in Mexico? I'd never feel at home there. I don't even speak any Spanish. Do you?"

"A few cusswords is all."

"I don't want to go to Mexico. I want to go home. I want to see my mother walkin' again. I want to see her movin' and talkin' natural."

Corey rode a while before he spoke again. "What happened to Josie was awful. I don't want it happenin' to you."

"It won't. My family would see to that."

"What about me? Chances are your brother James would kill me, or try to. Maybe you'd like to see me dead."

"No, I wouldn't. But I believe I could handle James."

"Think you could handle your mother, too? Clemmie's cut from pure rawhide."

"I'd tell them you're still my husband, that I still love you."

"Do you, or are you just sayin' that to get what you want?"

Alice fumbled for an answer that wouldn't come. "I did love you once. Lord knows I don't want to, but maybe I still do, a little. I don't know."

"There's a way to find out." He reined his horse in beside

hers. He drew her up against him and kissed her. She pulled back in surprise, unsure how to react. He kissed her again, longer and harder. She felt an unexpected flush of warmth. She found herself responding with an eagerness for which she had not been prepared.

"See?" he said. "It's still there."

She tingled, not yet quite accepting what had happened to her. "Maybe a little bit."

"I never got over you, Alice. Seems like you never got over me, either, even if you thought so. We'll make us a good life together. You'll see."

"But I still want to go home, at least long enough to see for myself that Mama is all right. Take me there, and then I'll go with you wherever you want. Colorado, California. Any place."

"Is that a promise? You're not just sayin' it to stall for time 'til you can get away from me?"

"Us Monahans were taught never to lie."

He reined up. "All right. You know the risk. But if you're willin' to take it, so am I."

"I don't understand why your mother is so bent on seein' me dead. If I intended to tell what I know about the Bascoms I'd have done it a long time ago."

"That's what she was fearful of at first. I have a feelin' it's gone way past that now. Us three sons are all she's got left in the world. She sees you takin' me away from her. She's jealous, and she's afraid."

"And maybe a little bit crazy."

"Maybe. Anyway, Oregon is way out of her reach, and they tell me it's a pretty country."

"Just one more thing. I don't want to spend the rest of my life dodgin' the law with you. Are you through with robbin' stores and banks and such?"

"Never was very good at it in the first place. There's other things I can do. I'm a pretty good carpenter and a damned good blacksmith. I could even farm if I had to. I'll make us a livin' and do it honest. I swear."

She turned her horse around and pointed toward the north star. "Home is that way."

Reluctantly he reined up beside her, pulling the pack mule after him. "You know what we might run into." He reached into his pocket and withdrew a small derringer. "Picked this up in Fort Worth a while back. Worst come to worst, you might need it."

She had been taught the use of guns ever since she was old enough to hold one. She had never handled one this small. "Looks like a toy."

"It's not. It can kill if you put the bullet in the right place."

She had never been far south of Rusty's farm. The darkness offered no landmarks, anyway. She trusted that if they rode north long enough they would come upon familiar ground. As she rode she puzzled over her contradictory emotions. She had believed any affection she once felt for Corey was gone, killed by his mother's cruelty and his own rough nature. But at least a remnant of it had survived, rekindled now by his presense. She found herself wanting him to take her in his arms and kiss her again. The thought made her ashamed, yet she took a guilty pleasure in it.

How could she hope to understand people like Corey and the whole haywire Bascom family if she did not even understand herself?

A glow in the east told her it would soon be daylight. Maybe now she could see a farmhouse and get some idea of where she was. She watched for chimney smoke. It was time for farmers and their families to be up and making breakfast. But she saw no smoke.

As the sun broke over the horizon and spilled early light across the land, she saw two horsemen.

Corey saw them, too. He said, "Damn. I hope that ain't Ma and Lacey." He drew his pistol. "Keep behind me."

The riders' faces were in shadow so that she did not recognize Rusty and Andy until they were within fifty yards. Rusty was hatless, a white bandage around his head.

She moved a little past Corey, trying to block him. "Don't shoot. They're friends."

"Not of mine." Corey brought the weapon up and drew back the hammer.

Rusty was quick to recognize Alice and Corey. He drew his pistol before he reached them.

Andy warned, "Careful. He's packin' as much artillery as you are."

Anger boiled up and strained Rusty's voice. "Move aside, Alice." He motioned with the weapon. "It's time for Corey to pay the preacher."

Her eyes pleaded as strongly as her voice. "You're wrong about him. He didn't kill Josie."

Rusty barely heard her. His hands shook with pent-up fury. "You don't owe him nothin'. I said move aside."

Andy had watched and listened, his mouth wide open. Now he pulled in front of Rusty and grabbed the hand that held the pistol.

"Hold on, Rusty. Hear her out."

"What's there to hear? He's lied to her and got her to believe it."

Alice said, "It wasn't Corey. He wasn't even there. It was his brother Lacey. He thought Josie was me."

Rusty did not want to believe. He had carried his hatred for Corey too long to turn loose of it easily. He jerked his hand free of Andy's grip and fired past Alice. Corey dropped his pistol and grabbed his right arm. He made a cry of surprise and pain.

Rusty saw that in his haste he had hardly more than scratched Corey. He leveled the pistol again. Andy grabbed Rusty's hand and gave it a twist. The muzzle pointed downward. Andy shouted, "Pull that trigger and you'll kill your horse."

"Turn me loose. Corey's got it comin'."

"By law I'm still a ranger, Rusty. I didn't resign. I just took a leave. I'm arrestin' Corey, and if you don't cool down I'll have to arrest you, too."

Rusty glared at him but found that Andy stared back with eyes that reminded him of a Comanche about to kill. Andy said firmly, "Corey's my prisoner. He's got my protection."

Slowly Rusty relaxed his grip on the pistol. Andy wrested it from his fingers and stuck it in his waistband. He said, "Maybe she's right, Rusty. Maybe Corey didn't kill Josie. And again, maybe he did, but it's up to the law to sort it all out. You were a ranger long enough to know that."

Rusty was confused, a hot streak of anger still burning. "First time you ever laid a hand on me, Andy."

"I oughtn't to've had to. You just lost your head for a minute. Once you've cooled off you'll see that I'm right."

Alice broke in, "Corey's bleedin'."

Rusty's bullet had cut a gash along Corey's forearm.

Andy said, "See what you can do for him." He stepped down to retrieve Corey's fallen pistol. He stuck it into his waistband along with Rusty's.

Alice ripped off Corey's sleeve, already torn by the bullet. She wrapped it around the wound. "That'll hold 'til we get to Rusty's cabin. Then we can fix it proper."

Rusty wrestled with his emotions. He looked in Alice's anxious face and saw Josie. He had faced the man he had searched for, then he had missed a chance to kill him. He felt uncertain and deeply frustrated. "I've ridden a thousand miles tryin' to find him. Now you're tellin' me I ought to've been huntin' for somebody else all the time." His hands trembled.

"I'm sorry, Rusty. We were all wrong about Corey. He's been tryin' to help me in his own left-handed way."

Rusty turned aside. He did not want her to see the turmoil he was going through.

Andy broke his silence. "Alice, how come you-all to be headin' back this way? Rusty came by and asked me to help him cut your trail. He figured Corey was takin' you to Mexico."

"That was his intention. I talked him out of it. I told him if he'd take me home first I'd go with him anywhere he wanted."

Rusty regained some of his composure. "You'd go with him willingly? Surely you don't still love him?"

"I didn't think so. I thought I was over him. I guess I didn't know my own feelin's."

"They're wasted on him. Even if he didn't kill Josie, they could put him away for life for what he *has* done. He's wanted for robbin' a bank over at Brownwood. Lord knows what else."

Corey complained, "I'm leakin' my life's blood. If you-all stay here talkin' all day I won't live long enough to see the jailhouse."

Rusty said, "It'd serve him right to just leave him afoot and let him die in his own slow time."

Andy said, "You know we can't do that. Even an outlaw has got certain rights."

Rusty shrugged, still conflicted. "Just so he doesn't get away. If he does, I'll kill him for sure the next time."

Rusty rode in silence, nursing his doubts, fighting confusion. His stomach was uneasy. His head still ached from the blow Corey had struck last night. He only half listened to Andy throwing questions at Alice.

"What you goin' to do about bein' married to Corey? The preachers say 'for better or worse, richer or poorer,' but they don't say what you do if your man goes to jail."

"I guess that's part of the 'worse.' "

"A lawyer could get you a divorce."

"I don't think a Monahan has ever been divorced, not as far back as anybody knows. It'd raise a scandal from here to Georgia."

Rusty saw his farm looming up ahead. He glanced at Corey, who had both hands clasped around the horn. He had paled from shock and loss of blood.

Alice said, "We're almost there, Corey."

Rusty said, "*He* wouldn't be if I was a better shot."

They stopped in front of the cabin. Andy dismounted and moved to help Alice down from her saddle, then Corey. Rusty took his time. He did not offer assistance.

Andy said, "We'll find some clean cloth and bandage him right."

Rusty grunted. "Do what you want to. He's your prisoner." He had rather have left Corey out there alone and let nature take its course.

Alice took Corey's left arm. "I'll help you with him, Andy." She started to move, then halted abruptly. Rusty saw shock in her face.

Two men and a woman stepped out of the kitchen and blocked the way onto the dog run. Bessie Bascom held her double-barreled shotgun. Lacey and Newley stood on either side of her. The old woman said, "Well, look who showed up. You people are the devil to find. Now you-all drop your guns on the ground."

Rusty had no weapon to drop. Facing the business end of those two barrels, Andy reluctantly placed his own pistol on the ground along with those belonging to Rusty and Corey.

Bessie's malevolent gaze fastened on Alice, then shifted to Corey's crudely bandaged arm. "What's the matter with my boy?"

Alice said, "He's been shot."

Bessie shifted the shotgun's muzzle toward Rusty. "Who done it? Him?"

Rusty swallowed, expecting her to shoot him.

The old woman stepped toward her son and reached out to touch the bandage. Most of the blood had dried, but a little was fresh enough to shine in the early morning sun. It stuck to her palm and fingers. She looked at her hand with revulsion and shifted her gaze back to Alice. "That comes from havin' truck with such as you. I told him you were a Jonah from the start." She swung the shotgun up into Alice's face. "You ain't puttin' a spell on any more sons of mine."

Corey stepped in front of Alice. He swayed a little but remained on his feet. "No, Ma, I ain't lettin' you."

"Get out of the way, boy."

"Before you can kill her you'll have to kill me."

The woman's eyes bulged with rage. "I'd kill anybody to protect what's left of this family."

"Not your own son."

"You've betrayed the family, just like your pa done. I killed him. I can kill you."

"It was the state police that killed Pa."

"They shot him, but I was the one told them where he'd be."

"You? Why?"

"I always kept this from you boys. He was fixin' to desert the family and run off with a saloon trollop. Now you're tryin' to run off with this piece of baggage."

Corey seemed shaken by the revelation. "She's my wife, and I love her. Killin' Alice will just make bad things worse. There's witnesses here, and one of them is a ranger."

"There won't be no witnesses when we leave." She laid the shotgun barrel against Corey's good arm and attempted to shove him aside with it. "Damn you, boy, I said move out of the way."

Corey tried to wrest the weapon from her but lacked the strength. He gave it a hard push instead, striking her chin with the barrel. She staggered. In attempting to regain her balance she let the shotgun tip down. One barrel fired.

Corey took the load in his chest and hurtled backward.

The old woman screamed. "Corey!"

She froze for a moment, choking down a rush of grief. Then she turned her fury back upon Alice. "You miserable Jezebel!" She brought the shotgun up again.

The tiny derringer flashed in Alice's hand. The shotgun

tilted toward the ground and discharged its second barrel. It raised a small eruption of dust. Bessie shivered, her confused eyes fixed on Alice. She protested, "I kept tellin' him . . ."

Blood trickled from the corner of her mouth. She leaned forward, then struck the ground like a felled oak.

Rusty grabbed up his pistol from the ground. Lacey shouted, "Ma!" He reached for the weapon at his hip. It had just cleared the holster when Rusty's bullet struck him. He teetered, trying to level his pistol. Rusty fired again, twice. Lacey crumpled.

Rusty muttered, "That's for Alice."

Newley went to his knees, sobbing as Rusty and Andy swung smoking pistols in his direction. "Don't kill me. Please don't."

Alice found her voice. "Don't shoot him. He's harmless."

Rusty felt his finger tightening again on the trigger. He had to stop himself from following through as Andy moved in front of him.

Andy said, "Maybe you know him, Alice, but we don't." He took Newley's pistol. "I hope you ain't goin' to give us any trouble, Bascom. Been killin' enough already."

Newley shook. He tried to speak but brought forth only a little jibberish.

Andy surveyed the carnage. "Lord, what a mess."

Wearily Rusty seated himself on the ground. He extended his arms across his knees and rested his aching head on them. He felt his stomach churning. He had hoped avenging Alice would give him satisfaction. It had not. "I thought I'd shoot Corey and that'd be the end of it. I didn't figure it would come to all this."

Alice knelt beside Corey. She could do nothing for him. She lowered her head and wept.

Andy said, "Looks like he did love you, after all."

She was slow to answer, her voice subdued. "In his way . . . I guess he did."

Andy turned to Rusty. "At least it was the old lady that killed him, not you. You don't have to carry Corey on your conscience."

Rusty looked at the still form of Bessie Bascom. He felt he should have some regret about the old woman, but he did not. His only sympathy went to Alice. "You don't have to report that Alice shot her. Tell them I did it. It'll save her some trouble and grief."

Andy nodded. "Trouble maybe, but not grief."

Alice held Corey's limp hand. A tear rolled down her cheek. In a thin voice she said, "I never saw anybody so poisoned with hate as she was. She always talked about protectin' her family, but she destroyed it herself."

"All but one." Andy nodded toward Newley, who was still on his knees, trembling.

She said, "He never was quite like the others. They always drug him along against his will."

Andy asked Rusty, "What do you think we ought to do with him?"

Rusty felt empty. At this point he did not care. "You're the law. You call it."

"I don't have a fugitive list with me. If he's wanted for anything I don't know about it." He approached Newley. "Stand up."

Newley arose on wobbly legs.

Andy said, "Get on your horse and see how far you can go before dark. Don't let your shadow fall on this side of the Colorado River ever again."

After a silent final look at his mother and brothers, Newley hurried to the barn where the Bascoms had hidden their horses. Shortly he rode out of the corral and put his mount into a lope, heading northward.

Andy returned to Alice. "Does that suit you?"

She nodded. "He's got the Bascom taint in his blood. It'll probably get him killed, but it won't be our doin'."

Andy said, "I'll have to go tell Tom Blessing about this. I'm still a ranger, but he's the local law."

Rusty raised his head and gave Andy a long study. He did not look like a boy anymore. He said, "You did good today. It's a pity you've decided to resign."

"I never said that. I said I was comin' home to heal up and to think about it. I'm still thinkin' about it."

Rusty arose, his legs weak. He walked into the cabin's kitchen and slumped into a chair. He felt wrung out, exhausted.

Alice followed him worriedly. "Are you all right?"

Rusty shook his head. "No. Maybe next week I'll be all right again, or next month. Right now I just feel used up."

Alice looked at him with sad eyes. It struck him again how much she resembled her older sisters. But she was not them, not Geneva and not Josie. She was Alice, just as Josie had been Josie and not Geneva.

Well, at least Josie could rest easy now, he thought. He wondered when *he* would.

Several days' ride brought a nagging ache back into Andy's shoulder, but he had no intention of telling anybody about it. He followed the San Saba River, hoping the cook had been out there with his pole and line. A mess of fresh-fried catfish would make for a tasty supper after all the fat bacon he had eaten on the trail.

He saw the tents ahead and was pleased that the ranger camp had not been moved in his absence. If he ever decided to get a place of his own and settle down he might very well choose such a pleasant spot on this river where tall pecan trees spread their heavy shade along the banks and the water ran clear and cool. It carried him back in memory to some of the better times he had spent with the Comanches.

The Comanches. Reports lately from the high plains had left him with mixed feelings. It was said the army had defeated them after an almost bloodless encounter in a faraway canyon and had run off their horses. They had no choice but to give up and start a long, sad walk to the reservation. That meant he would probably never be called upon to fight them again. The rangers could shift their main attention to lawless white men instead of Indians. Yet his sympathy went to the People, like his foster brother Steals the Ponies, afoot, confined, forced to accept the dubious charity of the federal government. It was too much for a proud race to have to bear. He grieved for them.

Len Tanner was on horse guard. He hollered and put his mount into a long trot to overtake Andy. "Hey, button, how's the shoulder?"

"What shoulder?"

"You back to stay?"

"If the captain will have me."

"He's been hopin' you'd show up. Where'd you leave Rusty?"

"At home. He's decided bein' a farmer is more restful than bein' a ranger."

"Rusty ain't gettin' no younger. The ranger life is for young men like me and you."

Tanner had some gray streaks in his hair, but Andy knew that to mention it would set him off into a longer speech than Andy wanted to hear. "Where are the Morris brothers?"

"On patrol. We been havin' a lot of fun chasin' after outlaws over in Kimble County. You'll enjoy it." He turned serious. "Did Rusty ever find that feller he was huntin' for?"

"Corey Bascom? Yes, that's over and done with."

"And Alice?"

"Rusty took her back to her folks. She's safe now."

"I sort of hoped her and Rusty . . . well, it would kind of make up to him for losin' Josie like he did."

"Who knows? Rusty took a mighty deep wound, a lot worse than what I got in my shoulder. Such things take a long time to heal." Andy looked toward the row of tents. "I'd better report to the captain. Let him know I'm ready for whatever he wants me to do."

A broad grin creased Tanner's freckled face. "He'll be tickled to see you."

The captain stood in front of the headquarters tent, watching Andy approach. Andy dismounted and gave him what passed for a salute in ranger circles.

The captain returned the salute in a manner even less military than Andy's. "I've been wondering about you, Pickard. Have you healed up?"

"Enough, sir. Reportin' for duty."

"Glad to have you. I'll put you back on the pay roster. And Mr. Shannon?"

Andy shook his head. "He won't be comin'."

"A pity. But we must all make choices in this life. If you're hungry, go ask Bo to fix something for you."

Andy saw a boy sitting at the mess tent, peeling potatoes while the black cook watched. He asked, "Is that . . . ?"

The captain nodded. "It's Scooter."

"I thought the Indians got him."

"So did we all. But when the boy saw they were about to overtake him he ran into a cedarbrake and hid. The Comanches hunted for him. They came so close that he said he could hear them breathing. He laid in the cedar all night, scared to death. But at daylight they were gone. He wandered around afoot for several days, hungry, dodging rattlesnakes. Finally some cowboys found him, fed him, and brought him to us."